NO SAFETY IN A POST APOCALYPTIC WORLD

CICADA

M.L. BANNER

BEST-SELLING AUTHOR OF STONE AGE

CICADA

(A Stone Age World Novel)
Stone Age Series Book 3

by
M.L. Banner

ISBN: 0-9908741-2-5 (Paperback)
ISBN 978-0-9908741-3-3 (eBook)
ASIN: B0137R8018 (eBook)
First Edition: 8/2015
Second Edition: 10/2016

CICADA is an original work of fiction.
The characters and dialogs are the products of this author's vivid imagination.
Most of the science and the historical incidents described in this novel are based on
reality, and so are its warnings.

Cover Art: Damonza.com
Editor: Karen Conlin
Proofreader: Sara Jones
Formatting: Polgarus Studio

Published by

Toes in the Water Publishing, LLC
www.toesinthewaterpublishing.com

The Stone Age World

An apocalyptic solar storm takes the world into a new Stone Age
"A great apocalyptic story!"

Stone Age (Volume #1) – The Event caught all but a few by surprise

DESOLATION (Volume #2) – Survival is the only option during the new Stone Age

CICADA (Volume #3) – No safety in a post-apocalyptic world

REMNANTS (Volume #4) – Coming soon

Stone Age Shorts

Short stories set in the Stone Age World

Max's Epoch –Find out what happens to Stone Age's favorite Character, Max Thompson

Time Slip – A scientist attempts to use a slip in time to save his wife, but ends up in a new Stone Age

Songs of a Dead Country – A survivalist fights to live and find his way in a new Stone Age

For more on the Cicada Series, go to:
http://stoneageseries.com/cicada

Want more about the Stone Age World?
www.StoneAgeSeries.com
Stone Age World facts vs. fiction;
what's next; extra material not in the books; more

Prelude
Kuwait City, Kuwait
1991

The RPG's explosion tore through the C130's wing, hitting it in the exact spot needed to disable the ailerons and send it helplessly to the ground. It was pure dumb luck that the bastards hit his plane, since most Iraqi soldiers couldn't hit the broadside of one of Sadam's palaces. This was his tenth time riding in the back of one of these big-bellied planes and lately, because the Iraqi troops were taking potshots at their aircraft with their AKs and RPGs, US pilots had adopted the custom of landing in a corkscrew pattern, making their moving target much more difficult to hit. This asshole scored a bullseye.

The side trip to Camp Doha in Kuwait was starting to look like a stupid idea. He was headed home in a few days and certainly didn't need to see any more action, now that the war—if you could call the trouncing delivered by Operation Desert Storm a war—had ended almost as quickly as it started. But this was his own mission now, not the Army's. And this mission would be far more important than any the Army could have sent him on: if this mission was successful, one day he would save the world.

Maxwell Thompson clutched the web-netting, bracing for the impact from their heavy landing—the insurgent who shot them down would tell his brothers it was a crash. Max wasn't too worried, though, as these things rarely exploded and most injuries or deaths were from unsecured equipment crushing its passengers; theirs was empty but for him. Just in case, he mouthed the words to a well-rehearsed prayer to God. It was entirely up to Him and the pilot, what happened next.

A few hours later, Max found the man he was looking for sitting alone at a small table in the corner of the makeshift bar, nursing a brandy. The pub was serious, like most drinking establishments in Kuwait City; it had sprung up quietly, without signage or fanfare so as to not piss off the local Muslim clerics who took offense to such public activities.

It was a small place and one he had never visited before; he had tried many of the pubs in this industrial city back when he found his solace at the bottom of the bottle. This one was new, having just opened a few days ago. Yet it was packed with mostly off-duty officers and contractors, foreign and American. It was murky and boiling inside, with two shafts of light shooting through the only translucent areas of a single, dirty windowpane. Dust from the dirt floor filled the air, kicked up by the boots of the pub's patrons.

Max quickly grabbed his order and the only unused chair and parked it and himself on the other side of the man's table, not asking for permission. He took a sip of his Iraqi coffee. The bitterness of its grounds, many still floating on the black liquid's surface, filled his senses instantly. His head started to pulse from the combo of the caffeine jolt and the bump he had sustained earlier in this morning's hard landing. But he didn't care; he found his man.

The man finally looked up from his brandy, still lost in thought and only slightly acknowledging his new guest. "Didn't think anyone but the locals drank that shit. You got something against alcohol?" the man said and took a small sip from his glass.

"Both are bad habits; this is the one I didn't give up. Are you Preston Tanner?"

Preston looked up again, this time scrutinizing the stranger, but he didn't say anything. He just stared.

Max continued, "I'm Maxwell Thompson, and I'd like to offer you a job."

PART I

"Cicada will be a new hope for humanity, combining the most robust scientific minds with the most robust technology and top-of-the-line security. Those living and working at Cicada will feel safe and enjoy an environment that will enable them to find solutions to the world's problems when the apocalypse comes."
- Maxwell Thompson 1989

An inscription marked on the capstone of Cicada's north gate's wall

1.

Cicada

One Year A.E.

"Welcome to Cicada!" Preston bellowed to the Kings, his voice a weak volley against the rapid gunfire's campaign being waged on the other side of the wall. He continued to grin, which seemed grossly disconnected from what was going on around them.

The guards retreated. Those on the wall refocused their attention outward perhaps on the next wave of oncoming squatters.

Bill King wrapped his mitts around Preston's offered hand, clamping down like a vise grip and pumping vigorously. "We're so glad to be here."

Max thought Bill might puke right then. The strain of their gunfight outside the walls must have been catching up with him.

Bill continued, "Max told us about this place and said it was safe…" His voice vibrated with tension.

Lisa, with tears streaming down her checks, pushed past him and threw her arms around Preston. "Thank you for letting us in." Realizing she was making a scene, she receded, wiped her face with her sleeve and tried to regain composure while looking back to Sally, perhaps hoping she was filled with similar relief.

"…and this is my daughter, Sally," Bill said, his voice raspy, no doubt dried by another day of scorching heat.

A dying scream, although muffled by the wall, made them all

stutter and gulp a mouthful of dusty air.

Sally remained stationary, silent and nearly motionless, staring past Preston.

Max's heart weighed heavy, watching this. They had been through so much already, and then he had convinced them to leave their other daughter, son-in-law and new grandson at a place they could have made a home, a safe place. The whole time in Mexico, then in New Mexico, and throughout their journey, he told them Cicada would be safe. Now even he was starting to doubt this after yet another gunfight, this time outside Cicada's walls.

A series of pops—distinctive of a 9mm handgun—erupted behind the heavy gate they had just come through, making Sally and Lisa jerk.

"We're going inside," Max announced and pushed Lisa and Sally toward the entrance in the large fence line surrounding the entire compound, separating it from the rest of Cicada's grounds. Bill followed close behind.

"Of course; let's go into Comms, at least until this episode is over." Preston's voice was steady, as if he were proposing nothing more than a momentary break from the hot sun.

Max glanced back and caught Bill gawking, first at the structure towering above them then at the whole complex; only now would he get a sense of the sheer size of Cicada.

Confirming his thoughts, Bill sputtered, "Wow, this place is enormous!"

Max had told them several times that it looked like the Roman Coliseum, although the Coliseum would have looked very small by comparison. "It's one hundred seventy-six acres and it's two and one-half miles around the oval wall," Max stated reflexively, like some bored tourist guide wanting to finish his tour and get home. It wasn't boredom, but hypersensitivity about their security that caused Max to scrutinize every square inch of their surroundings as he pushed his friends closer to the fencing. He sensed someone watching them from above and waved at the top of the tower.

An arm thrust out over a railing at the highest point in Cicada and waved back.

"Was that Shingles on watch?" Max yelled back.

Preston caught up and passed them, chirping, "Yep." He held open the single door in the thick metal barrier that bisected the guard tower, and they all walked through.

"How often are the attacks?"

"Two to three times a week."

Additional volleys popped from the other side of the wall, more muted than those from moments ago. Perhaps this episode was almost over.

"The Squatts were first congregating at the east gate. We thought you were part of a group headed to the north gate."

Max knew this was Preston offering his excuse of why they were almost shot because they were left waiting so long. His anger was boiling up, getting ready to explode. *Safety first.*

He steered the Kings into a T-intersection, past the tower and another large building called "Residences." They turned toward the tower and through a door that read "Comms" and below that "Managers' Offices." It was a rather plain-looking, white, two-story structure separated from the tower and Operations underneath by a pea-gravel road. Max had always thought that for a building containing the brains of the whole complex, it should have looked more... complex.

Once they were all inside, Preston closed the door behind them.

"So what the hell's with all the squatters on our land?" Max crossed his arms and glowered at his aide.

Preston walked by them, opened a mini-refrigerator, pulled out five bottles of water and handed them out.

"It's cold!" Sally moaned, pressing it up against her sticky head.

Lisa gulped hers down as she noticed the room was air-conditioned. "Mmmm."

"Where are the radios, and do they even work?" Bill took in the comfortable two-story space with welcoming sofas and inviting armchairs, worthy of an upscale doctor's reception area and belied by the complex's plain exterior.

"The Comms room and our offices are up the stairs behind me. This is the reception area, but I thought you would be more comfy here."

"So, explain the squatters," Max insisted.

"If you haven't noticed, they have guns," Preston answered sarcastically, apparently forgetting who was the boss and who the employee.

"That's why we have the sonic weapons among the many defenses *you* designed into Cicada for everyone's safety."

Bill, now relaxing a little, sat down and watched the fireworks.

"Mr. Thompson"—Preston sank into one of the couches—"I'm afraid that none of our high-tech weapons are working. When we step out of our shielded environments, most of our electronics short out when we try to use them."

"So shoot the bastards that come too close. Others will learn pretty damn quickly not to come close again."

"There's just too many of them to sit on top of the walls and shoot each one."

"Okay, fine. So, what are you doing instead?"

"We've just let them be, hoping they would grow weary and

finally go away."

"How's that working?" He was very close to losing his temper.

"Not very well, Mr. Thompson." Preston looked down, feeling the full weight of his boss' scorn.

Max realized he was losing control and all eyes were on him. He decided this was neither the time nor the place for this argument. "Who's manning Comms now?"

"A young man, Sally's age, named Webber. You wouldn't know him. He came to us by solving the Cicada puzzle: a computer and electronics genius."

Sally's ears perked up; she was interested in this part of the conversation, and at the mention of something normal, her frayed nerves calmed a little.

"He usually works with a woman named Magdalena. She's—"

"Magdalena Garcia's here?" Max sang, his face instantly changing from irritated to gleeful. "Is she in Comms now?"

"That's right; I forgot that you helped her with some trouble in Mexico."

The Kings' heads moved back and forth, watching the argumentative volleys like a verbal tennis match. The ball was now in Max's court. Since none of them had heard *this* story, they watched expectantly for his next swing.

Max forfeited the match and was already mounting the stairs along the west wall to the Comms room.

"She's not there right now. She had swing, and then was up late working on a project all last night. She's probably asleep. Would you like her room number?" Preston didn't even try to hold back a smirk.

Max snorted just a little. Truth was he would have loved to have seen Magdalena, just not in that way. "Hi Webber, I'm Maxwell Thompson." Max was sincerely interested in meeting Webber—the man who solved the Cicada puzzle—knowing what a vital role he played at Cicada. Mostly, though, he wanted to get away from being the object of their attention. He just didn't want to have to explain Magdalena. At this point, he was wondering about his feelings for a woman who was way too young for him.

Sally followed him through the door while her eyes took in all the equipment in the immediate room and beyond. Communications had a half-moon console desk at its center, bound by a dozen or so monitors, which looked out to another room separated by a floor-to-ceiling Plexiglas wall. This was where they kept the good stuff; it was a clean room, with probably the nicest equipment Sally had ever seen. And she had seen some nice gear, as she had often tested the latest gadgets with the most cutting-edge tech before anyone else. Back before the world ended.

Max felt sorry for her because until now, she had been out of place in this world without much technology.

"Holy shit, is that a Cray XK7?"

"I wish. It's a CS though. Still pretty powerful," Webber said, getting up from his desk chair to meet his boss and Cicada's newest residents, especially the pretty one.

"I should say so, with an Rpeak of six petaflops… I'm just amazed to even see a working computer, much less what was among the ten fastest on the planet before the Event."

"Mr. Thompson, I sure as hell hope she's working with Mags and me," said a beaming Webber. "Warren Webber." He offered his hand enthusiastically.

"Sally. Sally King." She shook quickly, a faint blush on her skin.

Preston was leaning in the doorway. "Let's give the Kings some time to get settled first, then maybe—"

The first bang sounded like a paper bag popping outside.

However, the second was a thundering boom that shook even the solid structure around them.

"What the hell?" Preston chirped, his head lifted, as he tried to get a sense of what and where the explosions came from.

"Preston, with me! The rest of you, stay here."

Max jogged outside with Preston in tow. Sally and Lisa nervously looked at each other, then at Webber, but they didn't see Bill, who had followed the other two.

Max ran toward the north gate, but Preston rushed ahead and veered off toward the nearest wall, using it for cover. One man stood on the top of each side of the gate, above them now, both firing their automatic weapons at the combatants on the other side. The massive gate was pitched slightly outward; the bottom was bent equally inward, one of its huge hinges twisted and mangled—the obvious focus of their blast. Max could see movement through an opening to the other side.

He started to follow Preston to a safe position out of the open, when he heard someone right behind him. Spinning around and seeing it was Bill, Max barked, "I told you to stay put in Comms."

Preston screeched a warning their way.

"I wanted to help."

Max had his back to the gate, seemingly uninterested in the affairs behind him. "You are my best friend and if something happened to you or your family, I don't know what I'd do."

"Hey, I know about the promise to ol' great-grandpa, but I'm good now, so let's drop the protective friend act and move on. You can't protect me twenty-four seven. That's obvious even here."

Max reeled from the verbal sucker punch.

More gunfire, and then someone yelled, "Incoming."

Max instinctively dove away from the yelling and tackled Bill, who was mid-sentence, finger pointed outward, when Max's full weight hit him, knocking all the air out of his lungs. Then there was a loud explosion.

Grenade. Close range. Thompson was no stranger to the sound. This one was so close that he felt the blast wave hit him, along with a heavy weight coming to rest on top of him. His ears screamed and he waited for the searing agony to hit the rest of his body wherever the shrapnel would have buried itself inside him. But there was no pain, only a heavy weight on top of him, his ringing ears, muffled shouting around them and wetness.

He realized his eyes were squeezed tight, and he opened them to see Bill coughing and pushing against him, hollering something he couldn't hear. More wetness, which now started to obscure his vision and dripped onto Bill's face. He winced, trying to keep it from his own eyes, whatever it was… *blood, a lot of it.*

Max felt the weight lift off them.

Freed now, he rolled off Bill and faced what was weighing them down; it was the body of some pudgy man, whose face—now mostly gone—and body had taken most of the grenade's blast.

If this man had not been in between them and the grenade, both of them would have been casualties. *Dammit, Bill, for disobeying my order.*

A shadow fell over him. Preston reached down and grabbed Max by his sleeves. His mouth said, "Are you all right?" but Max could only hear muffled sounds, like he had cotton packed in his ears, and loud ringing. He sure as hell hoped this wasn't permanent. These things usually only lasted a few days. Every time, though, he wondered if this would be the one that did in his hearing.

Preston shouted something else at him. His hearing was already coming back. *That's a good sign.* Max could almost understand what he was saying now. It wasn't a wellness check question; Preston was pissed.

"Sir, what the hell were you thinking?" Preston was still a little agitated. Max was cleaning the dead man's blood from his head, neck and face in the washroom of an empty apartment next to the two they had given the Kings, in a mostly empty wing of the Residences building—sort of a glorified dormitory. Max had excused himself while Preston showed the Kings their apartments, after which he suggested they clean up a bit too while he checked in on Mr. Thompson.

"You realize that Dr. Sampson died trying to save you because you were standing in the open? He ran after you when he saw that one of the Squatts had tossed a grenade through that damaged gate. What were you doing?"

Max was dumbfounded. He had been in the middle of many battles, yet he had ignored all that he knew and had been taught because of Bill. And because of his actions, someone had died? He splashed more water on his face.

He was going to say something to justify his actions, but there really was no justification for what he had done. His overt worry for his friend, originating from his great-grandfather's commitment to watch over Bill's family, had gone too far.

Max looked once more at his reflection and didn't like what he saw. He wiped his face with a towel, leaving more gore on it.

"Was this a normal attack?"

"No, this was more coordinated. And they purposely hit the north gate as if they knew it was the weakest point in Cicada's defensive wall."

"That explosion sounded like C4, and the one that killed Dr. Sampson… that was a grenade. Ordinary *Squatts*, as you call them, wouldn't have tools like those." He roughly rubbed at his beard, trying to get the blood out. The washbasin was a gruesome sight.

"I was thinking the same thing. Wish there was a way to find out where they're getting the military surplus," Preston said, leaning with a shoulder against the bathroom doorway.

"Maybe I can…" Max paused and looked up at his reflection; steam, dust and blood spray covered most of the mirror, but he could see enough. This was as good as it was going to get.

He walked past Preston, slapping his shoulder, and headed to the front door.

"Where are you going? I wanted to… talk to you some more." Preston fidgeted. Had Max been paying attention, he would have seen his manager acting like a child about to reveal something to his parents.

"I'm going to pay a visit to the apartment of the man I got killed. Then, I'm showing the Kings around. We've struggled to get here for a year. I owe them a few moments of enjoyment. Then, I'm going find out personally where this military hardware came from and maybe put a stop to these attacks. Can we talk later?"

Preston didn't speak, but nodded and smiled.

Max opened the front door but paused. "Please see to it that the gate's shored up. And for God's sake, tell the damn guards to shoot the next person that comes close to that thing."

Neither of them could have guessed the threat that would arrive at their gates next.

2.

Bios-2

One Day B.E.

Senator Brian P. Westerling was up for re-election in six months, but he didn't care; he wasn't even campaigning. When the world was about to end, running for a third term in the US Senate was a trivial matter. He just intercepted the notification—sent only to a few select scientists—announcing the Cicada Protocol had started. A giant solar flare would end it all. This was no surprise to him; after all, he knew what was coming and with it, he would be the one responsible for bringing this chapter of humanity to a close. It was a moment of pride for him.

Enveloped in the comfort of his supple leather lounge chair and the buzz from a bourbon and ice smoothing his pre-speech jitters, he took a drag from his Cohiba Robusto and released white swirling puffs of wispy smoke circles. He grinned at his airborne creations as they appeared to float out from the lonely confines of his office to the outside environment he created. Ringing beside him drew his attention.

"Sir, everyone is ready," the voice on his intercom announced.

"Thanks, Reynolds." Resting the freshly lit cigar on his polished stainless-steel ashtray, a gift from one of his many mistresses, Westerling popped out of his chair. Its butter-soft arms released their squeaky embrace. He stood, then straightened his tie and buttoned his jacket while walking across his vast office. Past his desk, he stopped in front of the giant floor-to-ceiling, forty-five degree angled windows that were his office walls; like the control tower of an airport, it gave him a view of everything. Looking down to a street polished and marble-like, he took note of the several hundred men and women who looked up at him, seemingly at attention.

He beamed a smile, one practiced from thirty years of politics, to the expectant faces below. They were all there because of him, and soon, they would be thanking him for their very lives. His pride was far greater than when they completed all the construction last month. It was now time.

"Greetings, men and women of Bios-2," he belted over a wireless microphone connected to the entire city's loudspeakers. "What started out as a dream for me, twelve years ago, has become a reality." His voice echoed off the smooth surfaces of the buildings and streets. "Many of you were here at the beginning, and some of you have just joined us; but we are all part of one family now."

He lowered the microphone from his mouth, dropped his head to appear pensive and then slowly lifted it along with the mic. "And now, I have news." Again, he paused for effect. Looking at the eager faces, now full of concern, his eyes started to well with tears. That skill had come in handy during debates.

"It has been announced that a giant X45 solar flare is about to hit the earth, together with an equally massive CME, which should strike sometime tomorrow morning. You know what this means. It is the technology killer our scientists have been predicting for years and one of the reasons we built this place so quickly."

The next part of the speech he had practiced, knowing their reactions, but it was necessary. He could almost hear the din of worried conversations, even through the thick bulletproof glass of his office walls.

"I know many of you have left family and friends behind to be here. I also know that you will want to warn them in one of your daily phone calls. I'm afraid we simply cannot allow this, which is why there will be no further communication with the outside world until tomorrow. As you know, after tomorrow, it won't matter."

He held up his hands, a physical gesture to quiet their disturbance. "I know. I know this may seem unfair, but because of what we are doing here, and to protect us from the outside world, we have to cease communications. If the world knew what we have here, they would all come and try to take it, and we cannot allow that. This place and its purpose are not known by anyone, except us. And after tomorrow, this one fact will save our lives."

His puffery knew no boundaries. It didn't matter who or how many people came to their impenetrable city walls, anyone attempting entry would be burned down in their tracks. Unless they were one of the scientists who thought this was Cicada.

All his skills from his years in politics couldn't hold back the curls of a smile that formed on his lips.

Westerling had kept the comms open on his phone, and he heard Lunder Gufstafson, his Security Director, join in. With the wireless mic flipped off, he asked his question loud enough that both Reynolds and Lunder could hear. "Do we have the green light, gentlemen?"

"Confirmed all clear, it's a go," announced Reynolds, his voice distorted over the small speaker.

"All clear. It's a go, sir," proclaimed Lunder.

Westerling once again faced the crowd, who was not sure if the announcements were over; without hesitation, he pushed a button on a small console on the credenza behind his desk. The office lights flickered just a little, and then the sky exploded in light. It was a momentary rainbow of colors, which became a dome of almost transparent grid lines of light that shot out from just above his head and arched downward to just outside their walls.

He flipped on the microphone once again. "You can see that we have turned on the Energy Protective Field, or EPF. From now on, nothing gets out and nothing gets in. You are dismissed."

He set the microphone down and walked briskly to his unfinished bourbon and cigar, hopeful it hadn't gone out. There was much to celebrate.

Security Director Lunder knocked on the door and entered Westerling's office, shutting it behind him. "Masterful job, sir." He wasn't just buttering up his boss; he genuinely believed Westerling couldn't have done a better job.

"Thanks, Lunder." Westerling swallowed the last gulp of his forty-year-old bourbon and beamed like the star quarterback who just had his way with the most beautiful cheerleader. He did love taking home the prize.

Lunder waited an appropriate amount of time, and then interrupted the senator's elation. "Sir, there's a call from Senators Gibson and Ferguson. They're headed here in a convoy of five cars less than five miles away. They wanted to let us know they're coming."

"Besides the senators, who's with them?" Westerling asked, resting his empty crystal tumbler on top of the latest personnel reports he had received earlier from Lunder.

"Their families, a security detail and a Dr. John Bevins—he's Mrs.

Gibson's plastic surgeon—and Bevins's wife." Lunder was reading from a small notebook, where he kept his observations and important scribbles.

Westerling beckoned Lunder to sit on the sofa opposite him.

Nose in his notebook, Lunder sat. "I think we should keep Dr. Bevins."

"Are the guards set up?"

"Yes, they're all ready. They're just waiting for your word."

"Do you know yet who's who in each car?" Westerling asked. He stood up and looked out to the front gate, the approaching fleet already visible from the south.

"We will in a moment. Do I have your authority?"

"Yes, of course."

Lunder pulled the radio from his belt and called the gate commander. "You've got authorization."

The radio blasted static, and then "Roger that. Will establish location of Dr. Bevins through cell GPS."

Even though the EPF was on, blocking every communication going out, they had an antenna array above this, which was still tapped into the world's communication's networks—at least until tomorrow when everything would apparently go down.

Lunder stood up beside Westerling to see the show. Five cars, ranging from black Suburbans to a Mercedes ragtop, rolled up to Bios-2's main gate and stopped.

The radio gave them the play by play they needed.

"Gate Commander, this is Operations, you have a go for vehicles one through four. Hold the Mercedes and apprehend its occupants."

The pulsating grid-light pattern of the EPF was turned off. Operations, below them, and Westerling had the only controls for the EPF.

"Roger that, Operations; confirm go on vehicles one through four. Apprehend occupants of vehicle five."

The first vehicle in the line was one of the black Suburbans, windows blackened and bulletproof. Its driver's side door cracked open and its driver stepped outside. From his suit, earpiece and impatient gait, it was obvious he was Secret Service; it was one of the perks of running for president twice. Although Gibson almost won the first time, revelations about hush money and mistresses scuttled any chance of a second run. The man was a prick of the first order, but he had been useful to his boss—it was Gibson who greenlit Bios-2 for Westerling, and both Gibson and Ferguson helped to keep Bios-2 hidden from everyone in the Capitol. They must have heard about the pending solar flare and were seeking safety.

Westerling opened his mouth, probably to ask when the operation was going to take place, when they both noticed the Secret Service driver's face change from annoyed curiosity to wide-eyed alarm. The driver then bolted back into the Suburban just as a missile blasted from the top of the gate, hitting the vehicle almost instantly. The explosion was a wonderful fiery blast that opened up the black SUV like a shucked clamshell and incinerated everyone inside. Three more missiles shot from different placements on the wall, their white trails of death following each to their targets.

The fourth vehicle, a stretch limo, exploded the way Lunder expected, like those he saw in movies. It appeared that the TOW rocket missed the direct hit, instead striking just in front of it. The blast tore through the grill, and then lifted the car up and over, where it hung—standing erect on its rear—for just a moment before falling backwards toward the Mercedes, which was already squealing its tires in a mad attempt to back away to safety. The ragtop was just getting some traction, but the limo, which resembled a giant exploded cigar, descended faster, matching its progression. Just inches before the convertible reached safety, the limo's twisted grill and bumper assembly speared its hood, stopping it dead in its tracks.

Several of Bios-2's security personnel raced from the gate to the Mercedes, drawing automatic weapons, and yelled something at the driver. Westerling and Lunder couldn't hear without the parabolic. Two of the security detachment broke from the group and fired rounds into the limo, already partially ablaze. The occupants of the Mercedes, a soft-looking man in shorts and a yellow polo and a slender woman wearing a miniskirt and a colorful hat that one might see at a Kentucky Derby, exited their car and followed the men back to the gate.

"Operations, this is the Gate Commander. We have acquired subjects and dispatched the other vehicles and their occupants. We're sending in cleanup."

"Good work, Gate Commander. Operations out."

Westerling sat back down, unable to hold back his grin. "That was fun. Good work, Lunder." He raised his glass, a sign instructing Lunder to get him more bourbon and grab a glass for himself as well.

"Thank you, sir."

"Do we expect any others?"

"No, that's it. The president is going underground at Camp David, and the VP is going to Cheyenne Mountain." The security director returned with two glasses, handing one to his boss.

"Shit, that old fool might actually make it there."

"I know." Lunder practically inhaled most of his drink, rarely tasting something so delightful.

"Tell me how we're doing on the scientists."

"Well," Lunder said, almost finished with his bourbon, ready to show off why his boss had so much trust in him, "we've already secured ten scientists who were headed to Cicada. But we expect to pick up many more over the next few days or weeks. We figure they would be slowed by the Event on their way here. So, the ruse worked very well." Lunder reminded him, lest Westerling forget, it was his idea to send the fake emails to the Cicada scientists and divert them to Bios-2.

"Indeed, I guess time will tell then. And with Cicada?"

"Well," he hesitated, not wanting to give him any bad news, "today, two doctors showed up." Lunder pulled out his notes. "A Doctor Merriweather, expert in particle accelerator design, and a Doctor Valdez, a micro-epidemiologist, specializing in apocalyptic viruses."

"So why didn't we get these guys?"

"Well, you'll remember, the database copy we stole from Maxwell Thompson was a little older. These two must have been some of their recent additions to the Cicada Protocol."

"So, this was definitely not a good thing?"

With his boss, it was all about the Ben Franklin list. Everything was broken down to a plus or minus, to check whether an action was a good or bad thing. "Well, it's not good for us. You might remember Merriweather was one of the scientists our contractor was chasing in Texas."

"Wasn't that Stoneridge?"

Dr. Stoneridge received funding from Cicada's grant funding organization. But Westerling's Euro-hitman stole the doctor's technology and burned down his lab to cover their tracks.

"Well, they worked together and then Stoneridge disappeared, but our guy got the plans for their accelerator that Merriweather designed."

"So what, we've got the plans, and we already have something so much more important from Stoneridge."

Add another mark to the plus column.

They both smirked at each other, and each took another sip of the smooth liquid.

"True, and the good news is that Cicada so far only has three other scientists. And by tomorrow, they'll be in the same boat as us," Lunder continued, "with those destined there getting slowed or stopped by the Event."

"The Event?"

"Well, that's what Dr. Reid calls it in his bulletin."

"Of course, the infamous Dr. Reid… did we get him yet?"

To Lunder, it seemed his boss looked at this as some sort of epic game of Fantasy Baseball, where his goal was to collect as many of the best players as he could, for pride's sake and to spite Cicada. Now he wanted Alex Rodriguez.

"He received our faux Cicada notice, so we'll see if he shows up."

3.
Bios-2
One Year A.E.

Dr. Melanie Reid looked up from the barrel of the Electro-Magnetic Accelerator, or EMA—she preferred ray gun—to see if the guard saw it too, or saw her: maybe it was a plant, put there to gauge her reaction. Yet the guard seemed uninterested in her and her activities, as he did most days. Instead, he was absorbed in an adult comic book starring big-bosomed women.

He licked his lower lip and turned the page.

Melanie excitedly reached in and quickly yanked out the folded piece of paper. It had the familiar infinity symbol on it. Carefully, she unfolded it in front of the barrel of the ray gun, so its bulk would obscure the note. *Well done.*

She restrained a smirk that threatened to radiate and give away their game.

Dearest,
In black ink my love may still shine bright.
And shine bright it shall, even in bondage.
I have little time, but when the clock strikes thirteen, you shall seek relief and yet find my love instead.
Carr

The first part was from one of her favorite Shakespearean sonnets. The rest was his code, in case the message was found. She looked at her watch. It was almost one o'clock. In military time that was 1300 hours.

"Hey, Simon, I need to use the can."

"Can't it wait?"

He was obviously up to one of the good parts in his porno comic book.

"Sorry, you know us girls can't hold it, and I would hate for it to get messy."

He didn't want that either, since he'd be responsible for cleaning it up.

"Okay, okay. Go ahead, but I'll be right behind you."

She walked out, with Simon following closely, down the long concrete hallway. Melanie likened him to a perverted puppy dog, whose eyes she could feel were fixated on her rear. Simon was the reason she wore baggy clothes. She often deflected comments about this to their colleagues by stating plainly, "Only my husband should know what I look like underneath."

Outside of the low rhythmic hum of the ever-running machinery below them, there were no other noises. They were probably all alone. It would be so easy to turn around and snap Simple Simon's neck and escape. No one would catch her. But then what? Where would she go? And it would be an infinitely more difficult task to break Carr out, even though his confinement was less restrictive than hers. She still had few ways of escaping this place, with the EPF almost always on. And they had been held captive for almost nine months now. No, her best bet was working with the other scientists; together they would find a way out. Hopefully that would come soon enough.

But now, she would get to see her husband.

At the hallway's T-intersection her pace quickened, forcing Simon a couple steps behind her to struggle to match her silent stride. His clunky feet thudded and echoed through the seemingly endless corridors, whereas her soundless footsteps would have been muffled by the sound of Simon's lumbering gait. Her size-eleven work tennis shoes had long ago worn out, having practically no soles left, and they certainly didn't have a Payless here. So she often slipped an old sock—Bios-2 had lots of those—over each of them. It kept her toes inside her holey shoes and gave her the added benefit of walking nearly silently. It also made her chuckle, considering she wore a pair of shoes that finally lived up to its name: sneakers.

At the ladies' room entrance, she slid to a stop, turned and looked back at Simon. He jerked up in a panic, caught staring at her. Even though he was a perv, he was a harmless perv. She almost felt sorry for this young man, who'd been dealt about twenty cards short of a full deck. "You coming in with me?" She couldn't help herself.

"Ah-ah... no! But, I'll be right here." He did his best to sound self-important.

"You make sure I don't leave or anything."

She stepped into the dank bathroom, closing the door behind her with a brief creak. Kneeling down, she listened and looked out under the stalls and the sinks. She could also see the fronts of each of the stalls through the mirrors. They were all closed.

She whistled softly, just a little chirp that only he would hear.

A squeak came from one of the stalls then a large boot appeared, and then another. Finally, the door to the third stall opened and a familiar form stepped out. Oh, she longed for him.

He wore a bright grin that busted through the murk of this place, otherwise lit by one small fluorescent—they were under strict energy usage rules. She was filled with his warmth. It didn't matter where they were, his smile made her feel like she was looking directly into the sun. She lived to be with him, wherever that was.

She flew silently to him and they wrapped their arms around each other.

Her lips found his; they were cracked and rugged, and minty.

She pulled her mouth away. "Why, Dr. Carrington Reid, is that a breath mint, just for little ol' me?"

"Dr. Melanie Sinclaire-Reid, I offer nothing but the best for my girl."

"I love what you did with the place," she said, looking into the stall. A white sheet hung from a dowel rod that spanned the back wall of the stall and draped down over the toilet and floor—his way of turning a disgusting bathroom stall into their own sanitary sanctuary.

This was the sixth time they'd met here, always being careful to not be caught. But they had been separated for almost a month now, so they had to find creative ways to be together.

"My dearest, our love nest awaits," he whispered to her ear, reminding her that they had to keep their voices down. "And we'll have to move foreplay along. I don't have much time before they change shifts and I'm considered AWOL."

"Skip the sonnets, you said the magic words," she breathed while hastily unbuttoning his pants, sliding her tongue into his mouth as he undid hers. In a tangle of arms and legs they shimmied into the stall, leaving their pants behind.

"Oh wait," Melanie stopped. "I almost forgot; today at dinner, I'm going to ask for a census of who will attend our next meeting. Will you be there? We can make goo-goo eyes at each other while we plan the overthrow of this place." She then started to kiss him again.

He pulled away. "Yes, I'll be there." He slid his hands under her shirt. "You holding it the same way, passing the message down the line?"

"Ugh hah." She pulled her shirt over her head and unclasped her bra, making it easy for him.

"One more thing"—he yanked his shirt off—"the EMA is fine. I was just making excuses to pass you the note. But our bosses expect it to be fully functional today, so be sure to make it obvious that you found the problem and then get it installed, today."

"Are you done?" She waited, breathing deeply, expectantly.

"Yes, but—" She put her hand over his mouth while she guided him inside her.

Simon thought he heard talking. But he always heard talking inside his head. He'd tell people, "On account my ears are so good." But they were better than good; they were amazing—he loved that word. Some even said they were like a "medical instrument."

He craned his neck and concentrated on their voices and what they said. Then he knew they were at it again, and he felt excitement spread from his groin.

He crouched down behind the door and pushed it open slowly, its creak almost imperceptible to anyone else.

Because of how the door opened, he had direct line of sight to the big mirrors over all the sinks, and most importantly, he could see into all of the stalls, except one. He fixed his gaze on the third stall, its closed door blocking his view; he could only see their feet. But he could hear them, and so he closed his eyes and listened to their moaning in delight.

He loved his job. He got to read his comics all day and make people do what he told them to. Most of the time, these people were boring; they did things he didn't care about, in laboratories he didn't understand. But sometimes, he got to see or hear people doing things they shouldn't be doing, and then he would tell his boss about it. Each time, he was rewarded with more comic books. This time, he would be richly rewarded because he had something big to tell.

For now, he just listened.

4.

Cicada

While the Kings relished every moment in the luxury of a soapy shower, Max used the time to make a stop on the floor above before meeting up with them later for a tour and food at the Rec Facility.

Max checked the door number and inserted his key, hoping he'd grabbed the correct master—apparently there were many—the click confirmed it. No one but Preston knew he was going here. But not wanting to have to explain himself, he checked both ways and then slipped in carefully, as if afraid of waking this apartment's resident. Of course, that was impossible, because this resident was dead.

From what Preston had told him, Doctor Raymond Sampson was a loner, making almost no friends in the nearly twelve months since he'd been here. He was a civil engineer, and his primary focus was on making their walls and gates stronger. *Looks like you had some unfinished work yet on the north gate*, Max thought.

Dr. Sampson was one of the many scientists they found through the Cicada Foundation Max had set up. Dr. Sampson had received a two-year grant for his work and just before it expired, he received the Cicada Protocol notice the day before the Event and arrived the same day, one of the first. And other than the tech Cicada was able to get from his grant work, they knew little about this man. Max wanted more, if only to satisfy his own conscience.

All the apartments were the same in the large multi-story building called Residences: a living area, two bedrooms and a shared bath. No apartment contained a kitchen, since everyone ate at the Rec Facility. From the entrance, he tentatively walked right into the living room, darkened by the drawn curtains.

He heard a scratching noise and unconsciously drew his weapon, wondering if there was someone in there with him. He tiptoed back and fumbled for the light switch. *Click.* Max gasped.

The entire room had been tossed. Papers lay everywhere; the mattress leaned up against the wall, sliced from end to end, with its stuffing pulled out like a gutted deer; drawers were overturned; clothes, toiletries, and various knick-knacks were strewn all over the floor. And on the top of the heap sat a dead microwave, its cracked door hanging open, revealing an empty chamber.

The noise again: this time a scratch, followed by a sliding sound. There was definitely someone or something in the room with him.

Max advanced into the living room and craned his neck around the corner. He switched off the safety.

Nothing. Just more debris.

That sound *again*. No question; something was moving, but it was smaller than a person.

Further into the living room, he spotted an overturned terrarium, one of its glass panels shattered. When he saw the gray, translucent skin in a wrinkled pile, he instinctively raised his gun and crouched. Now he knew what he was hearing. It was a snake, and he hated snakes.

Just to his left, out of his periphery, he sensed a slight movement.

Slowly, he turned his head and saw the reptile coiled on the floor right before him. It started to rattle.

"Shit!" he whispered, his lips—like his whole body—unmoving.

Gently, he backed up toward the living room closet, keeping his upper body and hands practically immobile. When he gauged he'd put at least three feet between himself and the rattler, his moves were more deliberate, but still trying not to startle the huge creature. Max found what he needed, thankful that Sampson was one of the few to still use wire hangers. After a minute he was ready.

"Got you!" he proclaimed proudly.

"Bringing your laundry on the tour?"

Max was happy to hear the levity from Bill, who seemed to be settling down. He only wished Sally and Lisa, their faces drawn and uninterested, could do likewise.

"Nah"—he held up the pillowcase tied in the middle with a large lump at its bottom—"just something I need to drop off at my residence. It's on the way."

Lisa eyed Max's shirt covered in Sampson's dried blood like some tie-dye experiment gone bad. "Hope you'll change that thing, too."

He would.

Max was very particular about his residence. He had decided long ago, while it was being built, that no one would enter. It would be his sanctuary, which would be especially important to him as a figure so public in this closed community. Only Preston had even seen the inside of his place after construction, and that had been years ago. Yet, it seemed that the Kings were the exception to most his rules and he certainly didn't want to carry a rattlesnake around with him all day. His primary purpose was to give them some comfort and help them gain a sense of safety. He hoped seeing where he lived would do that. So, while they jeered and jested about his living room's dusty decor, Max excused himself and dumped the six-foot snake into his empty bedroom hamper—just a temporary fix—and changed clothes.

"Let's go see some cool shit," Max bellowed as he motioned for everyone to head to the exit.

Lisa was the last through the door, when she stopped before the three pictures that hung on the entry foyer's wall. "I remember your great-grandfather, Russell Thompson, the guy who started Cicada, and of course I'm embarrassed and flattered to see our picture right there beside him, but who is this pretty woman?" She pointed at the smallest picture on the wall.

He knew the picture well, but he looked at it anyway. It was the one surviving photograph of the only woman Max had ever loved— his Fatima, who had died in Kuwait. She was looking up from an empty hospital bed where she worked. It was the very one he had found himself in after passing out in a bar and cracking his head open; when he awoke he was looking up into the same possessing eyes that observed him now.

Her picture, a testament to the epoch moment in his life, was there with the others as reminders of why Cicada was so important to him. That way, he would see these prompts every time he left and returned each day. The few times he stayed here, he imagined Fatima saying things to him like, *Have a great day, honey* when he went to his office in Comms. Or *Welcome home* when he returned.

But now, gazing into those captivating dark pools, he heard different words. This time he heard, *You must protect them!*

He reached in front of Lisa and pulled the door shut, nudging both of them outside.

"She was someone special. I'll tell you about her later." He locked the door and said, "Come on, let me show you what is probably, at this moment, the most advanced research facility in the world. And right after that, I have something wonderful to show you."

Magdalena walked in rubbing her eyes, her black hair pulled back into a ponytail. She dressed casual, as normal, wearing a loose muscle tee and shorts, clean and creased. Her step was lively, but her demeanor seemed sad.

"Hey, sleepy head," Webber said, pulling off his headphones. "Welcome to the land of the living."

"Thanks for letting me catch some Z's, Web." She smiled a shallow smile. "I heard Sampson bought it today from some Squatts trying to break in."

"Yeah, I wondered if you'd slept through that too... Not too many people knew him." He paused to see if she wanted to add anything, but she didn't; instead, she headed for the server room. "You hear who arrived?"

She stopped and mock-glared at him. "Do you really think that little of me? Of course I know who arrived. I'm going to meet up with Max and his friends in a few minutes to show them the Library." Her smile grew. She twisted the knob to the clean room's door. "Just have to do my daily check on the Crays."

"Now that you're here, I'm going to get a bite to eat. Can you lock up when you leave?" He left without waiting for an answer.

"Sure. I'll probably see you in the dining... whatever." She shrugged and headed into the entryway of the clean room. After putting on her anti-static booties and white, full-length lab coat, she strode into what was for her one of the two coolest rooms on earth, both figuratively and literally. Of course, what would compare. Cicada had the only working super-computers anywhere and it was certainly cold from the air conditioning.

She pulled out a drawer, unfolding the Cray's monitor and

keyboard. The screen instantly flashed to life. Almost as quickly, she started to type. In about ten minutes, after running all her tests, she would be done and she could go see Max and meet the people who meant so much to him.

The mole was sure that he had entered the Comms room without being seen. If he was caught, because of his position, he'd at least have a reason for being here. The clean room's lights were on, and he could see Magdalena inside with her back to him. She was running her tests, so he had enough time to do what he needed and leave before she would possibly look his way. Not that she could see him, as all the lights in the Communications room were off.

After making sure the door was secure, he walked over to the Comms console and sat. Reaching down to the bottom drawer, he inserted his key, unlocked it and slid it open. Inside sat something that would have seemed odd in the high-tech world preceding the Event. After the Event, it seemed odder still. In fact, he was one of only maybe two dozen people on the planet who knew it existed. Grabbing the receiver of the 1970s-style phone, he put his ear to it and depressed the clear plastic buttons for the fifth and sixth lines at the same time. Both lit up bright red, indicating he had a line. His receiver crackled, and then he heard something like a dial tone. Then, it rang. It always reminded him of the ringing sound in Magdalena's Pink Floyd's *The Wall* album—a quick double-tone, followed by a pause; another quick double-tone followed by another pause. On the third ring, someone picked it up but said nothing.

"Bios-2, this is Cicada Comms," he said into his receiver.

The other side, after hearing the correct words in the correct order, asked in a thick German accent, "What do you have to report?"

"Mr. Thompson and his friends, the Kings, arrived today. We also had another attack that badly damaged the north gate, but it is being repaired. The attack hurt Mr. Thompson, though not badly, but it killed Doctor Ronald Sampson. I checked Dr. Sampson's room and couldn't find anything incriminating. I will call in again tomorrow. That is all."

"What is your current scientist count?" asked the German voice.

"I have no update from the last report—minus one, of course."

"Thank you for the intel." The German hung up.

He nervously put the phone back into its cradle and shut the drawer.

A clicking alerted him that someone was about to come through the clean room's door into Comms. *He had to get out right away!*

"Webs, are you still here?" Magdalena thrust her head out the door and saw the Comms door swing shut, as if Webber had just left.

"This is the main research facility, where our scientists make their magic." They were standing in an empty foyer, in front of an elevator. Max pressed his thumb against a small, rectangular raised plate. A light flashed and the elevator doors opened. "This is a biometric scanner for entry and use of the elevator or the door to the first-floor offices and labs behind us—there's a stairwell through there." He waited for them to enter then closed the door.

"Although there are five floors where our scientists are working on various problems, I'm taking you to the top floor."

"How many scientists are here now?" Sally asked.

"I believe twenty-one."

"That seems lower than I would have thought," Lisa said, whose claustrophobia had kicked in almost as soon as the door shut.

"It is. We had planned on a lot more, but many didn't make it." He hated where this conversation was going. "Bill, you'll love Dr. Cockerell's lab. From what I understand, he's building some sort of new hovercraft using something called John-Teller metal, although I have no idea what that is."

The door opened with a *ding*. Quietly, they exited the elevator and walked down a long hallway with many doors to many labs. Max noticed that Lisa and Sally were looking down rather than into the labs like Bill was doing with interest. Seeing Rob Johnson standing in front of a lab door gave him an idea.

"Johnson," Max called out, "can we borrow you for a moment?"

Johnson hesitated then marched their way, looking distracted. As if on cue, he started to beam.

"Good to see you finally made it, Mr. Thompson," he gushed, shaking Max's hand enthusiastically. "We all wondered, since your last call."

Bill looked at Max curiously. *Call?* Cell phones hadn't worked since the Event.

After introductions, Max asked Johnson if he would escort them through the labs—especially Dr. Cockerell's—and then he'd meet them all in front of the Library.

"I'm sorry, but I have one task I must attend to first." Max excused himself as Johnson and the Kings headed for Cockerell's lab. When they left the hallway, Max went to Sampson's lab, door 4G. Interestingly, it was the same door Johnson had been standing in front of when he called him over. Max entered, turned on the lights and immediately started looking for Sampson's computer terminal, hoping what he was searching for would be near it. This lab was one of the largest, taking up three lab spaces. Immediately in front were several test displays of gray concrete-like blocks stacked on scales. At the far corner, Max found a likely spot for his objective: a lab cabinet with a monitor and desktop PC beside it. Below were multiple shelves and a single, locked drawer. He tried several keys until the lock clicked and the drawer slid open, revealing only two items: a small portable hard drive and a composition notebook with graph-paper pages and lots of mechanical drawings and illegible scribbling. Snatching a satchel on another table, he placed both objects inside. He locked the drawer, turned off the lights and headed to the Library. He would have to investigate those contents later and figure out who had been searching through Sampson's apartment—and why.

"Okay, now for the real cool stuff." Max flashed a wide grin.

He had met the Kings—Johnson excused himself, saying he was in a hurry—at the elevator entrance of the Recreational Center and School. They proceeded down one floor.

"All who reside at Cicada have biometric access to where we're going. I'll get you into the system tomorrow because you'll want to come down here... a lot. Also, this floor is only accessible by elevator—there are no stairs like in other buildings."

The elevator doors opened into an all-concrete hallway. Nondescript neon lights illuminated the small hall and its three doors.

"We excavated this area down three floors. Where we're going is the biggest open area in all of Cicada, other than the outside. The next floor down is much of our mechanical, electrical, ductwork, ventilation, etc. Below that is power storage."

Max stopped at a door marked *Library*. "So, here we are at—"

"—the Library," Sally finished, sounding sarcastic. "And me without my library card."

"You joke, but get a load of this." Max pushed on the door and held it open for them.

It was, in fact, a library… gigantic by any pre-Event measure. "We have over one hundred thousand volumes here." He looked at each of their faces and saw the delight he had hoped for. "Everything from ancient Biblical texts to best-selling fiction. But this is nothing compared to what you're about to see."

Max walked through a large reading area with tables and inviting chairs parked around them, each with stacks of books, piled in various configurations. At a glance, Sally thought it could have been any big public or university library. But then after the last table, there was a glass wall separating the Library from rows and rows of metal cabinets.

They walked through a glass door and into a much cooler temperature.

"Those are server racks," Sally said with enthusiasm. "Looks like fifteen rows, with twenty racks in a row, and maybe, what, twelve servers per rack. Oh my God, that's what, ten petabytes of storage?"

"Actually thirty," answered a woman's voice from the back of the room as she strolled toward them.

"That's over thirty million gigs of storage space." Sally continued her thought progression, not realizing that all eyes were on the woman coming their way. "You could store…" She thought about it.

"Everything!" the woman, now standing in front of them, answered. "Well, not literally everything; certainly all of the important stuff we need. We have the collective storage of all the public universities, the Library of Congress and thousands of information websites, including Wikipedia, all stored here. So when we figure out what the hell is going on outside and get back to normal, we'll have most of the important knowledge base of humanity stored here to start again," she finished with a big glowing grin.

"Damn good to see you, Magdalena." Max lifted her in a bear hug.

After a long moment, she said, "I'm so glad you're safe, Max. I thought I'd never see you again." Her eyes were watery and happy. "Hi," she said the others. "I'm Magdalena, but everyone here calls me Mags."

A large *clunk* sound echoed around the server room, and then they were plunged into darkness.

"Uncle Max, what happened to the lights?" Sally screeched, trying to sound strong in front of Max's pretty friend.

"It'll be okay; they'll come on shortly," Magdalena said resolutely.

A couple of beeping noises from the UPS, protecting the servers from shutting down, chirped its desire for more power in the darkness.

There was a crash and a thump, prompting shrieks from both Sally and Lisa.

"Pendejo! Sorry, my bad. That was me."

"Magdalena, are you all right?" Alarm tinged Max's voice.

A light clicked on. "Yep, I'm so clumsy." She was holding a flexible light plugged into the USB port of a laptop that rested on a worktable with several chairs. She shined it around the room—first on Sally and Lisa, who were holding onto each other. Sally was wiping away her tears before all could see them in the bright glare.

Next, on Bill, who was walking over to his wife and daughter to offer comfort; then on Max, who was already there, staring down upon her with concern. Last, straight down, giving them all a place to walk to. "You'd best come over here and sit down; it might be a few hours before the power comes on."

5.
Bios-2

"You mean, almost a year after the Event, Maxwell Thompson finally shows up in the flesh?" Westerling said, sitting in his favorite office lounge chair, Lunder on the couch across from him. It was their daily meeting where they discussed all of B2's security issues.

"Yes, sir." Some days, Lunder's German accent was so thick it sounded to Westerling as if he had just arrived from the old country. "And they came in right when some of the Squatts were attacking."

"Did any of them get hurt?" he asked, eyebrows raised, expectant.

"One of our moles bought it, a Dr. Sampson."

"Dammit! At least Sampson was expendable. Nothing incriminating left behind, I trust?"

"Our guy says no and will check in with us tomorrow, I hope with more details."

"No one else?"

"Thompson was only slightly hurt."

"That boy is sure damned lucky. Did the blast at least cause some damage?"

"The north gate is in bad shape; they're going to have to work hard to get that fixed, but it is definitely their weak point."

"Excellent. Be sure to get some more explosives into the Squatts' hands. They seem to be making good use of it. See what you can do to step up their attacks, lend a hand if we need to. I would sure love to see Cicada fall, before they figure us out."

"You got it, boss." Lunder wrote a note and checked off something else. "Next, the EMAs are all back up and ready."

"I love our ray guns."

"Yes, Dr. Reid said she found the problem, fixed it and we reinstalled them. I had one of my men test one out on some poor slob who was walking below the wall. It works great."

"I thought I saw the EPF go down this afternoon; now I understand why. Were all your men set for—"

"—Yes, of course. As always, everyone was on high alert when we took the EPF down. So, all five EMAs are back up and covering nearly 100% of the area outside the walls. We'll be ready if we have to service the EPF again. The Outsiders will stay back."

Westerling knew that the EMAs were vital to the protection of Bios-2, not so much as a first line of defense, but as a deterrent. Each was a truly awesome weapon that fired the equivalent of a lightning bolt. Anything it touched was instantly burned to a crispy marshmallow. But the damned thing had worse aim than a snub-nose .38. That's why they installed a Taser-like dart that shot out of a barrel mounted below the EMA. The dart would hit the target, and then the EMA almost simultaneously blasted its deadly bolt of electricity, now with complete accuracy, up to four hundred meters. They only had one dart per gun; after that, the EMA's electrical bolts would travel to the nearest ground in the general vicinity of the intended target. But the Outsiders didn't know this. They also didn't know that when B2's generator went down, taking their Electric Protection Field, or EPF, with it, they only had two or three shots from all five of their EMAs. All the Outsiders knew was when one of those things was fired, its intended target was about to experience hell on earth.

"Good. What else do you have for me?"

"Well, speaking of Doctor Reid…"

"Dr. Carrington Reid?"

"No, his wife. Melanie Sinclaire-Reid, the NASA astronaut." Lunder didn't expect his boss to remember all the details, although it was more important that he know the pertinent particulars. "If you'll recall, we separated the Reids and put her under guard for stirring the pot with the other scientists, trying to convince them to leave. Anyway, her guard"—he opened his notebook—"a Simon Washington…"

"I know the kid, big and stupid, but loyal for comic books."

"Yes, sir, that's him. Well, he caught them meeting up in the ladies' room again."

"For what purpose?" Westerling asked and immediately realized, making a smirky O with his mouth and nodding affirmatively. "So, what's the problem with this? They're married, they miss each other."

"Well, it's against the rules."

"They do good work, don't they?"

"Yes, but if everyone decided to break the rules they didn't like, we'd have chaos."

"Fine, throw her in the brig for a few hours, and then put them back together. They should not be separated. Keep them under watch, but let them have their fun together. Of course, she can no longer stir the pot, or she'll face longer jail time—or worse. Make it known to her."

"What about Mr. Reid?"

"Leave him to me."

"Okay, but—"

There was a knock on the door and Deanna—obviously tipsy again—stepped inside without asking for permission; she knew he hated this. Leanne broke free from her mother's hand, rushed the span of his office and jumped in his lap.

"Ooof. Geeze, you're getting big, my baby-girl," bellowed Westerling in his jolly Santa-like voice.

"Crapaw, I'm six now. I'm a big girl."

"Daddy, I'm sorry, but Leanne was dying to show off her new dress to her grandfather."

"We done here?" he asked Lunder while bouncing his granddaughter on his lap. She yipped with glee after every jolt.

"Yes sir. Everything else can wait until tom—"

"Thanks, Lunder." Westerling cut him off, not even looking back at him. His attention was on the only two people who mattered in his life.

Leanne hopped off his lap and spun around so her dress flared out in a perfect cone.

"Wow, that's beautiful." Westerling clapped merrily.

Lunder closed the door behind him, miffed that two girls, even family, came before concluding their business.

6.
Bios-2

A quick look around showed no one was paying much attention to her. Melanie drew one knee to her chest. About a dozen or so scientists were sitting with her at the picnic-style table, one of several in the dining room. She pretended to adjust the sock she wore over her shoe, leaned closer to the man nearest to her and whispered, "It's time we break out of this place, but we have to be smart about it. What I want to know is who is in. If you're in, just turn your milk carton upside down, and we'll count you and be in touch with you. Pass the word."

She rose abruptly and left the table, taking a square nutrient bar and her allotted murky glass of water from her tray and left the lunchroom.

A few minutes later, Carrington and Rush—a big supporter and friend for both of them—walked down the middle of the room as Carrington dictated to him the name of each one choosing to be a part of their scheme. Within a couple minutes, their census was done. Over fifty percent of the scientists and workers had announced their desire to break out.

Carrington smiled, remembering their interlude earlier.

"She's quite the planner," Rush said.

"Among other things," he answered and grinned some more.

When Melanie turned the corner of the hallway leading to their apartment, she knew she was up shit creek without a paddle. Two security guards, and not the usual dumb kind, were waiting for her.

"Please come with us, Mrs. Reid," said the larger of the two.

"Dr. Reid, please. I think I earned that title."

They said nothing, both glaring at her.

"Would you at least tell me where you're taking me?" Her heart was thumping. She knew she had been caught. She thought the plan would work great because only a few even knew it was her idea to conduct the census at lunch break.

"We've been ordered to take you to the brig, ma'am."

"What? For what?"

"Dr. Reid," said the shorter of the two, although he was still two inches over her, and she was nearly six feet. "Please don't ask us any questions. We have a job to do. Someone will check in with you regarding the reasons why you're in the brig."

"Just wanted to know what rights I have."

"Dr. Reid, you should know by now that you have no rights. So I'm asking you one last time to be quiet."

She may have been stubborn as a mule, but she wasn't stupid. She didn't say another word.

A couple floors below Residences was the brig. It was a small prison, with about thirty jail cells, almost half-filled. But unlike what she suspected of most pre-Event jails, this one looked fairly clean. They walked past several of the cells, and she prepared for the indecent catcalls which naturally would come from men who were locked up and now saw a woman parading into their domain. But there wasn't so much as a peep from any of the inmates. In fact, the prison was so quiet, it was downright eerie. They must be scared about what might happen if they spoke up. *Note to self: say nothing!*

They stopped at her cell and she took note of the number. *Oh, great, lucky 13.* She stepped in without a complaint then the larger of the two guards closed the cell and both left her.

She thought about all she did and said. She was very careful about everything. Where had she messed up? Glancing up, she saw a man standing in front of her cell, watching her. He set down the chair in his hands, positioned it precisely facing her and sat.

"Dr. Reid, I am Lunder Gufstafson, Security Director for Bios-2. Do you know why you are here?"

Oh crap, here it comes. You committed insurrection. You're a traitor. You're getting the death penalty. "Ah no, I'm afraid I don't."

"Come on, Dr. Reid, make it easy on yourself; admit to it and I promise we'll go easy on you."

"Okay, fine. I'm sorry. I knew it was wrong. But, I can't help it…"

"It's tough being separated from your husband, isn't it?"

"Ah… Yes," she stuttered, forcing herself to not say anything further which might betray her.

"Well, we of course understand why you and your husband would break the rules and find ways to be together."

Oh, thank God, that's what he's talking about.

"But, rules are rules, and we have to make an example out of anyone breaking the rules. So you are going to stay here for another few hours to give you time to contemplate the consequences of your actions. Then you will go home to your husband tonight. You will remain together as long as you don't break any more rules. Do we have an agreement?"

"Yes, that seems fair." Her heart galloped with a mixture of anxiety and excitement.

"Good. It's settled then." He stood up and grabbed the chair, but before walking away, he leaned into the bars and spoke softly. "And one more thing?"

"Yes?" Her heart skipped a few beats.

"No more stirring the pot among your fellow scientists. We're not kidding around with this one. If you're caught doing it again, ve vill expel you. You think it's tough here because ve have rules, but it's far worse out there." His accent often came out when he was being a hard-ass. "There" sounded like "zair."

Her heart was pounding. They had her dead to rights and there was nothing she could do about it.

"Finally, my boss, Mr. Westerling, would like to meet with you two personally at sunrise tomorrow. Just go to the top floor of the tower. Do you know how to get to the tower?"

"Ye-yes." Her head was throbbing.

"Good. And Dr. Reid?" Lunder said, again leaning forward like he had a secret to tell; one that involved her.

She felt nauseated, ready to vomit. "Yes?"

"Get some sleep tonight. Tomorrow is a big day for you both."

7.

Outside Bios-2

"I believe we're almost there, Teacher," John offered as he led them through a forest of mostly half-dead pines and aspens.

"John, this is good news. We will be patient," the Teacher reassured him, only a few steps behind. More than a dozen others surrounded the Teacher, wearing robes which had once been pure white, now soiled from their long journey. They listened attentively, waiting for more words. When they were sure that was all he had to say, two of the apostles, elected to that purpose, slowed from the pack and waited for the first cluster behind them to catch up. They spread the Teacher's message to a few of that group. "We're almost there. Be patient." The two apostles in their gray-white robes then raced to catch back up with the others and wait for the next Teacher proclamation. The message traveled to all in the cluster and from it, three or four held back to spread it to the next cluster, and so on, until all two thousand followers heard the same message. This was their message-delivery procedure every time the Teacher spoke, every day they traveled.

When the current message made it to a cluster midway through the multitude, a little boy near the front of the group looked up to his father, tugged on his red cloak and asked, "What did the Teacher say?"

Frank ignored him for just a moment, doing his part by telling the man behind him. The boy watched his father, a brawny man of honor within the Teacher's followers. His hair and beard were Santa Claus white, a stark contrast to his red robe, the lower third of which was stained black, like all the robes, from their many miles of walking.

Finally, he lowered his head to see his son's expectant eyes. In a move more graceful than his bulk should have allowed, he hoisted the eight year old into his arms, not slowing his pace with the cluster. As their guard, assigned from the heralded God's Army, his job was to keep them safe and make sure they maintained their pace. "My, my, you're getting big now."

Zachary furrowed his eyebrows and pouted, unhappy that his question wasn't being answered. He pleaded again, "What did he say, Father?"

"He said we've almost arrived at our new home, but we must be patient." His face was so full of joy that even the ugly scar that ran around his neck, just under his chin, looked happy.

Zachary perked up and gazed into his father's loving eyes. "Tell me again about the Teacher and our journey."

"Son, you've heard this a thousand times a thousand."

"I know, but tell it to me again." He loved this story, at least this version, when his father was willing to tell it.

"Okay, fine… It has been a long and hard journey for us, as you know. The Teacher's followers have been walking across the country for almost a full year now and we have suffered many great losses. Almost half of the followers perished at a ranch run by the devil's servants in Illinois—"

"Like Thomas," Zachary broke in, looking somber.

"Yes, Thomas, the Teacher's most trusted servant, was one of those who was taken by these devils, who poured their fire out upon them. Those who survived retreated to be with the Teacher, who was readying his troops to finish off the devils. But at that moment, the Teacher's God sent him a sign; most thought it was just a bright orange nuclear cloud, a sign of a nuclear power plant's destruction— also brought on by the devils in a futile attempt to get the Teacher's followers. But the Teacher knew it was a sign from his God, telling him to move on. The Teacher knew right then that instead of him and his followers, the devils would burn in a fiery hell reserved just for them."

Frank paused to look at his son, who was full of fear, as if he had never heard this part. He hoisted him up a little higher in his arms and held him firmly, enjoying this rare moment. Although he saw his son daily, the women of their cluster watched Zachary while his duties as a soldier took him away. He rarely had the opportunity to spend one-on-one time with the boy.

"But the Teacher and his followers moved on. They weren't running away; they were headed to a special place. A place he was told about in a vision, which was set aside for all of them, a place where they would be safe. So they set out on this long journey to Colorado, to a place called—"

"Shakayda!" the little boy bellowed.

"Yes. But there were many obstacles and many difficult times ahead. After six months, his followers were starving and everyone was filled with doubt, even the Teacher. Then, he was led to a cave by John for some rest and prayer. That was when the Teacher received his new revelation. It was there that the Teacher received the Book. And the Teacher told everyone, 'We are God's children, destined to be gods ourselves. God is within each one of us and as we become closer to our inner god, we become more like him. We are to persevere, in spite of—'"

"What is *per saver*, Father?" Zachary asked, his face scrunched to emphasize his confusion. Kids were so good at overdramatizing things.

"It means that when we struggle, even though it is hard on us, we become stronger and more like God. Each of us, even you my son, will become a god, in control of everything around you. You see, son, everything it is to be human, is also to be godlike."

Zachary thought his father to be the smartest man in the world, almost right there with the Teacher.

Frank continued. "This revelation changed everything, and pretty soon all the followers moved quickly and felt stronger…"

He paused because he could see another message was coming, and this time to just the soldiers in each cluster.

"…and in no time they were here, very close to our destination, that place called Cicada."

"Frank, you're needed up front," said one of the apostles, who continued down the line with this vital message.

"Wait, Father, you didn't tell me how we were found and that you were saved by the Teacher while you were swinging by your neck."

Frank put him down on the ground and said to him, "I'm sorry, Zachary, but I must work now. Stay with your Mommy-Sam here and wait for me, okay?"

"All right," Zachary answered in a whiny voice that he hated.

Frank raced forward, with others coming from the back. Most of the clusters were stopping, aware that something important was going on. Red robe joined red robe, until a sea of red robes washed forward and surrounded John, who delivered their orders.

Later, the troops emerged from the woods, into a large cut through the once dense foliage, onto a long road that took them up to a mesa less than a mile away. There were tents and lean-tos and shanties all around, on and off the road. The makeshift town had sprung up out of nowhere. A small path snaked along the road and through the myriad dwellings on it, along which John led his troops.

They were several hundred strong, all wearing red and all armed with automatic weapons, which they had acquired from a military supply facility along their way here. Marching together, their steps were thunderous and vibrated throughout the land, literally.

The shantytown's occupants poured from their shelters along the road or from the woods to see the source of this commotion. A worried buzz circulated everywhere.

At the forefront of the squatters another group formed, with a single man in front and another man on each side of him. This group was much smaller and looked less organized, but it was still a group of some unity. Most held knives, swords, clubs, and one even had a bow. The two groups marched toward each other until they stopped mere feet from one another and less than half a mile from the mesa, where a walled fortress stood.

"State your business," demanded the leader of the small group, a man wearing an old torn police shirt with a badge dangling precariously from a ripped breast pocket. He stood his place defiantly between the Teacher's soldiers and the walled fortress.

"We are followers of the Teacher, seeking refuge at Cicada," John roared.

"You're seeking what... where?" Police Shirt demanded.

"We want access to that walled city beyond, known as Cicada."

"I will be the one," the man belted out, "who will say whether or not you—"

Two shots echoed off the dead branches of the tree-lined road. Police Shirt jumped, startled by the noise and looked down, thinking he was shot, but he saw no blood. The two men on either side of him fell to the ground. The people, having at first crowded the road without being particularly worried, leapt off, anxious to get away from the slaughter they were sure was coming.

Police Shirt looked back up from his dead men, now visibly shaken. "Wha-what did you say you want?"

"Entrance to Cicada, will you give it? We will not ask again."

Police Shirt thought for a moment, and then said, "I'm not in charge of Bio... I mean Cicada. But it's late and they don't let anyone in this late. Why don't you and your men camp right there," he pointed near to where they had just come out of the woods, "and in the morning, I will see that you get into Cicada."

"Very good," John responded, turned around and walked through his men, who stood and waited for Police Shirt's men to leave. They did moments later, at least knowing they had met a superior army.

John returned to the woods to tell the Teacher that they were here and in the morning, they would have passage to their promised Cicada.

8.

Cicada

The flyer read:

> Rules for Squatters on Cicada Property:
>
> Anyone who comes within 1000 feet of Cicada's walls will be shot dead!
>
> If you have business with Cicada, go to the front gate, no more than two people at any one time.
>
> Our people are to pass freely, whenever they want, on our property, unmolested by any of your people.
>
> If you deviate from any of this, you will be shot dead!

"Maxwell, what the hell is this?" Preston asked, turning the black-and-white print over in his hands like a teacher just handed a single-page term paper from a failing student.

"It's our new policy. We're done with negotiating with the enemy or playing nice. I've made it simple for everyone: *you violate our rules and you're dead.* These people are trespassing on our land, yet we let them stay here, and they're attacking *us*? We're done playing around and putting all I care about at risk."

"So, if Grannie comes within 900 feet of our gate?"

"She's toast!" Max handed a ream of printed flyers to each of the "runners" waiting in Comms reception, where Cicada's only copy machine stood.

Preston looked at the copious use of their copy paper with equal scorn. It wasn't like they could pop down to Staples for more supplies, though he was surprised to see their copy machine still worked. He watched each of the three "runners" take a stack of printed flyers and a roof stapler. Each was escorted out by two guards wearing full combat gear. Three reams, or fifteen hundred pages total, should definitely get the word out. But Preston was worried where this would devolve to; likely, they would be murdering innocents.

After Max handed the last five hundred printed pages to the third runner, who promptly left Comms, he walked with all three teams as far as the south gate, where they exited. From the wall he watched as they fanned out and immediately began posting on trees, on lean-tos, on anything where their flyer could be stapled, and handing out one to every adult they could find. They would do this until all the flyers were gone and then return home. The two guards in each group of three were ordered to shoot any combatant, even if they offered only cross words. Snipers on the south wall and the watchtower were trained on each of the three groups propagating the flyers, providing cover fire if it was needed. It wasn't. Twenty minutes later, all three groups returned without any flyers and without an incident.

Preston preferred to sit out this event alone in his office, drinking a brandy and deliberating what was happening to his boss, Maxwell, and to Cicada. He had never seen Max like this. From the day he was hired over twenty-five years ago, until just after the Event, he noticed Maxwell had a benevolent presence about him that said "calm and in control." His actions were always selfless and helpful to others. That was why Preston had signed on and committed his life to this project. But in the last few years, Max's focus turned to protecting his friends and especially now, in the half a day that he'd been here, he seemed to have forgotten the big picture. It seemed obvious to Preston that Maxwell was definitely more worried about the safety of his people, especially the Kings, than he was at achieving the main goal of finding solutions to what ailed the world.

For almost a year now, the planet had received a daily barrage of coronal mass ejections, inducing electrical current everywhere and shooting all circuitry to hell. They had done a great job shielding themselves from most of each daily solar storm, but as long as the barrages continued, civilization would never be able to rebuild and chaos and violence would reign supreme. His biggest fear was that they would never find an answer and twenty or thirty or more years from now, mankind would be extinct. That was the problem on which their unified minds should be focused, not whether or not some two-bit criminal wanted to break in or whether some friends of Max's from the beach were safe.

He swallowed the last half of his brandy, holding his breath, waiting for the first shot by one of their guards killing some innocent. Instead, he watched the outside door blow in, followed by two scientists, their lab coats flapping as they bounded the stairs. They barged into his office without knocking or asking permission to enter—another sign of the lack of respect he'd been getting since Maxwell and his friends arrived.

"Where is Mr. Thompson?" Dr. Ronald Stoneridge demanded, out of breath and frantic.

"We really need to talk to him," added Dr. Montgomery Merriweather, more composed but equally winded.

This is what disturbed Preston the most. These two scientists, who would have come to see only him a day ago, were now demanding to see his boss. What the hell did Thompson know about Cicada's day-to-day workings? Sure, he may have built the damn thing and used his considerable fortune, but he was never here, instead spending his time at the beach in Mexico; it had been up to Preston to manage, to make and institute policy, to make the hard decisions when society was collapsing right outside their gates. *Then Maxwell shows up and these two nerds demand to see him and not me?* All the while, Maxwell has declared war on all the poor starving SOBs who just need help. What a hypocrite, a Christian that won't help his fellow neighbor.

"Mr. Tanner, we really need to see Mr. Thompson. This is very important. It affects everyone here at Cicada." Dr. Merriweather was insistent.

"Actually, it affects everybody in the world," Stoneridge corrected.

Max could have used a drink, bad. It was a feeling he hadn't had for many years now, not since Basra. He puzzled over where this urge was coming from. Thankfully, he had no time for either drinking or wondering why he wanted one. The runners had returned safely. And now that it was dark, the next phase of his plan was to take place. It would be the one thing that would remove all aggression from the Squatts.

He walked briskly down Cicada's main gravel road, called Russell Avenue, having just thanked the men and women who volunteered for what could have been deadly service. Rather than continuing straight to the watchtower and Operations below, where much of Cicada's arms and a fair amount of its munitions were kept and where Cicada's guards would usually suit up for an operation such as this, he turned right instead. He went around the Research Facility and marched straight up Max's Court to his residence across from the Rec Facility. He didn't have everything there, but he had more than what he and his partner needed to run his planned op quickly and quietly. The primary reason for the alternate prep venue was to avoid the scrutiny of others, especially Preston or the Kings.

He learned from both the Bible and the US military that to effectively control a population, there had to be a respect, which came from fear, which came from the rule of law, which must be policed absolutely by a higher power. This cause and effect was sometimes brutal and misunderstood by others who scrutinized their actions, believing a "kinder, gentler" policy was more humane. But that was always the opinion of a lazy few who were on a winning side. What Preston didn't seem to realize was that they were losing right now. Once he had them back on a winning side, they could argue what was morally right or wrong ad nauseam. Until then, the last thing he wanted was to have to explain himself. Once the results of his policy were visible, Max believed few would complain about it.

What Cicada needed was quick policy execution so that it could immediately reap its benefits and not waste its valuable resources on unnecessary skirmishes. How could his Cicada family work and play under the threat of constant attack? And with some luck, Max hoped they could find out how a hodge-podge group of squatters got their hands on military explosives.

He angled to his residence; cutting across the empty road named after him and approached his small detached home, right next door to an ancient adobe dwelling known as the First House. It had stood long before his great-grandfather added to it a hundred and fifty years ago. Today, it was maintained as a museum and reminder of Cicada's roots. The old mud-adobe building sagged from time and the elements.

Like a real-life demonstration of old vs. new, Max's residence—and many of Cicada's buildings for that matter—was made of a composite concrete block, consisting of a special polymer compound and concrete. The concrete was more for weight than anything else, as the polymer compound was as strong as steel and had an RF of 100 in the walls and ceiling. This construction turned out to be genius when the environment turned into 365 days of summer. Despite the unreliability of their power (and therefore their air conditioning), they mostly stayed cool.

Tom Rogers was already waiting for him by his front door: punctual, just like the military.

"Mr. Thompson." Rogers stood at attention and held his hand out.

"Max, please." Max shook his hand warmly. "Thank you for coming, Tom."

"You're very welcome Mr… Ah, Max," Tom responded and watched Max open his front door and walk in. "Don't we need to suit up at Operations?" he asked.

Max closed the door behind them and turned the deadbolt.

Tom wasn't sure that Max had heard him because he hadn't responded and continued walking to what looked like a bathroom door. Tom figured the man really had to take a leak. Max slid a long key into a lock that looked like overkill for a bathroom and opened the door. The room's lights flickered on.

"We have all we need in here," Max finally answered, beckoning Tom to come in.

"You ain't kidding," Tom said.

Max knew it was a prepper's wet dream: seven fully equipped M4s, a couple AKs, two Mossberg shotguns, multiple handguns with suppressors, grenades, tactical vests and helmets. In the middle of the small room was a table with shelves underneath. These were filled with C4, various comms equipment and ammo.

"Let's get suited up," Max said as he grabbed a vest and tossed it to Tom, "and let's go hunting."

9.
Bios-2

Westerling waited impatiently in front of an innocuous but very secure door marked *B216* and below that *Authorized Personnel Only*. He studied a thick multi-page document, which was heavily annotated and underlined; half of its pages hung by a single staple in the top corner. He reread the main points, not caring at all to decipher the tech-ese that made up most of the report. The result was what he cared about, not the technical reason why it occurred. And the result was not good. But he had a solution.

He closed the pages, rolled them up like a club and clutched them, punctuating his displeasure with a loud sigh. He really didn't care for it down here. Everything sounded hollow and the light was unnatural. Deep down, he felt he'd get sick if he stayed too long. He looked down the short end of the L-shaped hallway to B225 and the doorway to his bunker and winced at the thought of staying there for an extended period of time. If this necessary exercise doesn't take too long, he could get out of here and go topside where he belonged.

An electronic click echoed from the far end of the long side of the L, followed by two sets of boot steps and a large door closing. The boot sounds reverberated louder as they neared his location. As the two men turned the corner and headed his way, he could see that Dr. Carrington Reid was in front of one of his guards. Dr. Reid wore a smirk of confidence crowned by a fedora and an overall attitude of someone who was in control. This, of course, was a façade because Westerling was the only one in control of what happened here. He wanted to enjoy rubbing Reid's nose in his own self-righteousness, but his end purpose was greater. He needed this man, but he didn't want him to know it.

When they arrived, the guard nodded at Westerling, who nodded back. "Thank you, Jones."

"Sir." Jones stood at ease but clearly alert.

"Dr. Reid, I know you know who I am and I know you, so let's get down to why you are here."

Westerling turned and pressed his thumb on a flat-plate above a keypad, and the door instantly clicked its acknowledgement that he was "authorized personnel."

"After you." Westerling motioned Carrington inside and looked at the guard. "Stay here until I return." Jones promptly turned, back to the corner, so he could see down both hallways and stood at attention as Westerling closed the door behind them.

He was about to set into motion a plan that would have a disastrous effect on both their lives.

The first thing Carrington noticed was the humidity. It was sweltering inside, like being covered by a hot, soaking wet wool blanket. Breathing became difficult. As he struggled inhaling, he began to get a sense of the room's cavernous size. It was several stories of concrete-lined walls with massive machinery, some reaching up to and going through the ceiling of the room. Pipes, conduits and giant wires snaked up and down and around the space. Several huge conduits fed into what looked like a steam turbine in the room's center. A similar group of conduits on the other side ran out of his field of view. The walkway they were standing on wrapped around the entire circumference of the chamber. Just in front of them, an opening in the walkway led to a stairwell that went down and around to the next wall, and then opened up onto the bottom floor.

Westerling stopped at the very edge of the walkway, only a small railing separating him from what was at least a hundred-foot drop. Just for a moment, Carrington thought, *It would be so easy...*

"I even know what you're thinking," Westerling said, and Carrington jumped, feeling like he'd been caught, his thoughts somehow exposed. "You'll have ample opportunity to try that, but you'll want to hear what I have to say first."

It was the stifling heat, his sense of vertigo and perhaps the loud rumble of the machinery below that threatened to take hold of him and send him tumbling over; all conspired to knock him out at any moment. He said nothing and continued to stare forward and not down, desperately trying to get a firmer footing.

"Come here and take a look," Westerling said. He waited to say anything more until Reid ambled over; instead, the scientist remained where he was, a few steps back from the railing.

Westerling chortled. "I see, so the larger-than-life Dr. Reid is afraid of heights. This is something I didn't know." He smirked.

Smug bastard. Reid trudged over, not willing to let this man get the better of him.

"What do you want?" Carrington snapped.

He noticed the shaft that ran from the main piece of machinery topside, trying to think of anything but down. It occurred to him that they were right under the tower where this prick had his penthouse overlooking the whole facility. He guessed this must be the main turbine for a geothermal power facility and the tubes were channeling the steam through and away from the turbine.

"You noticed the most central piece of Bios-2. This is our power source. It supplies the almost unlimited supply of power that runs this entire facility. It's what gives us our lights, but even more important, our security. The length of conduit you are looking at, running through the ceiling, powers our EPF that keeps us safe by keeping all the cannibals out."

Carrington couldn't help but be intrigued with the brilliant design of the place. Feeling a little more confident, bolstered by his curiosity, he ventured a glance down the tube running from the shaft in the ceiling to the large turbine below. It hummed smoothly. On the other side of the cavernous room sat what looked like a bank of normal-looking gas generators. *Perhaps backup.*

"I can see you've figured out that our central generator is not powered by the diesel that runs our backup generators, which would be disastrous if it were to fail. Have you figured out how the main generator works and how it powers a small city of our size?"

Westerling obviously had some point to make, so Carrington patiently waited in silence for the conclusion of this insipid exercise.

"Fine, I'll tell you… it's geothermal."

Westerling started walking slowly, using the railing as his guide. "Follow me; I want to show you something."

Carrington reluctantly followed, interested, but still wondering what all of this had to do with him.

Westerling stopped where the walkway and railing elbowed left at the next wall that spanned a hundred feet or so until turning again along the next wall. "You see that?" He pointed to a large opening through the wall at the ground level.

Carrington looked and pointed to a closed door on the next wall, purposely being irritating. "That one?"

"No! There, where the tubes run from the generator into the next room. In there is an ancient volcanic vent that we cored out and tapped when we built this place. The superheated steam is channeled to the turbine you see here, to create our electricity."

"It looks well designed. So what do you need me for?"

"Simple." Westerling thrust at him the annotated document he had been studying earlier and holding the whole time. "Our scientists say we are screwed in a few months if we don't find another source of energy. Here's their report."

"Is your vent running dry?"

"So to speak. They suspect it was the earthquake we had a few months back and that it somehow is causing our aquifer to drain off. Regardless, it's just not outputting enough steam to fuel our generator to keep up with our energy demands. Even with our rationing, it slowly gets worse every month or two."

"Okay, so why me? What do I know about geothermal power?"

"You may not know a lot about geothermal"—

I know a whole lot more than you do, buddy.

—"but you know a lot about solar, and last I checked, the sun seems to be generating a lot of electricity lately. I'm hoping I can convince you to help us figure out what we can build to harness this unlimited energy and supplement or replace our geothermal power."

Carrington hadn't expected this conversation at all. Maybe he had this guy's intentions pegged all wrong. "Okay, fine, let's say I have an idea or two on how to do this. Why would I help those who have separated and imprisoned my wife and me?"

"Okay, we overreached a bit in our tactics—"

"Overreached? Are you kidding me?"

"Have you seen the world we live in right now? It is full of really bad people. Truly, you have no idea how bad these people are. If they were not kept out, they would surely kill each and every last one of us." Westerling carefully considered his next statement. "So here's the deal. We all need to work together, not against each other. I know you don't trust me, and that's expected. But, in reality, you and your wife are free to go at any time."

"You're telling me that Melanie and I could leave right now and you won't stop us?"

"That's correct. But know this: You will die out there, and those cannibals will as surely eat you two as you are standing in front of me. Instead, you could stay here and help us solve this problem. Yes, you will have to live by my rules. And if you do, I promise you that you both will be able to live safe and peaceful lives. Cross my rules, we will kick you out.

"You see this?" Westerling said holding up a picture he pulled from his front pocket, showing a young woman and a child. "It's a picture of my daughter and granddaughter, who live here, same as you and your wife. This was taken a year and a half ago at a house I own on Virginia Beach."

He snuffled and started to tear up rather convincingly. "Since my wife's death, they are the most important people in the world to me. Your wife is equally important to you, Dr. Reid. My men were wrong to separate you two. Two people who love each other should not be apart. When we're done here, you two will be together once more and I promise you that you won't be separated again.

"But there must be some conditions. I need you two to bring the other scientists back on board and have them use their collective efforts to help us all succeed. If you, or any of your scientist friends, don't want to stay, you can leave. Likewise, if you don't want to follow the rules, you'll be asked to leave.

"Finally, before you answer me, I'd like you to come to my office tomorrow morning and take a look at the world you and your wife would have to live in, outside these walls. That's it. Go now to your apartment, be with your wife; talk about what we have talked about. Then, tomorrow morning, I'll send a guard to escort you both to my Observation Tower and I'll show you what you probably won't want to see, but you'll need to see.

"Thank you, Dr. Reid."

Westerling didn't wait for an answer. He walked past Carrington toward the door they had come in.

Before he left, Carrington looked back at the other room and wondered what it was. A security guard stationed in front of the room's entrance looked up at him, a steady contact that seemed to say that he could read Carrington's mind. The guard's look was telling him, "Don't even try it."

When Melanie opened the apartment door, she wasn't exactly sure what she expected to find. She wanted to believe what Gufstafson told her, that she and Carr would be reunited. But she didn't really expect it to happen, assuming the worst instead: it was all a mistake; they found out what she was planning and changed their minds; she was delusional and imagined the whole thing. She became sure that they wouldn't allow Carr and her to be together.

So when the door swung wide to reveal Carrington sitting casually on their sofa in their small living room, working on some project—he was always tinkering with something—it was almost a complete surprise. She dropped the remains of her sack lunch in the entry. "Carr! My God, is that really you?" In just a few long strides, she closed the gap and jumped on top of him.

"You're… crushing… me." He smiled up at her and she backed off of him, sliding onto the couch. "Who did you think it would be in our home?" he asked.

"Is that what this is, our home?"

He dropped the two wires he was carefully holding and looked at her. "Melanie Sinclaire-Reid, our home is wherever we are together."

"Did you get told the same line I did?"

"You mean if we behave ourselves, we are allowed to stay here, but if we don't want to stay, we can leave of our own volition, and if we break the rules we're out? Then yes, I was told pretty much the same thing."

"Do you believe it?" If he did, perhaps she could, too.

"I figured we probably don't have a choice. But, I guess we'll find out a little more tomorrow."

"Yeah, we get to visit his palace in the sky and see for ourselves how bad it is out there." Melanie looked down. She wasn't sure what to believe anymore. The only things she was sure of were that she loved him and she'd do anything for him.

She looked up and saw that he had scribbled a note and pushed it her way. It read "Bugged?"

She lifted her shoulders as if to say, "I don't know." Then she grabbed the pencil and added "So we better be careful."

He nodded.

"What're you building?" she scribbled.

He grabbed the note and scribbled on the back, pushing it back to her.

She flipped it over. "A bomb!"

10.

Outside of Cicada

Max and Tom were almost invisible, walking silently, holding close to the shadows; no easy task, as the shadows constantly danced, being coaxed away by their malicious collaborators, the fiery aurora-filled skies above.

They had a name now and a general location. The Squatts called him Club because he carried a giant club with spikes on its end built to inflict maximum injury on its intended victims. Max pulled this information from an unwilling man who would probably never recover the use of his fingers after the interrogation. A well-placed gun butt to the middle of his hand and the fear of death was all it took before the fellow gave up Club's name and tree of residence. It was a lean-to in the woods with a British flag tied to a tree above it.

They entered the canopy of the thinning pine forest, leaving their shadows behind and finding easy cover in its darkness. The forest floor was thick with dead pine needles, a deep shag carpet of brittle spines crunching under their boots, making their progress less silent. Most of those who lived in the woods—hundreds of them—appeared to be asleep.

Each time they came upon a lean-to or something similar, Max pulled out a plastic flashlight and blasted its light up and down the pole, looking for a Union Jack.

They ran across several of Max's flyers; some were posted on the trees, but most had been discarded on the ground along with so much garbage piling up after a year of living here. The putrid smell of human waste was everywhere. These once-pristine forests were now no more than a dump of trash and humans.

After an unsuccessful hour, they were running out of campsites. So they doubled back and looked for any signs that a flag had once hung on a tree, assuming it must be taken down at night.

They looked again at one of the early lean-tos they had scrutinized, and because they had approached from a different direction, they had missed a piece of fishing line stuck into the bark. It was definitely used for securing something.

Tom was just about to kick over the lean-to when he heard a crackle of pine needles beside him. Pivoting, he saw a thick piece of wood coming down on him. It just grazed Tom's head, his movement surely saving him from death, and hit the tree instead. The truncheon thudded and bounced out of the attacker's hand. Max spun around and fired off a silenced round into the man's leg, not wanting to kill him just yet; it sounded like a small twig breaking and nothing more.

"You shot—" Tom brought the butt of his pistol down hard on the back of the man's head. This didn't knock him out but was effective in quieting him.

The man, known as Club and feared by many, shuddered enough that the bandana he wore as a protective hat slid off his head to the pine needle floor.

Max kneeled down face-to-face with Club and smiled, just slightly. "You were the one who attacked that place over there." He pointed toward Cicada. "And you tossed in the grenade. Good job, by the way; they had it coming to them."

The man wasn't sure whether these two were friend or foe but decided it was better to cooperate. "Ah, yeah… it's those damn scientists; they have food and water and we have nothing," he said, grimacing from the pain.

"I thought so. Now tell me where you got your explosives. We want some to take out that place—maybe we could split the spoils?"

Feeling a little more confident, Club told them, "There's a guy who brought these to me. He leaves me a sign when he's left me a new supply and sometimes instructions about where to hit the fortress."

"Where are the sign and the drop-off points?"

Club hesitated at first, and then gave up his only bargaining chip. "It's always at the same place: a split aspen, like from a lightning bolt, just off the road by the Cicada sign. I'm expecting a delivery tomorrow, just before sunrise. Maybe we could—"

Tom scooped up Club's bandana hat and shoved it into the man's mouth, holding it in place. "Do you need anything else?"

"No, I'm good," Max said.

As the sun broke over the rugged horizon, Beatrice Peters stepped out of her parents' tent to relieve herself. When she looked up from where she'd squatted, she fell back, as if her shock pushed her over. It was Club. He was as dead as anyone she'd seen, and these days, she'd seen lots of dead people. This was certainly ironic being that many of them died at Club's hands. He had even boasted last night about killing one of the people from the fortress on the hill.

She scuttled back a little, pulled up her pants and stood; she wanted to make sure what she saw was real, scrutinizing every hair and twig. And the knife. Club was strung up in the tree that made up his lean-to. His tongue was dangling out of his slack jaw, and his eyes were swollen in a permanent state of terror, forever staring into the ground. His hunting knife was sticking out of his chest. It pinned a bloody white piece of paper with words on it, as if he were some sort of community billboard. She recognized it as one of the flyers those men handed out yesterday, but someone had scrawled on it with a finger, using Club's blood: "G U I L T Y"

At long last, she screamed.

Squatters poured out of their tents, cardboard boxes and lean-tos. Within minutes, all received the message.

Bill King turned over again in his new bed, eyes wide open, thinking about the last twenty-four hours. He rose quietly, careful to not disturb Lisa, who was still unconscious from fatigue—they dealt with stress differently. He was exhausted still, but he couldn't sleep any longer. He threw on some clothes and left the Residence building, intending to go for a walk and to find Max. He had something he wanted to say to him.

It was that windless time, just before sunrise when everything was quiet and everyone was asleep, except for the auroras churning overhead, as they did every evening ever since the Event.

He stopped by Comms to see if Max was there.

Just inside, he found Webber—his Cubs hat permanently mounted to his head—and somebody else he didn't know. They were sitting in two of the comfy chairs playing cards.

"Hey there, Bill," Webber called out to him. "Care to join us vampires for a game of cards? If you do, you'll have to watch this guy. Like all Dodgers fans, he cheats."

"Hi, Bill, I'm Ray Johnson. Don't mind Webs, he's just saying that because he's gotten tired of losing like all Cubs fans."

"Hi, Ray, I'm Bill King…" Bill didn't really feel like socializing, after all. "Thanks, guys, I think I'll pass. Maybe next time… and Webs, we'll gang up, two to one."

"Ha, there you go; another suffering Cubs fan to keep you company," Johnson chuckled.

They both waved to Bill as he slipped out.

Outside the perimeter fence, Bill saw movement on the north wall by the damaged gate they had arrived through only yesterday. It was already mostly repaired, a miraculous feat since the explosion had twisted it and its hinges so badly. He didn't know why, but he felt an urge to be up on the wall and see the other side.

Working his way toward the northern wall stairs, he looked up and saw the man everyone called Shingles looking down on him, waving. Bill waved back. Magdalena told him that they called him that because he was always standing on some soaring roost somewhere: in the tower, on the wall, or on one of the roofs, like a roof-shingle. She couldn't ever remember seeing him on the ground.

His footsteps were crunching loudly on the gravel; he was aware of being exposed and visible in the light. He needed time to sort out his thoughts. The wall's peak beckoned him like a mountaintop needing to be climbed.

A piece of paper caught his eye, and he recognized it as one of Max's *You-Approach-You-Die* flyers. At least that's what Preston called them, and the policy had been the subject of everyone's conversation last night at the Rec Facility.

Bill ascended the long stairwell, taking two steps at a time.

Most were shocked about this flyer and its implications, but not so much Bill. He had witnessed Max in these situations firsthand and knew how he operated; like just before Max was abducted in Rocky Point, when he assigned Bill the task of killing the chief drug lord from a thousand meters away. It was awful, but it was necessary. Likewise, this action of Max's was forced upon the people of Cicada by these squatters who had no right to be here. Yes, they were starving, but if Cicada didn't do what it was supposed to, the whole world would eventually starve. And that might mean the end of humanity. As the saying goes, desperate times require desperate measures. He supported his friend in his decision. He just wanted to tell him.

Bill reached the top, panting. He had to brace himself so that he wouldn't stumble; that wasn't good at this height.

Wow, what a view.

"Morning," said a guard behind him, making him jump a little.

"Morning." Bill returned the sentiment. Not wanting a conversation, he said nothing further.

"Interesting development, huh?" said the guard, gesturing at Bill's right hand.

Bill was surprised to see that he still had the flyer clutched in it. "Ah, yeah, it is," Bill said. He definitely didn't feel like talking.

"You probably shouldn't be up here because it's not really safe. Mr. Thompson wouldn't like it," the guard—Bill wished he could remember his name—said in a quiet voice; no doubt part of that "keep Bill safe" thing. Perhaps he was right. Someone could shoot a person up here from below pretty easily.

A distant scream drew their attention toward the tree line.

Bill wasn't sure if his eyes had finally fully adjusted or if they had only now made themselves known, but he saw two figures coming up the hill, toward their gate. They were dressed in black and were almost invisible. This was obviously purposeful. The two figures looked up to them and flashed a signal, and the guard beside him turned and flashed a signal to Shingles in the tower. A large *clunk* vibrated below their feet and the gate opened slightly. Inside the wall, two other men pulled on the massive door to open it. The two figures on the other side waited, silent, but at ease.

One of the two figures in black looked back up at Bill and flashed a thumbs-up sign. *This must be Max.* Bill was shocked that he was outside, dressed like he was on a military mission or something.

Another two figures approached from the bottom of the hill. Bill could see by their shapes it was a woman and a man. The man was moving ahead of the woman, with his hand out. "Excuse me, sirs…" Bill could barely hear the beggar's plea.

The men in black spun around and pointed their weapons on the approaching couple, startled.

"Do not take another step or you will be shot," one of the two men in black demanded. *That was Max.*

Still the man approached, his hand extended. "We don't mean any harm; we just need some food. Please, would you help us?"

"Sir, you will not be asked again," the other man in black said. Bill didn't recognize him.

"But, all we want is food." The man kept moving.

The female behind him was fiddling with something as she followed the man up the hill, and then she released something from its coverings.

Both Max and the other man fired several times; their reports echoed off the walls and rolled down the valley below, like ripples in a lake after several stones were tossed in.

The man and woman were slumped over in their places, begging no more.

Bill dropped the flyer he was clutching and headed down the stairs. Sleep couldn't come fast enough for him now.

11.

Outside Bios-2

"Teacher!" John barked, waking him. The early morning air hung on them, just above a layer of sweat. He lifted his tired frame up in the bed he now shared with a naked woman taken from the village by one of his men. It was still dark, so he couldn't see what she looked like, but he remembered her dirty beauty. She was a pleasant enough diversion, but he found her less enjoyable from all the drugs they forced into her to make her compliant. He found those who were willing to serve him without the aid of drugs to be much more pleasurable.

"Teacher, please come. We need you now." John was unrelenting, just outside his sleeping chamber.

He swung his legs over the woman, pushed himself around her and stepped onto the carpeted ground two inches below. He grabbed his red robe and threw it over his nude form, first admiring himself. The walking these many months had not only been cleansing; it had made him physically stronger, leaner.

He ducked through the curtain that separated his sleeping chamber from the entry room of his very large two-room tent and found John with several of his men, standing over four other men on their knees. One of the four kneeling men wore a long, scruffy beard that looked like it was started years before the Event. He wore a police shirt with a police badge, and below the tarnished emblem was a nametag that said *Chen* even though the man sporting it looked more like a Jones or a Smith. Like the other three, he was bloodied, apparently from having been roughly handled by the Teacher's men. They must have had a reason.

"Teacher, I am sorry to wake you at this ungodly hour, but it was necessary. As you guessed last evening, this group's offer for us to rest was a ploy. Several of us, as you recommended, waited and surprised these men who were approaching our camp with the intention of attacking us while we slept. This"—John pushed the man in the police shirt—"is their leader."

"What do you have to say for yourself?" the Teacher demanded.

"I did nothing," Chen said. He lifted his shoulders upright but said nothing more.

The Teacher pulled the sash to his robe tighter and approached the man. "So, have you made arrangements with Cicada to let us in?"

"What? What the fu—"

John brought his rifle butt into the side of his head, knocking Chen to the carpet.

"You told my man here yesterday that you would talk to the ruler of Cicada, who would let us in this morning. Is that not true?"

Chen looked up. His eyes fluttered, dazed and far less prideful than a moment before. "What is Cicada? Oh, you mean the castle on the hill. Yeah, of course you're welcome to go in," Chen said and smiled, showing off brown, crusty teeth through his filthy beard.

"Ralph, please step forward." One of the men wearing a red robe walked around the group and knelt down. "Do you see this?" Ralph opened his mouth wide, showing a large space where there should have been a tongue. Chen's face contorted in confusion quickly followed by disgust.

The Teacher continued, "This is one of my most trusted men.

But a while ago, he told a lie to John here, also one of my most trusted men."

The Teacher strode to a chair placed in front of the captives, sat down and crossed his legs. "Our book says: *It is better to pluck out a man's eye caught lusting upon another's wife than lose the whole man to his sin; it is better to cut off his hand caught stealing than lose the whole man to his sin; and if a man lies, it is better to pluck out his tongue than lose the whole man to his sin.* You have been caught lying to us. You will now face your punishment."

Realization hit Chen like a bullet and he started to beg. "No, please. I'll get you into Shakonda. I'll do whatever you wan—" One of the guards dragged him out by his feet, heedless of his screams.

When they had left, the Teacher looked at the other three men on their knees. They had understandably become much more agitated. The scruffiest of their bunch, his torn clothes caked with dirt and other foulness, said, "I'll tell you whatever you want." He bowed to the Teacher.

"Good, son. What is the name of the castle on the hill?"

"They call it Bios Two. But you don't want to go there demanding anything or they will cut you down with their ray guns. You can go to their front gate, if you're not carrying guns, and ask to speak to them."

The Teacher looked into his eyes, as if he were trying to send his thoughts to him. He said calmly, "Thank you for your help, son. Because you answered truthfully, I promise you will not suffer." Then to John, "Take them and set up the display so that our new friends at Bios Two can see it. How long until sunrise?"

John looked up into the air, thinking. "Less than an hour, Teacher."

"You'd best be going then." The Teacher stood and returned to his sleeping chamber; he had a need to attend to. As he slipped through the curtain, he let his robe slide onto the floor and hopped onto his bed. He was filled with anticipation.

12.
Bios-2

It really is quite impressive, Melanie mused to herself as Westerling and Lunder spoke glowingly to her and Carrington about Bios-2 from this lofty perch. Westerling's office was entirely grotesque. It was gigantic, air-conditioned, full of plush furniture and looked out on a dying world through floor-to-ceiling windows. It reminded her of Gordon Gekko's ostentatious office in *Wall Street*, and Westerling was, in many ways, a carbon copy of Gekko: just a little too slick and seemingly in it for himself.

Carrington and Melanie had spoken last night after making love. They would be careful around these two men and not trust them. Even if the senator and Lunder were speaking the truth, which neither she nor Carr believed, they should never forget that they were forcibly separated, and she was placed under the watch of an armed guard for over a month. They had never been able to leave. They *had* been prisoners, even if Westerling and his security director tried to say otherwise. No matter what they said, it was never acceptable.

"You can see all of Bios-2 from here," Westerling bragged, a stinky cigar stuck in his mouth. "We built this place always with safety in mind, always to protect the men and women who work here."

Mel and Carr held hands and gazed upon the impressive sight of this mini-city on top of a Colorado mesa. The entire property was surrounded by a giant oval-shaped wall of block, topped with barbed wire and the tower they were in near the middle. The streets were a gray-white, the faux marble starting to darken in the short year since the apocalypse. But otherwise, the buildings and the city looked striking, without a doubt. Over the wall was a desolate world, somewhat obscured by a constant force field.

"As you know, from this tower we generate the force field that provides a barrier around this place so the natives cannot shoot bullets or arrows or toss stones at us. Now, let me show you what we have to deal with every day." Westerling walked to the opposite wall, mostly made of glass, separating his office from a conference room. Its only breach was a set of thick glass doors. He pulled on one of the two, putting his whole body into it, and then held it for the others.

Melanie and Carrington walked in, followed by the other two, as all moved to the window-wall that looked out at the other half of Bios-2 and the shantytown beyond their main gate. It wasn't so much of a town as hodge-podge clusters of tents, canopies, cardboard boxes and piled debris. It looked like a third-world country's poorest city. Melanie guessed that this was probably a common sight throughout what remained of America. Hundreds of people lived right outside their walls, struggling to survive, waiting for handouts from Bios-2 that would never come.

About a half mile away, a large cluster of people surrounded a raised platform where four men stood, bound to posts.

"What's going on there?" Carrington asked.

Melanie felt someone bump her shoulder and realized that Lunder had brought binoculars and handed one to each of them. She raised them to her eyes and focused on the platform. Two men, dressed in red robes, stood on each end of the platform, each with a military rifle slung around his neck, obviously ready to use them if provoked.

A single-file line of a dozen or so other men walked toward the platform from the back. One man, who wore a bright white robe, hopped up onto the platform and thrust his hands into the air, apparently to quiet the crowd, although the observers couldn't hear anything.

Lunder slipped out without them noticing and flipped off the EPF. The platform, its actors and its audience were at once brighter and more clear, like a giant set of stage lights were powered on.

"Is this display for us?" Melanie asked without averting her eyes. Almost as if in answer, the speakers in the room crackled and then static buzzed in the room. A voice crackled through the static.

"People, these men are yours, but they attempted to kill me and my men, so they shall pay. But first, you must get a foretaste of the justice that we serve, because our justice will be your master. For our book says, *thou may walk in the Valley of Death, but you shall fear no evil; for thine laws comfort me.*"

Melanie looked over to Lunder and saw that he was aiming at the platform what looked like a gun with a parabolic dish attached to its end.

The man in white walked over to a man in a police shirt with a police badge dangling from a pocket. He was bloodied, like he had been knocked around a bit. Now there were more men on the platform, all wearing bright crimson robes. Each seemed to sport a physical reminder that they had been through their own personal hell: two were missing arms, two had eye patches and she could have sworn one was missing his tongue, as his mouth hung open like his jaw wouldn't close.

"This man," he proclaimed as he pointed to the man in the police shirt, "broke a simple law. He lied to us. Our book says, *if a man lies, it is better to pluck out his tongue than lose the whole man to his sin.*"

Two men approached Police Shirt on either side of him and held his head to the post with gloved hands; his terror-filled screams could be heard even though the dish was pointed at the leader on the opposite end of the platform. Another man approached Police Shirt, holding a hook in one hand and a knife in another. The two men on either side pried his mouth open. The man with the hook and knife was swift. Smooth as oil, he hooked the man's tongue, pulled it out taut, sliced it and held it over his head for the screaming throng to see.

Melanie's stomach turned, and she tried to shut out the blood and muffled screams by closing her eyes.

"Can't you do anything about this?" Carrington begged.

"Why should we?" Lunder answered. "This is how savages deal with one of their own. Continue looking."

Melanie looked up again and saw Police Shirt writhing in pain, his hands bound behind him around the post. Each time he screamed, a gush of blood squirted out into the crowd, which stepped further back. The men in robes, except the speaker who stayed on the opposite corner of the stage, exited toward Bios-2, marched a few paces and then turned and aimed their rifles at the men.

The nearby crowd scattered like roaches.

The man in the bright white robe bellowed, "I will execute terrible vengeance against them and punish them in my wrath. They will know that I am a god."

All four slumped over, blood welling from bullet holes, still held to the posts by their bindings.

"Any of you who commit any sins against me or my men will be dealt with as harshly as these men." He jumped down from the platform and strode to his encampment in the trees, followed by the men in red.

"You see, that is life outside of these walls." Westerling was staring at Carrington and Melanie each clutching the other. "But in here you have safety. Please see that the other scientists hear the message."

13.

Bios-2

"They may be lying through their teeth, but I don't see any other option." Melanie looked up from beneath her wide-brimmed straw hat, lined for solar protection, and gazed at Carrington standing in front of her with his fedora tilted back, trying to read him. They had been standing outside the Recreational Facility for quite a while, letting the shock of the brutal quadruple murder wear off. God knows they had seen their share of death firsthand; hell, she had taken a few lives on her own. But they deserved it, and she'd done it only to gain her freedom.

At the root of the murders they saw today was evil: that same evil she had seen in Texas, then in Laramie, and now here. It was an evil that seemed to be in every man's and woman's heart. She felt that same evil when she took those lives. She remembered being shocked by the joy that came of taking revenge on those men who raped and imprisoned her. Oh, she'd seen evil in some of the men in this place. But it had rules to at least keep that in check. And by operating in community, they were working for a common purpose, a common good, rather than for selfish ends. Not so outside their walls, where that evil possessed everyone, like some sort of virus. And without accountability to God or the law, that virus turned men into monsters. Likewise, without the strong hand of Westerling, the same thing would happen here.

She saw a couple of the scientists she was supposed to meet with right about then hurry by. One glanced at Melanie suspiciously, probably wondering why she wasn't inside yet. "You and I might be able to survive out there, but the rest of the scientists, those who would follow us… I just don't think so." Melanie squeezed Carrington's hand so tight hers was turning white under the long cuffs of her sun-protection robe.

"Tell them to stay then." He smiled a determined smile, as if the decision had been made. But that's the way it was with Carrington; he would consider all the facts and when it was time, he would render a decision. Then he wouldn't second-guess it, unless some new set of facts came in. That made him a rock for her and was one of the many reasons she loved him so much. "We're together, and that's most important. The world may crumble around us, but we'll have each other. You need to go now and tell them your conclusion; they're waiting for you."

She knew he was right. She had made her decision, too. It was the same as his: They would stay and survive.

He kissed her softly but quickly, let go of her hand and walked away, knowing that she would procrastinate further if he stayed. She needed to convince them why her decision was best for everyone. But that also meant getting to the meeting in a timely fashion.

"Carr?" Melanie pleaded. He looked back. "I love you," she said before she marched into the lunchroom to try her best to convince them they had been all wrong—she and Carrington included—and now they needed to stay and be good servants to this community, even if Westerling was its leader. *I should probably start with Rush,* she reasoned; he was their go-to and had been for some time.

Carrington had his own near-impossible job to do. He was now responsible for coming up with an alternate plan to generate enough energy to power this entire place because the current geothermal system was failing; the report Westerling had given him from his science staff confirmed this. But something didn't feel right, and he needed more information to be able figure out why.

Westerling would soon be expecting plans for an electrostatic generation plant that used all CME-induced current from the sun's daily emissions. For whatever reason, their permanence was un-abating. He told her that he already knew what such a plant might look like, but it was reasonable for him to study what they had first so he could design around it. In truth, he wanted to see firsthand what was going on with Bios-2's power generation, see why he felt something was... off. Maybe it was because he knew he had to go back into that room and deal with his vertigo. Maybe he was afraid of being caught. Whatever reason, he was nervous as hell about what he was going to do next.

Carrington stood in the middle of the vast room and took it all in, from the ceiling and then back down. He followed the steam pipes from the open chamber, called the *Shaft Room*, where the steam came up from the geothermal reservoir through a filter system to the steam turbine in the middle of this room. Another set of pipes ran from the turbine and out, presumably to a condenser that cooled it, and then back down into the aquifer. He assumed the other room—the one he couldn't see but pointed at yesterday—was for cooling. Except that it was guarded and locked up; this had to mean something. He walked in that direction.

"Excuse me, you can't be down here," said a voice of authority from behind him. It was one of the guards.

Carrington's heart skipped a beat, but he took a breath and stated, "I'm Dr. Carrington Reid; Mr. Westerling has tasked me to work here on a project of his. I'm doing my research, under his authority."

"Wait here," the guard commanded as he pulled out his portable and made a call.

Within a few seconds, the guard was saying, "Yes sir, Mr. Gufstafson. I'll tell him, sir. Thank you. Sir? Right now, my replacement won't be down for shift change for another twenty minutes or so. Okay sir, I'll be right there." He stuck his radio back on his belt and said to Carrington, "You are cleared to do your work, Dr. Reid. You are welcome to go anywhere, except that room." Of course, "that room" was the locked room Carrington was headed for. "I have to go topside, but my replacement will be here right away." He trotted toward and then up the stairwell.

Carrington waited, walking around the main turbine, pretending to examine it. While he did this, he watched to confirm when the lone guard was gone and to make sure no one else was watching. After the guard slipped out, Carrington dashed to the entrance of the mystery room—the one he wasn't allowed to see.

"So you're giving in to them?" asked Sanchez. He was a bony computer nerd and not someone who would do well with cannibals lurking about.

"I'm giving into our condition," Melanie argued, trying to put as much passion as she could into what she said. But she hated politics, and she especially hated not being true to her heart; her heart said this was wrong because the people who ran this place were not good people. She tried to look at life as a math problem, and with math there was no wiggle room, although Carrington did a much better job of this. Her father said it best: "Life is what it is, and the rest is bullshit." She explained to them that this facility was their best chance at survival while society didn't exist outside of their walls and cannibals were allowed to run around unchecked. Furthermore, as long as the sun was bearing down on them so hard, killing the very cells of every living thing... All these factors made their decision pretty easy, even if they didn't like it. They would all survive together or die apart.

"Yeah, why are you singing a different tune now? Did you get something that you're not telling us?" That was Babinski. He was a prick, although a damned brilliant prick.

"Look, guys"—the only two women in the room looked at her sternly—"and gals. You didn't see what we saw; we watched four men get murdered in public. No, executed. Their dead bodies are still tied to poles, on display. It was a message to their people as well as to us. But, it's worse than that. From what I understand, their bodies will be gone by tomorrow morning, thanks to the many cannibals outside who will eat them..." She let this ferment with them. "Is that really the kind of place you're desperate to go to?"

A few heads shook.

"Me neither. We're not asking you to believe everything we're being told, but I believe that Bios-2 is our best chance of survival. Westerling and Lunder and the rest need us as much as we need them."

"But how do we know that they will do what they say?" Babinski continued his rant.

Melanie closed her eyes and hoped Carr was having more luck with his challenge.

Carrington ran into a brick wall of a guard at the entrance of the mystery room: they were all physical specimens, but this man was a towering hulk who must have been fed a diet of only meat and steroids. He appeared strikingly like a certain green comic-book character, only a bit more flesh-toned.

"This area is restricted," said the guard, in a higher pitched voice than expected.

"Oh, sorry. I'm Dr. Carrington Reid. I'm working on a project for Mr. Westerling. I need to get in here."

"Unless you get approval from Mr. Westerling and I have that approval in writing, you cannot go in there. No one is allowed in there," he said, solid as the building around them.

Another scientist in a lab coat walked past Carrington and said, "Hi, Harry. I'm just running a couple tests. I'll be out in ten minutes." He marched to the door's thumbprint access panel. Almost as quickly as he put his thumb on the pad, the door clicked open and he breezed in like he was walking into the public dining area to get water.

"No problem, Dr. Tenaka. We'll see you in ten," Harry said with a smile that morphed into a sneer when he glared back down at Dr. Reid.

Carrington tried to remember Dr. Tenaka. *That's right*, he thought. He's a nuclear physicist who kept to himself mostly, and until now, Carrington had no idea where Tenaka worked. *So, what was a nuclear physicist doing in a geothermal production plant?* And why wasn't Carrington asked to work with him? Something felt very wrong and he had to figure it out.

"Dr. Reid?" Harry called.

"Yes."

"If there's nothing else, get back to work."

He had a plan, but he wanted to run it by Melanie first. It was very risky and he wanted to make sure she was okay with it. If his suspicions were correct, it would be worth the risk.

"Yes, I'll get that approval from Mr. Westerling." He headed up the stairs, one step at a time. Each step lifted his level of anxiety.

14.
Cicada

"Come in," Max hollered at his front door. The pretense of this being his sanctuary was already gone. He downed the tequila, his first shot in many years, and felt it warm and burn his gut; it was the desired effect.

The morning's light burst through his front door, as if Helios crashed his chariot right there, setting fire to the earth and depositing Magdalena. She tentatively stepped in, with light appearing to seep from her pores.

Halting momentarily at the pictures on the wall, just long enough for them to register, she was visible from the living room. "Max?" she called out, not seeing him.

"Hi, Magdalena. I'm back here," Max said softly from the murky rear of the room.

"Why are you in the—"

A click, and a rush of sunlight spilled from the blinds behind Max. He sat at a desk, empty except for a computer monitor on one side and a tequila bottle and a shot glass on the other.

He rose, grabbed both bottle and glass and seized another glass from a bookshelf as he ambled over to her.

As he plopped into one end of the living room couch, a cloud of dust billowed up like a thousand little pinpricks dancing in the beams of the morning light shooting through the open door. He cursed himself for not letting someone in to clean this place in the couple years since he had last been here. He beckoned her to the other end and poured tequila into both glasses.

She accepted the glass. "Thanks, but—"

Max held up his hand. "Please, just one toast."

"Okay, then what shall we toast to?"

"Safety, or being alive, or"—he thought for a moment—"or how about to you for making it here, or hell, I don't care, let's just have a drink."

"I didn't think you drank."

"I don't, but I found lots of good reasons to have one today."

"Okay, let's toast to safety then." Magdalena extended her glass to Max's.

"To safety." He clinked her glass and drank his shot down in one gulp as she watched and took a sip. "It really is good to see you." Max smiled and poured another drink and held out the bottle to her.

She shook her head and took another small sip.

They sat quietly and without any awkwardness. He studied her and immediately realized she was more beautiful than he had remembered when he came to her aid in Mexico; also, she was older. Maybe it was because she looked similar to his beloved Fatima, and he wanted her to be unattainable, and therefore too young. Plus, she had been on her way to Cicada and he was off to find the Kings. Or maybe it was just the stress of surviving the ongoing apocalypse that made her look older.

But it wasn't stress. Her face carried the visible signs of someone who was in her thirties, not barely twenty, as he had assumed. The delightful lines around her eyes and the soft contours around her lips were of a woman and not the girl he had told himself she was.

Besides her age, Max had two revelations about Magdalena right then, sitting with her on his sofa. She didn't really look like Fatima. Magdalena looked like her own person: strong, wise and beautiful in her own way. He also realized at that moment that he could love her.

He was beaming, feeling the warm glow of the happiness that could be his.

Then the burden of his thoughts crashed back on him, crushing his momentary joy. He would have to worry about one more person at a time and place where he had little control.

Like a reflection of his mood, the sun hid behind a giant cloud, and just as quickly, the brightness faded from the room and from him.

She fidgeted in her seat, breaking his thoughts. She had something to say but seemed hesitant to speak.

"Are you okay?" she asked as she watched him drink another shot down as if it were water.

He didn't answer. Okay? Of course he wasn't okay. He had just executed a man and then gunned down two more innocents, all in the name of safety for Cicada and the people he cared about. He was again becoming that same person he had been in Basra. Yet, if he didn't do what he had to do, Cicada would eventually fall into the hands of the barbarians outside, who were receiving military-grade equipment from some outside source. Tom and he confirmed this when they swung by the split aspen and found the package of explosives waiting for the man who would never use them.

No, he was not okay. Worse, he was beginning to believe that this was his penance for past misdeeds; he had to be the protector of this place, regardless of what the future held. And he certainly couldn't open himself to the love of another woman.

"Yeah, I'm fine." He poured himself another drink.

There was a rapid bang on the doorframe followed by "Mr.

Thompson, are you in?" through the wide-open door.

She put her glass down and bounded up. "I'm going to go. Thanks for the drink."

A different voice called from the blazing doorway, the raging morning light still pouring through in torrents. "Mr. Thompson, sorry to bother you, but we really need to talk to you."

"I'll be right there," he yelled. To her, he spoke softly. "Please don't go."

"I think I have to," she faltered. "I don't want to see what happens next. I care about you too much." At the doorway, she stopped and turned to him. "I know you think you need to do whatever it takes to keep everyone safe, but consider the costs. The man I left in Mexico took the time to save several people, even though it meant he'd be delayed in meeting up with his friends and maybe helping them further. I'm not sure what happened to that man. I'd love to sit and talk with *him* for a while." She vanished into the light as the two men burst in.

Max was frozen in place, his shot glass poised at his lips. He held it there; for the first time since opening this old treasured bottle, the tequila's sweetness danced on his nostrils, never fully there, like her. But her words bit harder than the tequila's burn. He had had too much of both.

"Sorry, Mr. Thompson, but this is real important," one of them said. Max put the glass down and looked up at the outlines of two men in lab coats. His thoughts were already muddy from the alcohol and his fatigue made it hard to focus on them in the bright sunlight.

The older and shorter of the two said, "We've figured out why the CMEs never stop!"

15.
Bios-2

Westerling had stolen everything he needed from Cicada: the idea and plans for the Cicada complex, courtesy of one of his most senior people; then some of Thompson's land—seizing it by using a federal statute on grazing; and then just before and after the Event, many of their scientists. Now he wanted the prize, too. He wanted Cicada. It wasn't that he wanted to control the land or their personnel or even their resources anymore. He wanted them to fail.

There were many reasons for this, but the reasons didn't include a need. He didn't *need* them to fail for Bios-2 and therefore his daughter and granddaughter to prosper. It was much more of a want, a desire that gnawed at him, like regret did for most people; he didn't suffer regret. It was probably a pride issue for Westerling, and he had no problem admitting it. Cicada represented the one thing he couldn't yet control in a world in which he controlled so much, and that bothered him. They had control over the Outsiders outside their walls, and the crazy sun-drenched environment around them, but they couldn't control Cicada.

And yet, what bothered the senator most was Maxwell Thompson. Because Cicada was *his*, a hand-me-down from Thompson's great-granddad, along with his fortune, all the while Thompson played on the beach in Mexico.

For all of these reasons Westerling wanted Cicada to go down and he wanted it now. He knew they would eventually fail, but he was tired of waiting. He wanted them taken out and taken out immediately. And now that Thompson was there, he could strike down the two headaches at once. He had asked Lunder to come up with a plan that could be executed within a day or two.

"I'm sorry, sir, but I must disagree with the whole idea. Cicada will fall, and probably sooner than later. Why commit resources to a bold plan when under the current one we don't have to expend many resources at all, and we still get the same result?" The German's hands were flying around so much to make his point, Westerling would have thought he was an Italian with a German accent.

"I don't want to wait. We have them on the ropes. Now is the time to strike. We can take them down and take their resources to replace those we've expended. Plus, we'll get the bonus of maybe getting some more of their scientists. Most of all, I want it because I want to rub a dead Cicada into Thompson's face. Then, all that inheritance and planning will have been worth nothing. That's what I want and I expect you to make it happen."

Lunder realized he would lose this argument, if it was something Westerling really wanted, as he apparently did now. He'd have to follow orders. At least he gave it his best shot, but still prepared for this contingency.

"Okay, sir," he said while unrolling a set of plans on the coffee table. The leather sofa squeaked as he reached over and placed each of their coffee mugs on the first two corners of the plans. The final two points of the plans were held in place with Westerling's cigar ashtray and his own trusty Luger, given to him by his father from the War.

"There," he pointed to the coffee-mug side of the plans, "is our point of penetration. It will take us a while to get enough men through there. But, if we're careful and quiet, we'll take them by surprise. We'll also need to coordinate with our Outsider contact and have them mount an assault at the same time we arrive at their flank, to keep them busy. This should work, sir."

"Excellent. I love the idea. I knew we would use this to our advantage someday. When can we take 'em down?"

"Give me a day to pick our assault team and a day to get there and be ready for the diversion. So, in two days we can strike. It should take about an hour to take out their defenses and then we'll have them."

Westerling's intercom buzzed and he punched the button. "Yes?"

"Sir, there are three men at the front gate, asking to speak to the senator."

"Do we know who they are?"

"They're the ones who executed the leader of our Outsiders this morning."

Westerling took a sip of coffee and smiled at Lunder, who nodded in the affirmative. "Okay, Reynolds, let's give an audience to their leader only. I will only speak to their top leader. I'm counting on you to not waste my time with underlings. Once he's cleared, bring him to my office." Westerling punched the intercom button again, severing the connection.

"Is that wise, sir, bringing a stranger into your office?" Lunder asked, sitting back in the leather couch.

"I want to meet the man who has the huevos to put on today's display. Besides, we may be able to use him and his troops with your plan, if you can speed it up a day."

John, Frank, Stephen and the Teacher stood in front of the towering gate of Bios-2, waiting for the Teacher to be ushered inside. John had taken Frank and Stephen first and demanded an audience with their leader, the one who the settlers here called the Senator. Their request was granted, but this Senator would speak directly with the Teacher and only the Teacher. John didn't like it because it would be so simple for them to kill or hurt the Teacher without them there to protect him. Yet the Teacher insisted, saying he would be protected by his God and to have faith. John relented, as he always did, and so they waited, standing before this massive gate, in their finest red robes. It was their normal procedure to have the warriors wear red and the apostles wear white. Whether they were in battle or negotiating with an enemy, they wore red with the intent of striking fear in their opponents. Plus, their enemy would be less likely to be able to tell the generals from the soldiers with them all wearing the same thing.

Their robes were a gift from God after the Teacher received the Book; they were led to a hotel supply company and took more than a thousand white robes. One of their followers knew how to dye fabrics and made a blood-red dye for most of the robes, holding back fifty white ones. They then added their GA insignia where the hotel's name would have gone. The apostles wore the white as an expression of purity in their belief of the Teacher, and the warriors the red to show that they wore the blood of their enemies like a badge of honor.

A large rumble sounded behind the gate, shaking the very ground on which they stood. Then the gate cracked open, just enough for one man at a time to pass through.

The Teacher looked calm. "John, you and your men wait for me here. I will return shortly with exactly what we want." He then stepped forward and into Bios-2, the gate rumbling closed immediately behind him.

16.
Bios-2

Melanie, led by "Simple" Simon Washington, walked up to the entrance of Westerling's office and the Observation Tower. Simon was no longer watching her, at least that she knew. But he was detailed to their apartment building, where most of the scientists lived. So she asked him to lead her to Westerling's office. She didn't need an escort, but she thought it might still be good to include him. If he scored more comic books because of what she had to say, maybe Simon would be more predisposed to trusting her, and it would be smart to have a friend on the inside.

"Mrs. Melanie Reid to see Senator Westerling," announced Simon through the intercom button. "She has information she wishes to share about her meeting with the scientists." Simon spoke the words exactly as she had coached him.

The thick door buzzed open and she took the lead as they entered. Until now, she hadn't really paid attention to the security features of this entry area. Like much of Bios-2, the whole Observation Tower building was well designed from the beginning. It was entirely shielded against EMPs, as if they had known ahead of time that the Earth's atmosphere would become a raging electrical catastrophe for anything with a closed circuit. What she hadn't noticed, even during their visit earlier this morning to see the public execution, was the high level of security: six guards, the whole-body imaging scanner to pass through the second-tier entry, security cameras and lots of guns. All posed a nearly impenetrable barrier of protection for anyone wishing harm to Operations or Senator Westerling.

Melanie endured another over-the-top pat-down for weapons—in the pre-Event world, it would have been called groping—by a sneering guard, who was then able to see everything he felt in real-time color from the whole-body imager. She had heard some of her images were being floated around by the guards; she guessed this one would be added to their collection soon enough.

She was escorted to the elevator.

Just before the doors closed, she looked back and caught a glimpse of a tall man in a full-length red robe brushing by Simon; it reminded her of a hotel bathrobe but dyed in blood, and rather than bearing a hotel name on the breast, this one said *God's Army*. She knew instantly that this was one of the robed men who had put on the bloody display this morning. But his face was hidden in the shadows of his hood draped over his head. In the moment that passed when she saw him, she thought, *Maybe he doesn't have a face*, and then she saw only his blue, piercing eyes. They glowed like a wild animal's in moonlight. The doors closed and they were gone.

The guard behind her intoned his instructions. "You will sit in the Observation Waiting Room. Senator Westerling has an appointment before you…"

Melanie heard none of this; she saw only those two eyes gazing at her. She felt undressed… exposed. She folded her arms around her chest and hugged herself, trying to apply reason to her disquiet. She didn't know if it was the smug guards and their violations, the stranger in the red robe, or the fact that she was about to turn in several scientists who were not cooperating with their plan to assist— her mind cried out, *You mean 'aid and abet'*—Westerling and

Lunder.

She wished she could have spoken to Carrington again after her meeting with her colleagues, but she knew he was working on Westerling's solar power plan. She would fly solo on this and do what they originally agreed upon.

But it felt wrong. It was more than a feeling; her gut was telling her this was wrong. Telling her she needed to stop and go back. Her gut told her to not go through with this.

The elevator doors slid open and they spilled into the lush entry foyer with Westerling's office door on the right and the Observation Waiting Room on the left. The conference room connected them. There were other chairs in the foyer, but Lunder must have wanted her in the waiting room because she was deposited there by her guard. He released his claw-like grip on her arm and shut the door behind her.

It was a small room with a couple comfortable leather chairs and that same floor-to-ceiling forty-five-degree window, which looked out toward Bios-2's main gate and beyond that, the platform. The four dead men were still on display, like some crazy real-life art exhibit left to rot in the sun's burning heat. She blinked her eyes, as much to remove that image as to mitigate the glare, and then noticed the wall and door that separated this room from the conference room.

She tried the door—it was unlocked—and gingerly stuck her head through, confirming it was empty. She had forgotten how big a room it was; their eyes and minds had been on other things this morning. She was somewhat shocked to see the door to Westerling's office was open, remembering that he had to put his whole body into the heavy door to open it and that it automatically closed from a tension spring. She was about to shut herself back in the waiting room when she heard voices.

"Lunder, let's hold back on the plan to take over Cicada until after we know where we stand with this leader of that giant army outside."

That one word made her freeze. She dropped to her knees, not wanting to be seen but now desperate to hear more. She found a doorjamb by the door and shoved it under the door so it could close most of the way and not be obvious, but remain open enough so she could hear them.

"I was going to ask you about that, sir. I'll put it aside until you give the go command to bring Cicada to its knees."

She quietly hurried to the exit, wanting to get out and tell Carrington about Cicada. *It still exists?* She could hardly believe it, but believe it she did. A peek outside revealed the red-robed guy getting off the elevator with three guards. They strode through the foyer directly to Westerling's office. She shut the door and quietly returned to her listening position by the conference room entrance. Perhaps she could learn more while she waited for a chance to flee.

"Sir," said Lunder, "he's here."

It sounded to her like another door was opened, probably the one to Westerling's office, and then sounds of introduction between Lunder and she guessed the red-robed man, but she couldn't hear well enough. She stuck her head further through the door.

After a few seconds of listening to her staccato heartbeat in her ears, she heard Lunder again. "Sir, this is the Teacher."

"The Teacher, huh. They don't have real names where you come from?" Westerling chided.

"That is what my followers call me, so it is the name I use now," he said in a calm voice. Melanie pictured those eyes, blue and piercing, looking at her. She shuddered.

"I'm Brian Westerling, but you can call me Senator." Scorn dripped from Westerling's voice. "You now have an audience, what do you want?"

"Senator, I will be brief because you appear to be a man who is leading many people. My followers and I only need two things from you: some water and food, and information about Cicada."

Melanie's shoulders were in the way of the door and jamb as she craned her neck further through the crack in the door, desperate to hear what was said next.

"That's three things, actually. Hang on for a moment while I talk to my Security Chief."

A long silence and the fear of being caught made her pull her head back, like a bug going back into its hole, hiding. She heard a conversation in the background.

"I agree to your request," Westerling announced, "but let me show you something first."

Melanie craned her neck back out. Then she saw them coming toward the conference room, and she was so startled, she almost fell backwards. She softly pushed the door nearly closed, the jamb resisting, keeping it open only enough for sounds to get through and scurried back a few steps, out of view.

Westerling's voice now boomed, no longer muffled by the glass wall. "You can see a perfect panorama beyond our city walls right here. We had a great view of your display this morning, as you can see. Walk this way. So that you can understand who is in charge here, I need to show you something. Then, I'll describe our roles here and how we can help each other."

More silence. If she'd been a fly on the wall at least she could've seen what was going on.

"You see your men down there?" asked Lunder.

"Yes, of course," said the Teacher.

"Which is your least senior man?"

"Stephen. Of the three, he is the one furthest away, on our left," the Teacher stated, his voice still calm and resolute. "Why?"

"I want you to see"—it was Westerling now—"just what we are capable of."

Melanie rose only enough from her low crouch to see past an armchair between her and the floor-to-ceiling window. She could see three men in red robes, just like the one the man calling himself Teacher wore. They were alone at the other side of the gate, waiting.

Some activity on the wall to the right of the gate drew her attention. One of the guards, manning one of the five ray guns, swung it toward the farthest of the three robed men. A blinding bolt of electricity blasted in his direction.

She pinched her eyes tightly shut, but it was too late. She knew from working on these damned things that you could not look right at the energy blast or you would be blinded for a minute or two. It was like looking directly at a lightning strike.

When she opened her eyes, she saw only white light and a small patch of her vision. She caught a glimpse, and it was clear enough. The victim was now a blackened smoldering heap, over twenty feet from where he originally stood. She closed her eyes again, waiting for her blindness to pass. She didn't need to know what he looked like. Carrington and she had perfected these awful weapons, an offshoot of the concept of a Taser, shooting an electronic ground into the target at the same time that the lightning bolt was released, ensuring a precise hit on the target. Her contribution was the timing mechanism that enabled the Taser-like dart to hit its target an instant before the bolt.

The results were the same. The target was killed instantly, leaving an almost unrecognizable, torched husk of a human behind. More importantly, those around the victim learned to not screw with Bios-2. What only a few people understood was that these great weapons had only one dart. After that, the bolts of electricity would fly in any direction to the nearest ground. And the electrical charge was limited to maybe two or three more bolts before it was spent and needed to be recharged, which took some time with their limited power supplies. It was mainly a weapon of show. But the show was both awesome and awful.

"You see, Teacher," Westerling continued haughtily, "I chose to let you and your two most senior men live, because of what you can do for me. But I could burn you all to hell if I felt like it."

"Will... will you kindly tell me what you want from us?" asked the Teacher. His words skittered and wavered, his voice frail.

"Your followers will receive the food and water you need, and I will show you where Cicada is located. I'm even going to show you how to take over Cicada and kill everyone there. They have an abundance of food and resources. But you will remain at Cicada. Cicada will be yours to do with as you please. And you will never return here."

Melanie sprang up. Her face drawn, her mouth locked open; she breathed out a long breath. It was far worse than they had suspected. They were being lied to about Bios-2, of course. But she never expected to hear that Cicada was still functioning and its people were alive. When they had first arrived at Bios-2, thinking that they were at Cicada—that's what Carr's invitation showed—they were told that Cicada was dead and that all of the scientists were being diverted to this second facility. They had accepted this because it made sense. But others speculated that Cicada might still be more than a dream, especially after the heavy-handed treatment they all received. Now she knew, Cicada did exist… but for how long? Westerling had just arranged for everyone to be slain and the facility sacked by these red-robed killers. And no one else knew about it.

She had to stop them.

"I agree to your most generous offer."

"Wonderful. Mr. Gufstafson here will show you how to get there and will arrange for enough food for you and your people for your journey there. You should be able to make it by tonight."

She had to leave now.

"I'll be back with you in a couple of minutes, but now I have to attend to another matter." His voice sounded closer.

Melanie dashed for the exit. She leapt through the door and into the elevator. "I'm sorry, but I completely forgot my notes, which the senator needs," she yelled to the guard. "I'll be right back." The door closed. She didn't need to see how the guard responded, and she didn't want to see Westerling.

The senator walked past the conference table to the door to the waiting room. He pushed on it, noticing that it was already slightly ajar, blocked by a doorstop.

"Thank you for waiting, Dr. Reid…"

The room was empty.

17.

Cicada

"Wait!" Max yelled. The two doctors made their announcement and ran out the door without saying anything further. "Hold up!" he hollered through the opening. They stopped.

He was startled when he saw Magdalena had waited outside, apparently equally intrigued by the two scientists spouting craziness. "You're still here," Max mused for just a moment. "Great. Get Preston and bring him to their lab… You know where that is, right?" Nodding, she burst off in the opposite direction.

When Max caught up with Merriweather and Stoneridge, he asked, "So, what's with the CMEs?"

"Follow us to our lab and we'll show you," Monty said, and they both jogged to the side entrance of the Recreational Facility and School, rather than Research, where Max thought all the scientists had their labs. Although both buildings were similar four-story ultra-modern structures, it was Research where, as Max had told his friends during the tour, "most of the magic here happens."

"Your lab is above Rec?" he asked.

Dr. Stoneridge was doubled over at the entry threshold, unable to move, completely out of breath. "No… below… by Library."

Dr. Merriweather was about to open the door, when Max signaled a pause. "Let's hold up for Preston. In the meantime, hello. Doctor Stoneridge, I presume?" Max took the doctor's clammy hand.

"Oh sorry, where are my manners?" he said, recovering from the short run. "Mr. Thompson," he puffed as he shook Max's hand, "Ron is fine, or Dr. Ron. Many seem to like that, but I don't have a preference."

"Okay, Dr. Ron, I'm Max." He turned to the other and said, "Dr. Merriweather, right?"

"Monty; pleasure to officially meet you. Great place you built here."

"Thanks, Monty. And your lab is by the Library rather than in the Research building?"

"Oh, yes, I can see why that's puzzling. It's because of the computer power and the resources for research—we're tapped directly into the Library's servers."

"And the Library's space." Dr. Ron smiled. "I like to go there for a break. Maybe it's just a need for people. And yet it's quiet." He seemed to be composing himself.

"So, is there nothing you can tell me about what you've found while we wait for Preston?"

"It's better if we show you," Dr. Ron said adamantly.

"Fine. Until then, please tell me where you come from and what led you to Cicada." Max really hated small talk, but he wanted to know more about these two men who he was sure were about to rock his world.

She blew into the reception area of Comms and bounded up the stairs to Preston's open office door.

"Hi, Mags," a voice softly slipped out from beyond the partially open door of the dark Comms room.

Magdalena slowed at the doorway, squinting to see inside, but she had just come out of the sunshine and it seemed black as a pre-Event night in there. "Webs, is that you?" She knew it was but didn't expect him. "What are you doing here on your day off?" she asked but still stepped toward Preston's door.

Webber appeared in the doorway. "I was waiting for Sally King. She came in yesterday with Max and his friends. She's a techie from the outside world and showed interest in what we did. She even knew we had Crays." He spoke like a happy child, anxious for his scheduled time to go play in the sandbox.

"It says Cray on the side of each supercomputer," Magdalena said playfully.

"Don't worry, Mags, no one wants to replace you."

She was already in front of Preston's door, but when he said this, she whipped her head back to him, not understanding what he meant. *Funny, I wasn't even thinking that.* She shook her head and resumed her mission, knocking on Preston's door. "Gotta go, Web. Enjoy your new girlfriend." She hid her smile and walked in.

"Mr. Tanner," she offered apologetically, "sorry to bother you, but..." She noticed someone else in the room. "Oh, sorry, Johnson. Please excuse me," she said to both. "I need to borrow Preston Tanner.

"Sorry, sir, but you're needed right now at Dr. Ron and Dr. Merriweather's labs; they're waiting with Max for you. It's very important."

"Johnson, are we good now?" Preston asked, rising from his seat.

"Thank you, sir, we're good now," Johnson replied meekly, much as if he were a puppy who'd just had its nose whacked with a rolled-up paper. Magdalena wondered if Mr. Tanner had tongue-lashed him.

"Let's go," she insisted, and they rushed out of his office. Just before they turned the corner to the stairs, Magdalena caught a glimpse inside the darkened Comms room, the door now closed.

She leapt down the stairs but still mentally chewed on the image. Other than what splashed through the clear door with the fluorescents off and no outside windows to provide illumination, the room, except for the first few feet in and the console, was dark. Webber was sitting alone at his console. It was not uncommon for him to be in the dark; he often told her he liked the solitude and listened to his music on headphones. But he didn't have his headphones on. Instead, he had the large drawer in the console opened—one that was always locked—and from that drawer, Webber was holding what looked like a telephone.

"Have you all met?" Preston asked Max.

"Yes, of course," Monty responded. "Please, Mister… I mean Max, let's go; we need to show you this."

After passing the Library, Monty fiddled with a key to a wood door protected by metal bars. Then they greeted another door, all metal and very solid looking. Dr. Ron stuck his thumb on a flat shiny plate above the door handle. A red light flashed and the door clicked open.

Max didn't remember seeing this on the plans.

Dr. Ron already wore his lab coat, and so he waited for Max, Preston and Magdalena to grab one each out of a closet full of them, and then walked them through a fairly large laboratory.

Two women stood up as they approached. Monty announced, "These are our wives, Stephanie Merriweather and Dr. Betsy

Stoneridge. Ladies, this is Maxwell Thompson." They exchanged quick handshakes. "Both are quite adept in a laboratory and have been instrumental in—"

Dr. Ron, who was standing in front of a set of five computer monitors, some showing line graphs and some a series of numbers, cleared his throat and said loudly, "You see, my specialty is new power generation."

Monty jumped in. "Yeah, you should have seen his last project; it was cutting-edge stuff."

A longhaired Siamese cat rubbed up against Monty's leg; he hoisted him up and they all walked to Dr. Ron.

"A long time ago, before that, I created a fission-type reactor. It was pretty amazing because it generated 1.05 times the energy it consumed." He was looking at them with his back to the monitors, which continued to move, lines being drawn, sequences of numbers being splashed across the screens. It was calculating.

"Wait, you mean a perpetual motion machine?" Max asked, thinking he misheard what was said.

"Yes, I guess you could call it that. It was supposed to be a solution to the problem of efficient energy generation."

"Why haven't I heard about this? This should have changed the world."

Preston remained quiet, listening attentively.

"Well, for a couple of reasons. First, all my research and my lab, including the prototype reactor, were burned in a freak accident and my backups went missing. Second, there was a problem with the device."

"Okay, I'll bite. What was the problem?" Preston chirped in, hands dug in his lab coat's pockets.

"Gamma rays!"

"Gamma rays?" Max asked.

"Yes, I didn't realize it at the time, but the generator produced off-the-charts excessive amounts of gamma radiation. We were lucky to have survived the one and only test we ran. Anyway, when I lost my lab, and subsequently the funding, I abandoned that project, until recently.

"With our current project, we have been testing a new version of this fission reactor, but we've been very careful to monitor gamma ray emissions. One day, we noticed spiked readings even though we knew it couldn't be coming from us. Shingles helped us raise an antenna on the tower and another on the far wall. With these, we were able to triangulate the source of the emissions."

He turned to face the monitor screens and bent over to tap a few commands on the keyboard. One of the two largest screens flashed and then started to resolve a topo map. Max and the rest of them leaned closer to see.

With each second, it became more defined until it was completely clear. "Here," Dr. Ron pointed to a red "X" on the center of the screen at what looked like a large, elevated mesa, "is the origin of the gamma radiation."

"Is that us?" Preston asked.

"No, this is us," Max corrected, still facing Dr. Ron, listening. He had pointed to the lower left corner of the screen, to another mesa that looked similar but was a little smaller.

"So, what could be producing gamma radiation on top of a nearby mesa?" asked Magdalena.

"No, not on top of the mesa," Monty answered. "Inside it."

Preston looked jittery when the topo map first showed, and now he was unquestionably flustered. "So, what does this have to do with our permanent solar storms?"

Max had wondered this too.

"From seismic readings and some research you retrieved from the University of Colorado's computers, that mesa is right over some old volcanic vents, which are believed to be still active. Okay, so some have posited that if enough gamma radiation was released so that it would reach our core, it would damage the magnetosphere. And as we all know, we rely on the magnetosphere to protect us from the sun's damaging rays and plasma. Without it, we would be like…" Dr. Ron searched for the analogy.

"Venus," Monty offered.

"Yes, Venus gets scorched daily by the sun; so much so that even if Venus had all the other elements necessary for life, nothing could survive the radiation."

"And since the Event, our magnetosphere seems to be breaking down, more and more," Monty finished his thought.

"Is that why," Max chimed in, "our atmosphere is electrified and the sun's radiation seems to be getting worse every month?"

"Yes, we believe so," Dr. Ron answered, and Monty and their wives nodded.

"Are you telling me that the problems we have currently are because someone is generating gamma radiation using a machine like the one you developed?" As the question rolled out of Max's mouth, he realized the enormity of what this meant.

"Yes, we believe so," Monty said. "We believe this is the reason our environment suffered so badly this past year, and why what should have been a one-time event is actually a seemingly permanent series of smaller events with each solar emission."

Preston looked sick.

"Wait, who would do dis?" Magdalena's latent Mexican accent mingled with her otherwise near-perfect English, as seemed to happen when she was anxious.

"We don't know who. We only know where."

Max grabbed Preston's lab coat sleeve and pulled him aside while the others loudly discussed their theories.

"Are you all right?"

"It's just too shocking." Preston's head was pointed down, as if he were trying to prevent himself from tossing his breakfast.

"I know who is doing this."

Preston's head snapped to Max. "Who?"

"There is a copy of Cicada out there. And we need to stop them."

"But maybe they don't know what they're doing. Maybe they're just trying to create power… wait, how did you know who?"

Max looked at Preston curiously, not sure why he accepted the premise so quickly.

"I know, because I have their plans back at my office. They call themselves Bios-2."

18.

Bios-2

Slowly, she inched her head past the edge of the wall and peered down the hallway, and then drew back. "Dammit!" she whispered. She had to get into her apartment and talk to Carrington, if he was even there. Yet, in front of their apartment, stood Simon, the comic-book-reading sentry.

Her mind fishtailed like a Formula One racer losing control in the curves. *What could she do now? How would she get into her apartment? Then what? Westerling knew that she had been at the office waiting room and left, but would he know that she heard anything? If he didn't, then why the guard? Oh my God, this is real!*

She still couldn't get over the revelation that Cicada was active, when they had all been told it was a dead zone. Then Westerling made a deal with the red-robed man to march his army to Cicada and kill its inhabitants, and she couldn't even decide how to get into her apartment. She needed to do something, rather than helping these murderers as they had been for the past year in exchange for safety. At a minimum, they could no longer stay here, and they had to get to Cicada while it was still there. But how? She had to confer with Carrington and with her colleagues. She felt the bile rise up in her throat as she almost turned in these same colleagues.

First things first… She had to get Simon away from their apartment door. *But how?*

Carrington walked briskly to Supplies, conveniently located on the same floor as the entrance to B216. He was a little out of breath, even though he was in pretty good shape from a combination of lots of walking and lean eating. A far cry from the junk-food-fueled sedentary lifestyle he lived pre-Event.

Almost there, Carrington continued to look behind him to make sure no one was following. Although he now had carte blanche to patrol most of the areas while he was supposedly working on his plan to provide a power generation solution to Bios-2, he still didn't want to come under their scrutiny. At least not until he could find out what was in that mystery room and hide the bomb he was carrying. This was their fallback. If they found out that they were being lied to, as they still suspected, or if they believed they were unsafe, he would blow the CPF turbine and they would leave. But leaving a bomb in their apartment was too risky.

He had thought of the Supplies room this morning, and Mel agreed it was the perfect place. The room was vast, actually comprising many rooms. It was guarded, with many authorized personnel coming and going all the time signing in and out with the supplies they needed or were returning. As one of the "authorized personnel," he could place the package where it would lie undisturbed until they needed it. And if it was ever found, no one would know its origins. He would also grab what he needed to get into the mystery room.

At the entrance, an older man with discerning eyes sat behind a barred window reading a dog-eared copy of *Lucifer's Hammer* by Niven.

"Hello, Mr. Richards, I'm Dr. Carrington Reid, number S227A, here to pick up one notepad, an electric motor and a nanovoltmeter.

Also to drop off an electric clock I repaired."

"Sign in, Dr. Reid, and I'll need to check your backpack both in and out," Richards said in an almost disinterested voice. He slid open a small door beside the barred window.

Carrington unslung his backpack and pushed it through the door. Hopeful that neither the bag nor he would be scrutinized much, he hastily printed his name and community-assigned ID number/room number, and signed his name on the clipboard; Richards had already filled in the date and time. Beside the Drop-Off box was written *clock* and in the Pick-Up box was written *Nano-Meter, motor & notepad.* He slid the clipboard back through the opening under the bars and his backpack was pushed back through the small window.

An entrance door clicked open, and Carrington grabbed his backpack and walked through.

Richards bored holes in Carrington's back, watching him march down a long aisle between large shelves, until he turned out of sight.

"Washington!" she yelled through her cupped hands, in her deepest male-sounding voice. "Washington, get your ass down here. I need your help in the men's latrine."

Footsteps slowly approached. "Sir, I'm com—"

"Now, Washington; get your ass down here," she projected into the hall, and then ducked behind the ladies' room door and waited.

His running *clomp-clomp-clomp* rumbled toward her, and then squeaked to a halt before the men's entrance banged open. "Sir?" A muffled voice asked, unsure.

Melanie cracked her door, satisfied the bluff worked, and sprinted silently down the hall to her apartment.

After grabbing what was needed and depositing his package at a place near the back on a dusty bottom shelf, Carrington turned the corner to face the security door and felt assaulted once again by Richard's scornful gaze, like walking into the sunlight without protective clothing.

Richards kept scrutinizing his backpack, as if he were sure Carrington was hiding something.

He was. Carrington clutched his side, attempting to suppress the bulge of a stolen radio and handheld Taser hidden under his clothes.

"Okay, you can go. Sign here," he said, handing him the clipboard.

Two swishes of the pen, and Carrington tossed it back and hurried out the door before he did something that would somehow betray him further. With long strides, he returned to the turbine room via the innocuous B216 entrance. As he slowed his pace down the steps, he wiped away the wetness that streamed down his face and moved the radio and Taser to his backpack before they shorted out.

Because one of the guards was standing where he had intended to stand and observe, he instead walked to the Shaft Room, looking back at Harry, who was there guarding his mystery room's entrance. Carrington turned and checked around for others. It was empty. He checked again and Harry was still there, so he strolled to a doorway at the end of the room—maybe it was another way to get into the mystery room? Inside, it seemed considerably cooler. He would have to explore this further, when he had the time.

He pulled out the notepad and pretended to jot down copious notes about his research. But he was more interested in the personnel and guard traffic marching back and forth in the rooms. He walked back to the stairwell and stood for a while in a nook, watching. It was a perfect spot because he was somewhat hidden by the shadow of the nook, and the bathroom was there. Very inconspicuous.

In his notebook, he wrote, *Shaft Room door!* on the first page, along with a couple other observations. Then above this, he sketched the infinity symbol.

Because the machinery was pretty well designed, it didn't appear to need much maintenance. So, other than the occasional scientist racing to lunch, there weren't a lot of personnel down here. The guards were pretty stationary. Only one rotated every half hour between the turbine room and the Shaft Room and back. Guard #2 just rotated out of the main turbine room and was now out of his field of vision. That left Harry, the mystery room's guard.

Carrington reached into his backpack and pulled out the radio, identical to the ones the guards and other Bios-2 personnel use. He clicked to channel five, remembering that was Harry's radio setting.

He'd overheard many conversations over months, so he knew what to say. "Henderson, this is Andrews; we need you in Operations in five minutes. Mr. Westerling wants a detail and requested you for point. I will take over your watch." Carrington let go of the talk button and listened.

"I'll leave as soon as you relieve me," said Harry.

"You're wanted now. I will be there as soon as I finish my rounds in less than two."

Carrington waited patiently, knowing he would reply "Roger that."

Harry raced up the stairs, barely noticing the scientist wearing a fedora scribbling notes on a note pad.

Melanie closed the door quietly behind her and slid the deadbolt home. She looked for Carrington in every room, but he definitely wasn't there. "Where are you, my love?" she said softly to the empty apartment.

In their designated hiding place, in front of a vent grate, behind a table, she found a note. She looked around; it was force of habit, even though she knew there were no cameras, only bugs.

Dearest Mel,

I wanted to tell you this in person, but you weren't here, and I didn't have any time to waste. I hope you'll forgive my actions.

I have already started my project down in the basement of this facility today. It's possible that what they are telling us is correct, but something is just not adding up in my mind. And I just don't trust these people. I found a room that is restricted, even to me. It should be part of the geothermal production, but it isn't. So, why the secret and what is it? I don't have any idea what it might be, but it is so suspicious, I have to check it out. You know me, "trust but verify."

I'm worried though if I am caught sneaking around this area, especially since it is guarded, what might happen to me, or us. Please know I wouldn't take this chance unless I thought it was important to both of us. If we need to escape, then we need to know right away.

Please keep your eyes open, and be aware for anything, especially some sign from me.

I love you with all my heart and soul.
Carr

"Oh, no," she worried out loud. She shoved the note into her pocket and moved to their bedroom. In a box in the closet is where he kept the bombs, and she was hoping they were still there. Moving away the few pieces of clothing from on top, a natural cover for the box, she unfolded the edges and looked in.

She stood up, but her head drooped like she had no ability to hold it up. She walked to their living room and fell into their couch, reading his note again, and cried. She cried for her husband and what she was forced to do, what she had to do.

19.
Cicada

Max paced back and forth in the back of the lab. Preston was practically slumped over on a stool, staring at his shoes and occasionally at Max. The rest of them argued openly about who was responsible and why this was happening. Magdalena noticed Max wasn't participating in their discussion anymore, and she wanted to confirm a suspicion. Watching him only made her more anxious. What was he thinking?

Max wanted to kill something. He had been mentally avoiding the other Cicada, focusing instead on the chaotic crisis of the day. After changing their policy, leaving the message with the Squatts outside, and taking out the man responsible, he felt a small sense of relief, like he had some control over the threats outside of Cicada's walls.

But now, the evidence was unavoidable: theft of their scientists, by guiding them away from Cicada to another location; the plans of the other facility, which were a virtual copy of Cicada's; the mystery phone taps when he communicated with Cicada from his Mexican ranch; the military hardware getting into the hands of the squatters outside their gates; and now the revelation that the other site may be the cause of the apocalypse that was slowly destroying their world. All signs led to one conclusion, and that conclusion was that Bios-2 was their enemy. And that enemy had to be stopped.

Stopping Bios-2 would be the only way they could be safe. What's more, stopping Bios-2 might even stop the permanent solar storms, which might just give the Earth a fighting chance before time ran out. Stopping them meant killing them all. He would make them pay for all the death and pain they had caused and were causing to the billions of Earth's inhabitants.

The more he thought about it, the more anger consumed him.

He felt a soft tap on his arm.

"What!" he yelled.

"I-I'm sorry." Magdalena reeled back a few steps, afraid of the violence in Max's face.

The others all looked up at Max.

"Wait, Magdalena. What do you want?" he offered more calmly but still seething inside.

"I just wanted to know what you were going to do, now that you know who's causing this."

His eyes went black. "I'm going to kill them all!"

Magdalena backed up a few more steps. "But what if they don't know what they're doing? Are you still going to…"

"Kill them? Yes, I am. Someone needs to pay for what they've done to our world."

Max couldn't take it any longer; he got up and strode to the back of the lab. "Preston, are you coming?"

Preston didn't say anything. He just hoisted himself up and trudged after Max, out the door, dreading what he had to tell his boss next.

Max headed to the Library to see if he could find Bill. Lisa told him that he had left early that morning, saying he wanted to help out the scientist working on the hovercraft. She added that Sally was getting a tour from that nice young man, Webber.

Max thanked her and then walked briskly with Preston, who was very quiet.

"We need to get everyone to Comms in two hours. I think it's time to tell everyone what we're up against and to ask for volunteers."

"For what?" Preston asked softly, still staring at his feet.

"For the assault teams, of course."

"Isn't that a little... aggressive?"

Max just glared at Preston, not believing this was coming from him and angry that he had to justify his actions to someone who should be fully supportive.

"I'll also need all the personnel files. We need as many bodies as we can get with military or police or even hunting experience."

Preston nodded.

"Preston, what the hell's wrong with you?"

He stopped in the middle of Max's Court, halfway between Comms and the Library. "I need to tell you something." He looked up at Max, shoulders sagging. Then, seemingly jarred by something, he looked around like he was sure someone was watching, "But not here; at my office." He marched forward, and this time Max followed him.

"I did it!" Preston blurted out after Max had closed his office door on both of them.

"You did what?"

Preston dumped a stack of folders on Max's desk: the personnel files Max had asked about on the way here. Then, he sank onto the side chair.

He swallowed hard. "I sold Cicada's plans to a man named Lunder Gufstafson over fifteen years ago. I didn't keep the money and in fact donated it to the foundation, making it look like it came from an anonymous source. At the time, I didn't think you really cared about Cicada. I thought your only concern was the Kings. Plus, I was worried that if any of this came to pass, there should be another Cicada in the US. I know there are other facilities around the world, but I thought the US should have another one.

"He approached me and knew all about our facility and threatened to report us. Then, he said that they had the resources to build something similar and duplicate our efforts. I did a little investigating on my own and was pretty sure that his boss was a Colorado senator. But I never found out which one. I also suspected later that they were trying to take our scientists, but I had no idea they were so close and that they were causing the problems with the sun.

"I would have told you sooner, but I thought for the most part they were benign."

Max was very quiet for an uncomfortably long moment. Then he smiled and said, "Preston, I knew all about this a long time ago." He held up a rolled set of blueprints. "How do you think I got a copy of the plans to their facility?"

20.

Outside Bios-2

"I don't trust them," John announced to the Teacher and the remaining ten apostles sitting in a circle in the entry room of the Teacher's tent. The Teacher had just described all that he had been shown and told by the leader of Bios-2. He often didn't reveal everything in these times when he convened his apostolic counsels, which were designed to help him make and carry out big decisions for his followers; he usually saved his doubts and worries for his private counsel times with John. Prior to this session, he'd made his decision, but he wanted his apostles to speak freely before he had them commit their lives to it. Free will was important during these times because his fighters needed to fight with passion and be completely invested in the cause to ensure victory.

"We have no choice, with weapons like theirs," said Frank, his face drawn and serious. He replayed the image of his friend Stephen being charred like a piece of meat and looking like he had been tossed onto the hottest fire for many hours. He could still feel the prickles on his skin as the lightning from this devilish device came so close to him.

"I know, Brother Francis. I'm sorry about Brother Stephen." The Teacher's eyes were watery, seeming genuinely moved by Stephen's martyrdom. He shifted his attention. "Brother John, I agree with you about these people. This is why Francis and I will take three-quarters of my warriors and go to Cicada."

Frank nodded but surprise and uncertainty clouded his features.

The Teacher uncrossed and re-crossed his legs and turned back to Frank. "You will lead our forces to conquer Cicada."

John fidgeted where he sat, betraying his unspoken discomfort with the Teacher's plans. "John, I know you want to lead the takeover, but I need you here. Your job is to protect our women and children; all of us will depend on you for this, and no one would I trust more with this task. But you are to watch them and be ready for their treason."

"Where will you be, Teacher?" Frank asked, still a little unsure that he heard this correctly; he was shocked that the Teacher wanted him to lead their advance on the Promised Land, the home the Teacher had been prophesying about.

"I will be with you, of course. Cicada has been given to us by God and I must be there when they fall."

John punched his fist into the carpeted ground. "I'm sorry, Teacher, but why are we going to do nothing about these petulant infidels at Bios-2? They murdered our brother and they stand against us. They must pay with their lives."

"John, they will, in time. We must first secure our home at Cicada. Then we will assimilate the people we choose from Cicada. Finally, we will plan to take over Bios-2. But that is why it is so important that you watch what they do. They will show their weaknesses, then we will conquer Bios-2, and Brother Stephen's martyrdom will not be for naught. This I promise you."

His apostles were quiet; they were pensive but seemingly satisfied.

"If there is nothing else, I want to try out some more of the flesh from this tribe." The Teacher rose and all the apostles looked up, waiting for their sign to leave. "Go and be with your wives and families. We will leave in two hours."

He peeled open the curtain leading to his bedchamber to see what awaited him. Two women lay naked in his bed; one had passed out from the drugs she had been given, the other was bound and gagged. She looked at him as he stepped in and let his robe slide off him, and she tried to scream. Tears poured from her already red, swollen eyes.

As Frank watched Zachary play with his other children, he couldn't help but beam. All were from different women, but he loved them as if they had all come from him. His wife was barren, and so they raised others who were orphans alongside the children of his two mistresses. Camilla was a fiery red-haired beauty who had been following the Teacher since the beginning. She had been one of the Teacher's mistresses as well, but when she became pregnant with the Teacher's child, the Teacher asked Frank to care for Camilla and the child too.

Frank loved Camilla, just as much as he loved his wife, Sam, and his other mistress, Zoe, but in different ways. Camilla and Zoe were children really, barely in their twenties, whereas Sam was mature and his equal in most ways.

Camilla was not only fiery in look and personality; she was bright and took on the responsibilities of teaching his now eight boys and six girls. She also organized (at John's suggestion, Frank figured) some of the other women to copy pages of the Book so that others could read it and feel its importance. Because of the ongoing nature of the revelation, they were told, this was a job that would never be complete.

Daily, Camilla would teach from one of the copied pages.

Zachary, Frank's middle child, was the brightest of her students; he always asked questions, always wondered whether something was right or wrong and he always loved stories, often play-acting them out in front of the rest of the children. Zachary could read as well, which was pretty good for an eight year old. He even read difficult texts, like the Bible. Unfortunately, this text was forbidden, so it was the one secret they kept from the other followers.

After the Book was established as the sole sacred text of God's Army, the Teacher declared that all other religious writings were forbidden: "There is only the Book; No Follower can be in possession of or quote from any other religious text." Frank and others collected up the Bibles, Torahs, Korans, Books of Mormon and other religious-based texts and gave them to John, who burned them all.

Frank kept his portable military Bible for himself. He hadn't opened it in years, but he couldn't let it go, as he had written notes in it and read it so many times. It was more of a keepsake—he'd stopped believing. But he just couldn't part with it. So, he kept it hidden, until one day Camilla found it and asked if she could read it. Frank allowed it, but said she must keep it quiet. And she did.

Today, with his stomach grumbling as he prepared his mind and body for war, he watched with pleasure as Camilla gathered his children and had them sit in a circle around her as she taught from the Book.

"She's great with our kids, isn't she?" Sam asked as she sat by him on a fallen tree stump.

He put his arm around her and squeezed. "Yes, she is."

"You're worried about the battle?" She always knew him better than he did himself, and by the time he got back to his family, word had already reached their cluster and Sam.

"Not really; this shouldn't be much of one. The devil leader in Bios-2 has someone on the inside who will make it easier for us, and they do not have defenses like Bios-2."

"So what's troubling you, husband?"

He didn't answer right away. Just as she opened her mouth to speak again, he took her hand and kissed it, saying, "Do you ever question whether or not you chose the right path?"

Without hesitation she answered, "Other than marrying you, all the time. But, do not worry yourself, my husband. Our path is currently the right one; it is the one we were meant to follow, right now. And in the future, I am sure you will choose the right path again. And if you don't, you will find the right one and get back on it." She squeezed his hand and slid her arm around him.

He rested his head on her shoulder, and they watched Camilla and Zachary argue.

"So, if all of us will be gods, won't heaven be crowded?"

"But heaven is limitless," Camilla responded.

Frank felt someone walk up on them quietly; he turned, his hand on his sidearm, ready to defend his family, and rested. It was Peter. He leaned over to Frank and said, "It is time, Brother."

21.

Cicada

"There's another Cicada out there, and it's very close to here." Max was standing on the first step of the stairwell in the reception room of Comms. He had personally greeted everyone before beginning, thanking them for being a part of Cicada, and then he stepped up so he could be seen and began speaking to the forty-five in attendance. Most were scientists, including Dr. Ron and Monty. A few were in IT, one was an auto mechanic, there was a plumber and one schoolteacher. Other than Tom, only two that they knew of had any previous military training or combat experience. Preston was there; so was Magdalena, who flashed a quick smile when he looked her way, and of course Bill and Lisa. He hated for them to hear what he was about to say, but it was necessary that they knew what was at stake.

There were maybe a dozen others not in attendance—all performing various duties vital to Cicada—including five manning the wall, and Shingles. Sally had opted to not be a part of the meeting, saying she wanted to jump right into the work inside Comms and the server rooms. Yet, Max heard the door open when he first addressed the group and knew that she sat just inside the Comms room's doorway, behind him, listening and looking out at the room and everyone's faces, which changed from nervous fear to wonderment. A few dialogs rippled through the room.

Max held up his hands and patiently waited for the buzz to die down.

"I always suspected this, when I found out that someone had made a copy of my plans for Cicada. Then, when the Protocol message was sent, we found out that some of our scientists were somehow being redirected away from Cicada and sent to this Cicada copy. That told me someone was purposely trying to disrupt our plans, but I had no idea why.

"Earlier today, Dr. Ron and Dr. Monty, right there..." He pointed to them sitting on the largest loveseat. They were looking at a set of plans rolled out on the coffee table, pointing at a structure, when they heard their names called and they looked up. They raised their hands and then ignored everyone again, focusing on their assigned task.

"...these two scientists approached me with some disturbing news." He paused to make sure he chose the right words. "The Event that occurred almost a year ago continues almost every day... with solar storms, disruptive electrical discharges throughout our atmosphere and a perpetual summer. Some of you know that our magnetosphere has not been protecting us the way it should. Until today, we didn't understand why—until Dr. Ron and Dr. Monty discovered why.

"Someone has built a device, the purpose of which we don't know, but it is most likely destroying our magnetosphere." Conversations erupted everywhere. "And that..." Max projected his voice and waited until the din died down and he could be heard again. "...and that device is located at the other Cicada. So now we know there is another group of people, occupying a copy of our facility, who not only have malevolent intentions for Cicada, they are intent on damaging the entire world.

"The Event was real, but these people appear to be the reason why our magnetosphere hasn't recovered. So, they are the ones who are causing the problems we're experiencing now!"

Sally had been inching forward from inside Comms, drawn into the room by Max's speech. First into the Comms doorway, until now she was out in the hallway, directly behind Max. She heard some of this earlier, but not all of it. She had heard about the other Cicada, but not the rest. As she heard it and absorbed its ramifications, dread began to creep back into her. She really had thought she would be safe here at Cicada, believing from Max that the outside groups—so-called "Squatts"—could be controlled. It was one of the main reasons why she left her sister's family in New Mexico. That and she didn't know spit about farming, nor did she have any interest in that way of life. She worked with computers and was offered a chance to use her technical skills here at Cicada. But most important, was feeling safe, something she hadn't felt in almost a year now. It just occurred to her that most likely, no place would be safe as long as those people in the other Cicada existed. *They had to be stopped!*

"Let me have your attention!" Max's voice boomed, like a lighthouse's horn in the fog. Everyone almost swallowed their words. Max had been calm and reasoned, full of compassion, until now. He was speaking as their leader; what he was going to ask was important, and he needed them to understand.

"Now that we know all this, we also know what we have to do. This device and the people who built it must be stopped."

Most heads nodded in the affirmative. Even Dr. Ron and Monty, who had looked up from their papers.

"I'm putting together two assault teams and we're going to do our best to take this device down."

Silence.

"Most of you know a little about me, but what you may not know is that I served a tour in Iraq, just before Iraqi Freedom. I have led men and women into combat before. Also joining us will be Tom Rogers, who you may know works with Preston to manage our security. What I'm asking now is, are any of you with any military or police training willing to volunteer for this very important mission?"

If there had been any crickets in the room, their chirps would have been considered loud.

"If we succeed, we not only give Cicada a chance, we will potentially save our world. Keep in mind that all of our own personal safety will always be in peril because of this threat. The sole purpose of Cicada, and our common goal, is to find the answers to and solve the problems that led up to and caused the apocalypse. We now know the reason why and how to fix it. I need your help to carry this out. Failure may mean the end of all of us."

Max paused to let all of it sink in.

"All who are willing, please meet us over there at the coffee table, where we will be planning the assault. Are there any questions?"

"When will this assault happen?" asked a disembodied voice within the crowd.

"Tonight. Thank you." Max stepped down from the steps and walked over to the coffee table.

When the room cleared out, the group at the table numbered twelve. The Kings (minus Sally, who'd left to clear her head with a walk, or so she said) stood alongside Preston. The two scientists remained, standing next to Tom and Max. Mags, and four others neither of the Kings recognized, stood a little bit apart from them.

Max looked straight at the Kings. "You are welcome to be present at this discussion, but don't think you're coming tonight."

"Look," said Bill, "I know neither of us have any military training. But you know we know how to handle a rifle and"—he looked a bit perturbed—"we've been through a lot of crap this past year. I think we can handle it."

"I appreciate the offer, but even if you were both members of Seal Team Six, you're still not coming."

"But—"

"But nothing. End of discussion."

"Fine," Bill snapped, noticeably pissed. "We'd like to at least see your assault plans."

"Agreed."

Max turned to another face in their small group and smiled. Magdalena smiled back, warm and inviting. "Let me guess, in between taking care of your mother and fixing computers, you had a stint in the Mexican military?"

All eyes turned to look between the pretty woman with a dark complexion and Max. *Was this a girlfriend we didn't know about?* they wondered. Bill and Lisa, having met Mags and seen their interplay, winked at each other, enjoying the brief respite from the stress they all felt.

"Ha! No, but my father was a hunter and took me and my brothers out hunting for deer every year. I, what was the term you Americans use—*bagged*! I bagged more deer than my brothers and father then. I'm a good shot, and you know I can handle myself."

"Magdalena, I mean this sincerely. I really do appreciate your volunteering, and I know anyone that went up against you would have a bad day, but I really want someone with combat or hand-to-hand training or experience. So, I'll say the same thing I told my friends; you're welcome to stay, listen, even offer your opinions, but you're not coming."

"I understand. I'd just as soon not kill anyone anyway." She smiled sheepishly.

"Okay, let's get to the matter at hand." Max clapped once and looked around the table, gesturing toward Tom. "This is Tom Rogers. Tom and I have already spent time with each other. Suffice it to say, he is battle ready and will lead one of the two assault teams. Thank you both, Sue and Rob, for volunteering. I know you've had some time in the services. And thank you, Felix and Pel; although not military, you've both had some other weapons training." He was careful to not mention that neither had any military or police training, so that he wouldn't slight Magdalena, based on the reason he'd given for not including her in this op. "So that makes six, which is actually a very good number. Let's talk about the plan, and then just the six of us will go to Operations.

"Monty? Ron? Please tell me you found a point of entry and approximately where the device is located?"

The mole slid by everyone without them noticing—they were focused on Mr. Thompson—and carefully let himself into the Comms room. This was very risky, but once Bios-2 knew, they would see it was necessary. Making sure the door was secured, he sat in the console chair, unlocked the drawer and pulled out the phone receiver. Once again, he punched the fifth and sixth line buttons, illuminating both, and waited until he could finally say, "Bios-2, this is Cicada Comms. "

"You should not call us this often. You cannot risk getting caught. Vas is zo important?" The accent was thick. *Lunder must be stressed.*

"Mr. Thompson is leading an assault on Bios-Two tonight!"

"Do you know any details?"

"No, in fact they're discussing it outside this room right now. I have to go before I'm discovered."

"Thank you for the intel." Lunder hung up.

The man nervously put the phone back into the cradle and shut the drawer.

A clicking and a shadow alerted him that someone was about to come through the Comms room door. *He had to get out right away!*

The Comms room door opening and closing caused Max to look; he hadn't realized anyone was here. While Monty was pointing out their best guess of where the device was, Max watched Webber bound down the stairs and across the floor past them.

"Sorry to interrupt." He shot a guilty look at Max. "Forgot something," he said, waving a USB flash drive, "for Sally." He scuttled out the door and out of sight.

Max refocused his attention on tonight's assault plan. Their lives and the lives of perhaps everyone on Earth depended on their success.

22.
Bios-2

Westerling was in a celebratory mood. They had already planned to take down Cicada, and now a religious nut and several hundred of his idiot followers would do all the heavy lifting. Both Dr. Reids were on board and they would soon convince the rest of the scientists that it was futile to resist him. Everything was falling into place nicely.

Topping off his glass with an extra-large measure of bourbon from its decanter and sinking into his leather chair were his reward. After another puff from his cigar and a large gulp, he stared out the window and thought about what still needed to be done. At the top of the list was killing Cicada and that sonofabitch Thompson.

He put his glass down and fumbled with the buttons of his intercom, feeling a little light-headed from all the alcohol and smoke. His fingers, acting fatter than normal, punched what he thought were the office speakers—he wanted to hear it better and not have to scrunch over like some feeble old man and listen to the intercom's little speaker—and heard a crackle in the conference room. Then he banged the button beside it for the office, both buttons depressed together, the static telling him the office speakers were on as well. He punched the call button and the number one.

"Found you, sucker," he told the box of wires, winning another battle over one more object. He waited impatiently for Lunder to answer.

He started to suck on his fourth cigar of the day while taking another large swig of his giant bourbon and ice. He should feel at least a little guilty. Not that it was his health or that he was living high off the hog known as Bios-2 that bothered him; he was just a little worried that at this rate of consumption, his cigar and bourbon stock was going to disappear in a couple of years, maybe quicker if he didn't slow down a little. It wasn't like they were making the stuff anymore.

Where is that Kraut?

Lunder was busy with his normal juggling act, now directing Operations, when the phone started ringing. His boss couldn't help himself and often had to call him about something insignificant. He wondered what it was this time. At least it saved him the trouble of calling Westerling with the good news.

"Yes, sir," Lunder answered, turning the volume on his radio down so he could hear.

"Have you found the Reids yet?" Westerling belched, sounding very toasted.

"No, sir. But they'll turn up soon enough. I wouldn't worry…"

Lunder's radio squealed at him; Operations was reporting back.

"I have something more important to tell you." He purposely sat back and made his boss wait, relishing this last morsel of information, which he knew would make him happy.

The radio screeched some more. "Hang on; I'm speaking to Mr. Westerling."

"Got it," Reynolds at Operations answered. "Call when you are done. Out."

"Well, are you go… oing to make me wait all day?" Westerling's words were sluggish from alcohol.

"Sir? Oh yes, of course. You don't have to worry about killing Thompson at Cicada. He's coming here, tonight," Lunder happily announced.

"Tonight?"

Lunder could hear him take a long draw off his cigar and exhale little puffs—no doubt he was trying to blow drunk-happy white smoke rings, with little luck.

"Datsgoodnews!" he bellowed in one breath.

"Yes, that is the good news."

"Lunder, good work. Are we set up for him?"

"I'm briefing Operations and the wall sentries now. We're going to draw him in and make him feel like he's snuck up on us, and then we will let them have it with at least two EMAs and our snipers and we'll finish them off with automatic weapons fire. He won't stand a chance. You'll be rid of him tonight, sir."

"Lunder, I'd kiss you if you were here." Then Lunder heard Westerling's phone drop, followed by a cheerful, "Whohooo!" Westerling yelled unintelligibly away from the phone, "Take that you fu—" Then the line went dead.

23.
Bios-2

Melanie knew now what she must do. She had to kill Westerling and Lunder.

Part of her wished that Carrington was part of this, but maybe it was better this way. The consequences of what she had to do were not something she wanted to share with him. He was a good and decent man, and she didn't want him to go down that path of killing someone like she was forced into; it changes you, and once you do it, you can't take it back. She hoped that she would be able to put that horrible incident in Texas behind her. And except for the occasional nightmare, she had been able to do it. It wasn't her though; it was Carrington. He did that for her. He made her whole and gave her a hope she didn't have after she took the lives of those men. He not only saved her physical life on that road to Laramie, he saved her whole being. Until now, she had enough hope to ignore what happened to them.

Both of them were acting, pretending that everything was all right. Carrington did a masterful job, acting like he was fully accepting of their captors. But she knew he wasn't. He was ever hopeful, but he was ever vigilant as well. It was why he built the bomb; this was a complete surprise to her, but when he explained his reasons, it made complete sense. "Trust but verify," he told her. And if promises weren't kept, they'd blow the EPF and leave.

It was not the life they had wanted to choose, but at least it was a life. Then those plotting, backstabbing scumbags, Westerling and Lunder, made even that impossible.

There was only one course of action for her now. She was going to have to kill them both. She was going to have to be that person who killed in Texas: cold-blooded, full of hatred, and exacting in her revenge for what they did against her. Westerling and Lunder were no different. These two had taken away the lives that Melanie and Carrington could have had together at Cicada.

Perhaps, she thought, lying with her head back on their couch, *perhaps, if everything went right, Bios-2 would be rid of these two evil men, and we could still be together.*

That was hope speaking, and it was dangerous. She quieted this most dangerous impediment and mentally went through each step of her plan.

Carrington waited just another moment to make sure the guard was clear and considered what he was about to do. They had been promised lives of peace within a community, if they would just work with Westerling and his people. The alternative was living outside of Bios-2's walls in a destroyed world occupied by misery and ruled by maniacs and cannibals. So what if Westerling and Lunder were evil men? Wasn't his and Melanie's safety, and the safety of everyone in Bios-2, worth the price of turning the other cheek and not doing what's right?

If it was, then what the hell was he doing? He was about to violate their rules, only hours after being told not to. They were holding all the cards, and if he was caught, he and Melanie would be cast out or worse.

But his gut told him that he had to take a chance. There was something deeply wrong with this place; he knew it to his core. It was why he built the bomb; that was their post-apocalyptic insurance plan. If the powers that be went against their word or threatened them, he would use the device to take down the turbine, and therefore the EPF, and they would all escape. Hiding a bomb was easy, but getting into a restricted area and not getting caught was not.

What the hell is that place? he wondered as he glared at the secured entrance to the mystery room, where the guard should have been, and then ducked back. He knew enough about geothermal power production to know that room was not a piece of the geothermal puzzle. They were hiding something and he was about to find out what it was.

He checked once again, clumsily knocking his fedora off his head. But Harry the guard was definitely gone. Carrington had, at most, ten minutes before the next guard or worker appeared.

He grabbed his hat and scrambled across the vast turbine room, looking up to the walkways many stories above him, making sure there wasn't someone else who would see him. The coast was clear. He dashed the rest of the way to the secured entrance to the restricted room and pulled out of his backpack a handheld Taser. He held the Taser up against the thumb-pad and gave it a long jolt, until it gave a welcoming click. He quickly slipped inside.

Melanie breathed slowly and deeply, closed her eyes and visualized her plan. She could see every detail, what could happen and the risks of each step. When she was satisfied, she stood up resolutely. She grabbed the knife she had pilfered from one of the guards several months ago and went to her front door. Her heart was beating rapidly, but steady. She loudly unlocked the door and pulled it open. *A foot or so ought to do it.*

"Hello? Dr. Reid, are you there?" called Simon's voice behind the door. He put one foot through the gap.

She waited patiently, calmly, knowing precisely when to spring. She was that person she needed to be once more.

She was a killer.

The room was not at all what he expected.

The first red flag was the black and yellow triangle posted just past the doorway, indicating an ionizing radiation hazard. But it wasn't a warning sign to keep people out, since only a few were allowed inside. The sign couldn't be for prevention. It must be a real warning, but of what?

Then there was the whole purpose of this room, which didn't make any sense. There was some sort of well, which he expected. He knew the Shaft Room was where they captured the superheated steam from the aquifer below them, which was naturally heated by a magma chamber. Then, he expected the cool water had to be injected back into the aquifer somewhere; otherwise, the aquifer would run dry. Of course this was the reason for their needing an alternative energy source: the aquifer *was* running dry, and that meant no steam for their turbine.

He had assumed this room was where they would inject the condensed water. But there were no water pipes anywhere. And over what appeared to be an injection well was some sort of very elaborate machinery. It looked like a kind of electric generator. There were certainly moving parts inside it; he could feel the vibration. But it was remarkably quiet, not like any generator he had ever seen. Over the vent and connected to the machine was a beautifully designed conduit system with a multitude of tubes snaking out of every square inch of the conduit. These were either to cool whatever was going in... or keep it from coming out. But what was it, if not water?

An electronic display on the machine flashed numbers. Carrington looked around, again making sure no one was there and he remained unseen. He was the only one inside.

The display showed a bar graph with 1.00 on one side and 50.00 on the other, and the red bar was a little more than two-thirds, or a reading of around 30. The unit of measure was MeV.

Megaelectrovolts?

Carrington's mind raced. This couldn't mean what he thought, could it? This machine was generating radiation of some sort, perhaps gamma radiation. A huge amount of gamma radiation, in fact. Cobalt-60 could produce maybe 1.5 MeV, but not 30 MeV. And to what purpose? And why have some sort of gamma ray generator on top of a vent going deep into the earth?

His face sagged, and he quavered, faltering as the weight of it all pressed down on him.

"Oh my God!" His voice cracked. He felt faint and very scared.

He turned and stumbled from the room. He had to get out of here now. Halfway through the turbine room, a voice yelled from the other side, "Stop! Dr. Reid, you were not supposed to go there." It was Guard #2, coming from the Shaft Room early. "Stop!" the guard yelled, jogging to him now while pulling out his radio.

Carrington didn't wait; he bounded up the steps three at a time.

24.

On the road to Cicada

The Teacher took a big drink of water, but it didn't satisfy his thirst. He thirsted for something more. Ever since he saw it in a strange vision that day when the bright orange nuclear clouds erupted over that shitty little town in Illinois, he yearned for that city under the dome below the three-pointed mountain. He even saw the image of the cicada. It had taken the better part of a year, but tonight, they would reach the place he prophesied. By morning Cicada would be his.

It'd been a difficult journey.

He guzzled some more water and continued the trudge forward with several hundred of his finest warriors. Each step along this deserted road brought them closer to the end of their long journey. His mind wandered to what had brought him to this point: his early preaching, the crowds of followers, the miraculous healings, the visions, the end of the world and then the arduous trip to Colorado with over two thousand people. But it had been more than his talents and efforts that brought them here. He believed that John and the Book were the "game-changer" for them. It was John who led him to the cave after a hike in the woods, and there they found the Book. John said that a god, not the God, directed him to this revelation, to write it down and to give it to the Teacher to give to the world. It took a week, but they arrived from the cave with the written revelation. And what a revelation it was.

All who followed the Book would one day become gods themselves. It was the ultimate secret and yet the epitome of the human condition. It was why we were wired the way we were: to be in control, to be selfish, to have so many wants. But we could never get what we wanted because we had not yet achieved that next evolutionary leap. The Book provided the catalyst for this leap. By focusing our energies inward, we would one day achieve this perfection that we were meant to have.

The Book changed everything for the Teacher and his followers, as epic as—or more so—than any of his visions or preaching. They now had a purpose to go along with a place.

He knew that John had designed this from his own mind, using his own education and experience to write the Book, but where did the concepts come from? Where does any creative thought come from? Are we the creator or was someone else prior to it the originator? It didn't matter; he and his people had an answer to whatever their question was.

Meanwhile, John continued to have revelations. And that was the Teacher's only concern. Would John one day lose sight of his purpose and attempt to usurp the Teacher's rule? This worried him because the Book was bigger than any one person. It was even bigger than him.

First they would take over Cicada, and then he would reveal the Book to Cicada's residents and their settlers outside. Then, he would deal with John.

He repositioned the satchel resting against the small of his back, its straps digging into his shoulders, with the Book safely protected inside. He wished that the Book was just a little smaller.

John couldn't help but wonder if he made a mistake with the Teacher and the writing of their new bible, which he coined the Book. There was a great need for a new kind of purpose to lift up the Teacher and his followers from their doubt. They already had the Teacher's great preaching and his visions, but they needed something more. As it had been for most of his life, John's own purpose was to make other leaders great. He merely needed to find what would work for the Teacher. John himself was not best at being the leader, but he found that he could raise up others to be remarkable ones.

He did this in his Catholic high school, when he chose the school president. Part of his desire was to be part of the "in" crowd, and part of him just wanted to see if he could do it. So he recruited a popular football player and convinced him to run; John would get him the presidency. They became friends and he introduced John to all sorts of pretty people in the school, while John worked his plan over the entire school year to lift him up to the role. It was a landslide; he received one hundred percent of the vote. Of course, the new president promptly forgot who put him there and belittled John publicly. So, naturally, John did what any spurned leader-maker would do: He arranged for a convenient car accident, which ended the president's term and life.

The Teacher was an entirely different story. Paul Agabus Fairhaven was already a great speaker with creepy visions that often seemed to come true, but he was functionally illiterate. So, having a degree in religion from Notre Dame, John gave Fairhaven the words to speak. Later, as Paul became the Teacher, John witnessed the man's ability to embellish with each sermon and his belief system evolving didactically; and the crowds grew. John didn't have a plan, until then. He reasoned that so many men and women were willing to release their coin, and so many women would release themselves to a preacher and his followers who gave them what they wanted. It was a great run before and just after the Event.

But then the food started to run scarce, and their followers were starving and everyone was losing hope. John remembered the Mormon and Muslim faiths, how they grew out of God handing down a text that they could follow. Both tribes flourished through indoctrination, often by physical or psychological force, and at their root was their faith in a made-up text, written not by a god, but man. Taking from science fiction and a little bit of L. Ron Hubbard's *Dianetics*, John contemplated how he might craft the Book. It didn't have to be complete because the Teacher didn't really read, and John would control it and add to it over time. And then providence set in.

John and the Teacher were hiking in the woods. They split up to see if they could rustle up some game and John found a cave, already occupied and turned into a home by some kind of metaphysical writer. John killed him and read some of what he was writing. It was a masterpiece. It was there John decided a god would deliver the Book. If everybody had a purpose, a reason to move forward, other than to get somewhere safe, they might not just survive, they might thrive.

He moved all of the writer's pages into his backpack, hid the body and made up the whole story to the Teacher about a vision and revelation. John copied from the Mormons, telling the Teacher that when John sat behind a curtain in the cave's bedroom, he received the revelation from a god. The Teacher didn't believe at first, but when he wrote the first ten pages of what would become their Book by hand and read it to him, the Teacher believed. For John, it was a combination of plagiarism from the man's manuscript, liberally sprinkled with John's own words, to personalize it to their situation. Most of the be-your-own-god doctrine had already been written down by the dead author; John just made it better.

When they emerged from the cave and wandered back to their camp a week later, they amazed their followers with this new revelation. And it was the Book that brought them this far these past six months. Now they were at a precipice. The Teacher had taken three-quarters of their troops, and they were headed into a trap; John was sure of this. Meanwhile, John was left here with maybe two hundred of their troops to play babysitter to their women and the children, and of course "watch for their treason."

He was sure that the treason was in their show. Like the Great Oz of *The Wizard of Oz*, he believed there was a little man sitting behind the controls of a giant smoke screen. John just had to find a way past those controls. Regardless of what happened to the Teacher at Cicada, he would find Bios-2's Achilles' heel and he would take it for his people.

John lifted up the telescope, its tripod firmly planted in the middle of the road, his men protecting him. He scanned the walls of this place called Bios-2 and considered this version of Oz. It wasn't a scary smoke cloud they used to maintain control of its people… *It was their weapons!* These gave them their advantage over the settlers here. These had to be their weak point.

He looked at each of the five weapons, studying them carefully. He thought of how Stephen had been burned to a blackened crisp and knew it was an electrical discharge, but couldn't figure out how they controlled it. Then he remembered a strange shiny glint from what looked like a long strand of hair leading to Stephen.

Could it be? he wondered and then concentrated on the weapon. The gun to the right of the gate was turned down and gave a profile image, while the other looked at him straight on. Then he saw it, the dish that must focus the beam of electricity, but the small barrel below this must send something metal, like a bolt that would keep the beam from jumping to ground.

John moved his hat up and looked with unaided eyes at the small city. "You sneaky devils you. You only have one good shot, don't you?"

A plan started to come together.

25.

Outside Bios-2

Max and five other volunteers waded silently through the pines and aspens that only a year ago made up a majestic forest of green. Now dead or dying, they were all victims of no rainfall for almost that long during a perpetual summer. He wondered how long it would be before all plants and animals would perish, and with them humanity.

Tonight's auroras were very mild, only a dusting of the usual green luminescent clouds, barely giving them enough light to avoid a hidden ditch—or worse, a cliff. This was why Tom was leading. His eyesight was much better than Max's and he was a good tracker, as well as a great soldier.

A pine branch whipped back and slapped Max in the face, digging its needles into his cheek and threatening to do the same to its next victim walking behind him. With not so much as a flinch, he grabbed it and snapped it off.

Max veered off left so as he wouldn't be following the two rookies in front of him. Tom was a pro and had seen many battles, but his two recruits were very green behind the ears. Sue was thirty and was former US Army but had never done anything more than Basic when it came to using a weapon. She left the service as a food inspector. Rob had no formal military training but was a bit of a prepper and had taken some defensive tactics training. He was a little more hardened than Sue, having had to defend himself several times before making it here. Max's two recruits were not much more seasoned. Felix, at least he knew, having trained him a little to accompany Magdalena from Mexico to Cicada. Pel had some hunting experience and that was about all.

There was a whistle to his right; Tom's signal for "eyes open."

Max looked up and clenched his teeth to keep his jaw from dropping. There it was: their nemesis, Bios-2. It was huge— definitely bigger than Cicada. In many ways, it was like Cicada. It was on top of a mesa, accessible by an elevated road, and its complex was surrounded by a massive wall. But there was something peculiar over it and around it: a delicate transparent dome.

"It has some sort of resonating field above it," said Pel, a particle scientist. "I'm guessing it's a protective force field."

"Great. Now what, boss?" asked Tom.

"Let's move closer and observe. I'll take the lead." Max eyeballed Bios-2 and wondered how they would break into that.

Patrice Lazarro normally hated wall duty because it was so boring. No one could shoot at them with the EPF on and few of the Squatts ventured closer than the five-hundred-meter Death Zone, for fear of getting fried by one of their five EMAs. So her job of announcing any potential breaches to the Zone was superfluous, at best. Tonight was at least a little different only because the stars were out. It had been rare to see more than one or two stars at night; the brightness of the auroras that rolled in at twilight each night obscured the sky.

Patrice used to love watching the night sky and learned many of the constellations. For the first time in almost a year, she could see Ursa Minor with the North Star at the tip of its tail, and The Big

Dipper as well. *How beautiful,* she thought. *Based on the time of year*—she drew her binoculars to her face—*and the clear skies, I should be able to see Jupiter and maybe Ven—*

To Patrice's left, a small pop and a fire erupted about three hundred meters away in the open field. The fire quickly spread in a line, along a trail for maybe twenty feet. Then it appeared to go out a foot before a hunk of metal that used to be a car, which had long since been picked apart.

The car exploded, the boom thundering around them.

"Operations, I have a disturbance at three o'clock. Car fire. Reason and source, unknown." Patrice lowered the radio from her mouth and thought about what else she could report. "Please advise course of action."

Since all Bios-2's sentries would be familiar with it, Max and Tom chose the abandoned car as their diversion. With all eyes on it, they would sneak in the back way.

Pel pointed out that they could see the dome with their night-vision goggles. It was blue-green and pulsated with electricity, similar to most auroras, only it was perfectly convex. The dome stretched in a nearly flawless hemisphere over almost all of Bios-2, except for where it ended just inside one corner of the wall. That was their entry point.

Max tossed a grappling hook up onto the wall while the guards were trying to figure out what to do about the exploding car. Sue held it for him while he shinnied up. Tom was going next and the other four would maintain a perimeter around the rope so that Max and Tom had a means of escape. It would have been nice to have some more bodies coming with them on the inside, but he didn't trust them without being completely trained.

Their goal was to take a guard alive and force him or her to tell them where the device was and how to get in. It was a risky plan, but it was the best plan Max could come up with at the moment, and they had to do something.

He was halfway up the rope when he could see a guard running along the wall, past his location, probably to get a better view of the burning vehicle.

Max clung to the wall like a bug so he wouldn't be seen.

Lunder heard Patrice's announcement from the eastern wall and knew that Thompson had started something. Assuming he didn't know any of the other entrances from below, he would scale the northeastern edge of the wall, where the EPF barrier didn't quite reach it. It was the only place someone could breach their facility. But Lunder had a surprise waiting for them.

"Light 'em up!" he announced on his radio while he bent over the wall's lip to get a better look at his operation unfold.

"This is Operations, you have permission to engage the enemy." That was the official word to everyone waiting.

First, the EPF was switched off. Then there was a single shot and he watched the man on the rope fall to the ground. Then, one of the EMAs blasted its bolt at what looked like a man training his rifle on their shooter. Lunder closed his eyes before the corresponding flash and then waited another second before he opened them. He saw a smoking heap on the ground and two others scrambling. The automatic gunfire from their other guards cut them down before they could run far.

Lunder scoured the ground below for movement and saw none. "Thank you, Operations. Mission successful. Enemy has been neutralized," he told the radio and then descended the stairs.

He glanced up and caught Westerling in his office, watching the whole thing behind his window.

Webber mouthed the words to "Hold On Tight" by ELO, part of a mix that included Chicago, Boston and Little River Band. During the chorus, he felt the console vibrate and saw the red flashing indicator on his smallest computer monitor. He slipped off his headphones, the tinny sound of violins still resonating from them, and opened the drawer.

It was definitely ringing, he confirmed. But who in the hell would be calling them?

He reached around and banged on the wall separating Comms from Preston's office. "Preston! Come here. The phone is ringing. Preston!" he yelled at the top of his voice.

Preston blew through the door and huffed, "Who is that?"

"How should I know? Who else has a phone and is connected to us?"

Preston ignored the question. "Answer it."

Webber hesitated, not sure what to say. He clicked on the speakerphone so Preston could hear and then picked up the receiver. "Hello?"

"This is Senator Brian P. Westerling, the leader of Bios-2, or what you might refer to as the other Cicada. Let me speak to Preston Tanner."

Webber spun around in his chair and looked up at Preston, his face an image of stunned confusion. "How…" He couldn't even finish the sentence.

Preston grabbed the phone, stretching the cord to its limit. "This is Tanner. What do you want, Westerling?"

Webber was perplexed. It seemed obvious that Preston knew this man who led the other Cicada.

"I wanted you to know that Maxwell Thompson and the other men you sent to attack us have been stopped and killed."

"Uncle Max?" Sally King yelped in the Comms doorway. "Oh my God." Behind her was her father, holding her, trying to provide comfort.

Webber turned pale and looked nauseated.

"Assuming I believe you, what do you want?" Preston asked, the phone in his hand shaking.

"I have an army of over one thousand men headed your way now. They will give you one chance to surrender. If you do not accept it, they will destroy Cicada and everyone in it. Goodbye, Preston."

The line clicked off, leaving only static.

Preston hung up. The room was silent, but for a few sniffles from Sally and Bill.

"I wish to hell we had some way to confirm if this madman was telling us the truth. If only we could get recon and then plan accordingly…" Preston paused, and then as if he had a thought, looked to the doorway. "Hey, Bill?"

Bill King was gone.

"He said"—Sally sniffled and blew her nose in a rumpled tissue—"he said he had to go see a scientist about a hovercraft."

26.
Bios-2

"Simon Washington here, bringing back Mrs. Melanie Reid to see Senator Westerling," he announced at the door's intercom while looking down to confirm that the pressure on his side was, in fact, still his sidearm, now held by Melanie.

"Remember, Simon, I won't kill you if you do what exactly what I say." She pushed harder, signaling him to move forward.

The door buzzed open.

There were two guards by the entrance and one behind a barrier that would close if she took out the first two guards right away. She had to get through that barrier, and before that, take out the camera pointed at the door so Operations couldn't see, before it was too late.

The two guards approached and she walked past Simon toward them. He made a gurgling noise and fell to his knees, grabbing his neck, pretending to be choking. This wasn't the plan.

The two entry guards turned away from her and ran to Simon's aid, as unsure about him as she was. One was trying to administer the Heimlich. The guard at the barrier stood up from his seat and hurried past her, yelling "That's not how you do it."

While all attention was focused on Simon, she pulled out a small perfume bottle and aimed at the camera, spritzing a gooey dark paint-like substance on the lens.

Only the barrier guard remembered Melanie was there and looked up to find a gun pointed at the three of them.

"I don't want to kill you, but I will if—"

"Put down your weapon," said the barrier guard, now reaching for his sidearm.

"I mean it, I will drop you where you stand."

The other two abandoned Simon. The one doing the Heimlich dropped him to the floor, where he writhed with some unknown pain.

All three were slowly reaching for their weapons.

"Please…"

She reacted without thinking, aiming for the center of mass as she was taught.

A hollow ringing followed.

One of the guards was still moving and looked like he was moaning, but she couldn't hear him.

Simon was no longer feigning illness and slowly rose, semi-slouched above the injured guard—the others were no longer moving. She walked calmly up to the moaning guard, held the gun up and would have pulled the trigger, but she caught Simon's face. His eyes begged *why?* They were almost child-like in their innocent plea, not quite understanding what it all meant.

She couldn't do it.

Instead, she lifted the gun higher and brought it down upon the back of the guard's head with all her strength. He stopped moaning. She grabbed his radio and the other then tied up Simon, so he wouldn't be in trouble. Again, she felt a little sorry for him.

Lunder ran the last few steps, his boots squeaking on the concrete outside S227. The door was wide open, and a small amount of blood streaked the floor, indicating signs of a struggle. One of the guard's radios lay against an opposite wall, by their sofa. He bent down to pick it up, but then remembered their hiding spot where they passed notes, hoping she had left one there. Reaching behind the table up against the wall, he couldn't find anything.

He then pulled the note he had found left under a rock by Dr. Rush's door. Of all the scientists, he should have expected Dr. Rush to be involved in the Reids' scheming. In spite of Westerling's belief, Lunder knew they couldn't be trusted. He opened the note and read it once more.

They've been telling us lies. Cicada IS a reality. Westerling & Lunder took us from Cicada and are keeping us prisoner. They never intended to let us go. I'm going to stop them. Wait for my sign and we'll meet at the rendezvous point.

Mel

Lunder scrunched the note up in his hand, angry that he couldn't figure out where this traitor was. He thought he might get lucky and that she would meet Carrington here, but she'd been and gone. Then he thought she might try to take out their power, but now he realized where she was going. He tossed the crumpled note and darted out the door.

"Operations, this is Lunder Gufstafson. Dispatch security to Westerling and the Observation Tower immediately. I will meet them on the ground floor. Apprehend Dr. Melanie Reid. Consider her armed and dangerous."

"Mr. Gufstafson, I read you—"

A piercing squeal bellowed out of the radio. Lunder yanked it away from his ear and turned the volume down to minimize the hit to his already painful headache. He dashed down the stairs and out the doors into the morning sunlight. There were already a few guards in front of the tower's entrance; at least that part of his message had gone out before the loud noise. He turned up the volume, and the squeal still blared. Angrily, he turned it off.

"How the hell did you disrupt our radios too?" he said as he jogged. They had all underestimated Melanie Reid.

Carrington had been listening to the broadcast and knew he had to think quickly, before Lunder could give more instructions. He had been waiting for the right moment to carry out his plan, his resolve fading, when he heard the transmission and knew the window had opened but could slam shut without warning. Hiding behind a desk, he grabbed some tape from a drawer. Then taking two radios he had collected from two guards he had disarmed earlier, he taped them together and slid both mic buttons into the "On" position. With both transmitting at the same time, he whistled. The sound picked up and transmitted, resulting in both radios echoing a loud high-pitched feedback. That would take out all the radios on that frequency.

Now he had to wait for the time to spring.

He wished he could have told Melanie why he was going to do this. Of course she wouldn't understand, and she would have talked him out of it if he told her. He wished their lives could have gone in a different direction. He wished they had more time.

The elevator door opened up and he shrank further behind the desk, gun ready.

"I wanna see Crapaw," cried a little girl. It was Westerling's granddaughter.

"We're going to see him now," said Deanna.

"I wanna show him my new necklace Mrs. Reid gave me."

"You will. Here we are."

There was a knock on the door and the sound of it opening.

"Crapaw… Crapaw. Look at my new necklace."

Carrington peered over the desk and saw a woman and beyond the doorway, a little girl hugging Westerling.

"Dammit," he breathed. He would have to wait longer.

The elevator door opened again.

Melanie slid out of the elevator and peered into the reception room. There was no one there and Westerling's office door was open. He could hear voices inside. She slipped into the waiting room, and then slinked into the conference room, crawling underneath the long table, until she reached the end.

Lying sideways and boosting her head out, she scanned his office, clutching her gun.

He was standing right there and looking away from her, talking to someone out of her view. He was less than fifteen feet away from her: easy shot.

She slid the gun along the floor and brought it up slightly, acquiring a perfect sight picture. She aimed right at his head. *Apply pressure to the trigger. Wait for the shot.*

She took a breath and unwrapped her finger from the trigger.

Westerling held up little Leanne, his granddaughter, and spun her around. She was joyfully showing off the necklace Mel had given her. She couldn't shoot and risk hitting the child. And even if she had a clean shot, could she shoot the child's grandfather right in front of her?

She sighed, at a loss.

There was a commotion coming from the elevator. The waiting room door burst open and so must have Westerling's office as he looked in that direction and let go of Leanne, who ran to her mother's arms.

It was now or never. She fired.

"I'm sure glad I followed your recommendation and had the window walls hardened to withstand a bullet."

"Well, as you can see, even these pacifist scientists can commit violence," Lunder said proudly.

"Speaking of which, can you get my daughter and granddaughter down below and out of harm's way?"

"Yes, of course." Lunder turned to the guards and said, "Take them to their residence and post one guard there until I tell you otherwise. And leave me with Mr. Westerling."

"Yes sir," they announced and left, ushering Leanne and her mom out of the office and closing the door.

"What are we going to do with her?" Westerling motioned toward the conference room, where an unconscious Melanie lay on the floor, her hands and feet zip-tied.

"Until we find her husband, I'm going to do nothing. I'll take her to my office and hold her there."

27.

Outside Cicada

Flying a hovercraft was completely different from flying an airplane. Its inventor, Dr. Cockerell, said it would be the same, but he was wrong. Bill had had a few hours' flying experience, courtesy of a close friend of Max's who owned a private plane in Mexico and was certified to give flight lessons. Flying his Cessna was easy; this was not. All the controls in a Cessna were intuitive, designed by many engineers over a hundred years of trial and error; but the hovercraft's controls, designed by a generous mad scientist and with no trial and error, took practice. Unfortunately, that was a luxury Bill didn't have. With an airplane, there was an element of "feeling" the controls when you maneuvered. The hovercraft, shaped like a toaster, took lots of thought, which was not good for split-second decisions. He prayed that he wouldn't make the wrong ones and burn himself to a crisp, as he often did with toast.

It would have seemed to the casual observer—who would supposedly think a flying blue toaster was normal—that he was on some suicidal quest during the toaster's inaugural flight. Twice he almost crashed into the forest's canopy below. He had brought the hovercraft so perilously close to the treetops that a couple of them slapped the craft's underside.

Bill found that when he wanted to bring the hovercraft lower, a very light touch with one thumb on the stick caused it to descend very rapidly. But when he wanted to ascend, he had to pull. Side to side was easy, although he had to be careful not to toss himself off the damn thing. After getting the hang of the controls, maybe halfway to Bios-2, his next worry was being seen by the troops he was attempting to scout.

The oversized toaster was painted blue, not as some ode to a giant Smurf, but because Cockerell thought it would blend into the sky. He forgot that people on the ground would be looking up at its bottom, which was black. However, when he was closer to the ground, the blue made him very visible against the brown trees and gray-brown mountains. Fixing that was for another day, if he made it to another day.

Yet, in spite of the significant learning curve, the hovercraft was an amazing vehicle from its quiet hum during operations to its propulsion method, which Bill still didn't even comprehend after several attempts by Cockerell to explain it to him. He was pretty sure if this machine had been constructed before the Event, this scientist would have been a billionaire because everyone would have wanted one. Or, he would have been bankrupt after the first crash and subsequent class-action lawsuit.

He could see a few specks on the roadway ahead of him. He decided if they were the invaders he was trying to gather intel on, he was too visible flying over the road. He pulled up on the stick and took her up above the treetops and then maneuvered to the left, about twenty meters in from the tree line, hoping that would be enough cover. He was getting the hang of this now.

Within a few minutes he slid—completely unobserved—past hordes of men and women in red robes. There were hundreds of them, marching like fire ants heading to their next leafy conquest. Except these red ants had automatic rifles and a few carried larger-caliber weapons.

"Shit, the threat was real," he said to the wind, which instantly puffed up his cheeks with warm dryness. He knew he should turn back and report this to Preston, as it was his sole purpose for being out here, but when he looked up, in the distance he could see the oval walls on top of a mesa that he guessed was Bios-2. He needed to check this out too while he was here. Then he would zip back hours before the marauders arrived at Cicada.

With his friend Max... missing... He had difficulty even considering this, and forced himself into not accepting the story of his death. Either the story was false, which would make sense, or somehow Max would survive, as he always seemed to do. And maybe, he would find Max and help him, return a favor that had run its course way too long. Regardless of whether he found Max or not, he *knew* he was alive. And, Cicada (and Max, when he returned) would need Bill's intel. His efforts were much more important now. Everything pointed to his checking out Bios-2.

He pointed the toaster-craft directly at the mesa-top complex shimmering on the horizon.

"I want to speak to Francis alone," the Teacher told the six apostles who accompanied him on this journey to Cicada. The other four remained with John at their camp outside of Bios-2.

"But Teacher, you haven't yet chosen a replacement for Stephen and we wanted to give you some options," whined Stanley.

"That can wait. We must now prepare our minds and bodies for the battle that may come at Cicada. Sometime after I have taken Cicada and I've had a chance to discuss it with Brother John, I will announce my decision. Now, tell Francis I wish to speak to him alone."

Stanley said nothing more and rushed forward to get Francis, who was leading them toward Cicada. The other six slowed their pace from the Teacher's, to give him privacy with the soldier.

While the Teacher waited for him, so that they could discuss strategy, he thought about their march so far. They had been walking in the brutal midday sunlight for a couple hours now, right down the middle of the road, where no shade existed as the tree line's cover was too far off on each side. Walking closer to the tree line was not an option since each side was littered with abandoned cars and nature's own detritus, all of which would only slow their progression, and only for the benefit of a few moments of shade. But they would have to stop shortly to give everyone a rest so they would be stronger when they arrived.

"Yes, Teacher, how can I serve you?" Frank called out, hesitant to interrupt his Teacher deep in thought.

"You understand the plan, Francis?"

"Yes, Teacher, I do. We'll arrive at Cicada in the evening, when we'll make our demands. They will have already been contacted by that fork-tongued devil at Bios-2, so they should not need time to think. If they do not open their doors to us, we will attack them using the explosives we have been given. I will have all our men and women ready to take their north gate when it is time. Then, if we were told the truth and we are able to open the other gates, you'll march in with the remainder of our warriors and we will take Cicada. The siege should only take a couple of hours, assuming they resist."

"Excellent. I knew I was correct to place my faith in you. I have no doubt that your transition to a god like me will be a short one." Teacher grinned as if he was offering him the golden pot at the end of the rainbow.

Frank didn't know what to say to this part, which was just so weird. He had been raised a Christian, and although he didn't have a strong faith, he believed there was only one god, and that was the God of Abraham. When the Teacher saved him from the noose and his family from the knives of cannibals, Frank would have probably followed him at that moment if he had said he was the chief duck priest from a cult of duck gods. Instead, this man they all called the Teacher spoke words from the Bible, albeit a little twisted. They seemed to be walking down a path of order and justice in a very orderless and unjust world. It was during this time that the Teacher had come to trust him because Frank believed in always speaking the truth when he was asked, never candy coating his answers to what he thought the Teacher wanted.

When the group had been struggling, John and the Teacher returned after being gone for a few days, talking about gods, and not the one and only God, but many gods. They started preaching from the Book, which was the genesis of their mutual revelation. Through it they preached the doctrine that any one of them could be a god; they just had to focus their energies inward and follow the Book. Frank had a feeling that John had written the whole thing himself, knowing that the Teacher was not very literate, as he admitted to Frank. Everyone bought into this, but he hadn't. Now what could he do? His life and his families' lives were dependent on the Teacher and the Teacher's fortunes. They were connected to this man, no matter how screwy his beliefs were.

"Now," the Teacher continued after a long pause, "let us have all our warriors stop and rest in the shade for a bit; we wouldn't want to be exhausted just before the battle."

"Yes, Teacher."

Frank excused himself and jogged ahead to the front of the group, where he told his lieutenants and steered them into a clearing, just inside the tree line cover.

There they rested.

Bill never knew he was in trouble until it was too late.

He arrived at Bios-2—the other Cicada—quick enough. The size was amazing, a little bigger than Cicada, and laid out very similarly. Their walls were taller and seemed more fortified. They had giant cannons with weird dishes at the end of each. They reminded him of a 60s sci-fi movie's ray guns. There was a tower in the middle, practically a skyscraper, with antennas on top and a large smokestack in the middle that bellowed rippling white clouds. And above the tower, he saw something perplexing.

The whole time Bill kept rubbing his eyes, trying to understand what he first thought was the shimmering effect of the heat or the tiring of his eyes. The semi-visible dome was surely a mirage, which would disappear when he got closer. Yet, as he closed the distance to less than a mile, the form looked more solid. He had to see it from above. Maybe he could even do a quick pass overhead at the craft's max speed. He should be safe because they wouldn't expect him to fly over; no one would be staring into the intense light of the sun above him. They would expect threats to come from the other side of the walls, from the ground.

He pulled up hard on the yoke and gained altitude. When he was high enough that he could go forward and down to gain the most speed, he pushed the accelerator button—stupidly placed by his left knee—and lightly pressed on the stick. Just after he passed over the wall he noticed a problem.

The hovercraft lurched a bit and then sputtered, and he quickly lost some valuable altitude. He pulled up, slowing himself, but it didn't help with his dropping. It then lurched violently, as if his propulsion system was cycling on and off. He was falling like a big, blue brick. It lost all maneuverability and all Bill could do was hold on and go down with the ship. He doubted he could survive a drop of at least three hundred feet.

He watched as he torpedoed toward a large open space in the complex; people were scrambling. So much for passing over unnoticed. One of the people on the wall turned his ray gun-cannon toward him. He was screwed.

As he approached the dome at literally breakneck speed, he marveled that it was both solid and yet translucent, seemingly made up of gridlines of pulsating light. Would he pass right through and splat on the ground, or just smash into the top of it?

He couldn't close his eyes.

The hovercraft then hummed to life, for just a moment, shooting him forward and up so quickly that his body crashed into the craft hard and he almost let go and fell out. Like a stone skidding on the surface of a placid lake, the blue toaster with Bill clutching it desperately skipped across the pulsating light-dome that protected Bios-2.

Maybe it was the impact with the craft, or the g-force, but he had a sense of being in an old Warner Brothers cartoon, with all the silly animated noises. "Boing... boing... boing." Then he was falling again, now past Bios-2's far wall, over a vast smoldering field of black and brown.

A thought popped into his head: *reboot!* Bill punched the "on" button twice to turn it off and then on again, hoping it was like rebooting a computer, which had solved almost every computer problem he had in the past. It seemed to work as he felt the hovercraft fight against gravity's pull. But it wasn't enough thrust. He hit the ground hard, just outside the wall.

He might have been unconscious for a bit, because his eyes flicked open and he saw people standing over him. They lifted him up and carried him, and then everything went black.

To say the atmosphere around Cicada was electric was a laughable statement of the obvious. Everyone ran around as if they were on fire. Most were seeking information, going from residence to residence or building to building, asking about the coming invaders, or trying to confirm that their founder was actually dead. A few like Sally sought solace alone, in their own way, in a place where they felt comfortable. For Sally, it was the Library. Preston had added the Kings' thumbprint data into the system. And although she had experienced the power outage once, she still felt safe down there. It had technology and books, her two favorite things on earth; and it was quiet. She rationalized her decision by figuring at this point, all she could do was worry, and she had been doing that almost nonstop for the better part of a year now.

She brought along Max's crazy-looking flashlight, one of the type he called "Frankensteins" because of the protective covering. It was perhaps overkill in an underground building, which was heavily shielded against EMPs, but she was no longer taking chances getting stuck in the darkness like before. Although, even the darkness and its solitude would be comforting at this point. She just wanted to have some control over the light. More to the point, she was hoping to escape her worries by reading a new novel. She didn't want to deal with these newest crises; Uncle Max maybe being killed and an invading army about to strike were too much for one person to take. She was numb.

She pretended for a moment that she was back at the university, searching the library bookshelves for a new hidden gem to get lost in. Looking up and down the aisles, she finally found an interesting shelf, stocked full of several large tomes by Stephen King. She wasn't into horror stories, but then remembered Preston had a copy of *The Stand* on his desk and said there was another at their Library and she should check it out. He had told her very strongly, "It reminds me of the struggle we are constantly involved in, every day of our lives: a struggle between good and evil. We don't have to look very far for evil these days, but good is a lot harder to find. This book is about that good and how with God's help, good will win the day over evil. Mark my words, we all will have to make our stand someday."

Okay, it wasn't light reading and didn't exactly take her mind away, but she wanted to be reminded that good could win over evil. She spotted the dog-eared paperback, its blue-black cover hanging by a few fibers. She snatched it.

Then she found a soft chair at a table with a bunch of books stacked like some chaotic game of Jenga, sat down and started to read.

As she read about the Walking Dude, the book's evil antagonist, a man burst through the Library door, searching for someone. She slunk behind the bramble of books and held hers in front of her face, like some shield of protection against the world's intrusion. Every few seconds, she peeked over the top as casually as she could. When the man looked her direction a jolt of recognition hit him, and he hurried in her direction. She didn't recognize him at all, but as he came closer, he seemed surer that she was who he was seeking. She held her book up higher, completely obscuring her face, and pretended to be captivated by it.

"Sally King?" he asked from the other side of the table.

She put the book down. "Yes."

"Your mother, Lisa King, is looking for you. She's with Mr. Tanner in the infirmary. Mr. Thompson is alive and being treated. They're asking for you and your father. Do you know where he is?"

She leapt from her seat. "Uncle Max is alive? Ah, no I haven't seen him since this morning." Also, she was wondering where her dad was. She wanted to run and follow this stranger to see Uncle Max, but then she looked around, trying to figure out what she needed to do to officially borrow her book, when the man spun around and hurried away. She hollered, "Wait. Are you going to show me to the infirmary?"

"No," he hesitated, "I've been asked to find Bill King after I found you. Infirmary is upstairs on the second floor." And then he was gone.

28.
Bios-2

She woke to congratulatory voices. Men full of their pride and their own self-validations. They were loud and boisterous and they were inside her aching head. Melanie's eyes flicked open. The assault of light was like a splash of acid on each brain cell of her pounding head. She squeezed them shut and collected herself, her head pulsating pain with each breath. The last thing she remembered was… shooting Westerling. She let one eye squint open, letting in a bearable amount of sunlight from the outside window-wall. The voices continued: Lunder and Westerling, but the bastard sounded no worse off for her efforts.

Lying on her side, she was hog-tied like some prized pig ready to go to slaughter. Her rage built up again, their laughter lighter fluid to its fiery coals. Melanie had been working hard to keep it in check since she had been in Bios-2's captivity, and with Carrington, she was able to hold it back. But she no longer desired that. Now, she wanted to embrace her rage.

She couldn't see them, but she could hear them as if they were standing over her. A quick look confirmed they weren't there, and she realized that she was pointed in the wrong direction, with her back to them. Carefully she rocked onto her other side, facing into Westerling's office. He was definitely unharmed, even though she remembered having him in her sights and squeezing the trigger and feeling the release. Then somebody, she guessed it was Lunder, had knocked her out. A little blemish on the window-wall separating her from them, told her the answer. "Shit, bulletproof glass," she whispered.

Westerling and Lunder shared looks of adulation. These two men acted like they controlled the world. She hated them and wanted them dead more than she wanted anything. Then she thought of Carrington, and as if cooled by a momentary cloudburst of calming rain, her rage simmered.

She hoped that he'd gotten the note she left for him. But if he didn't make it to their apartment, perhaps he found out from Rush. She wanted him safe.

What was in store for her couldn't be good. They would probably make an example of her to the other scientists and the other workers of Bios-2; she now knew they were in fact all prisoners here. Regardless, she had to find a way to escape. She reached down to the back of her shoe and pulled out the small knife she had hidden there. Carrington joked about it, calling it her James Bond knife, but he would have thought it smart now. After getting it free, she was about to slice at the zip-tie binding her hands but stopped.

She looked back at the two men who didn't yet notice she was conscious. She was in plain view of them. Even if she could free herself, how far could she get before being caught again? The hallway, the elevator, certainly not the building exit. No, patience had always served her well in the past. She would wait for the right time. And if she was lucky, she might be able to surprise and kill one of them at close range. She had done it before, and she would look forward to doing it again. So she closed her eyes, clutched the cool comfort of her knife in her palm, listened to them and waited.

Carrington had been waiting for so long behind the secretarial desk outside Westerling's office, his legs were cramping up. He figured that someone else had a similar idea, because that person had already taken out four guards at the tower's entrance door, left wide open. He had been able to walk right up to Westerling's door, but then he had heard the voices and ducked behind this desk. Deanna and Leanne were escorted out of Westerling's office; they all walked to the elevator. Still, he waited. Now he heard only two voices in Westerling's office: Lunder's and the senator's. It was time.

He peeked around the desk in both directions and saw just one guard standing between him and the door. This guard was playing with his radio, fumbling with the volume and squelch control and then the talk button. No doubt, he was frustrated by the disturbance Carrington had created. Each time he depressed the talk button, it would squeal. Unfortunately, so did the two radios he had bound together and later placed in the drawer of the desk he was currently hiding behind. The guard studied the desk, trying to figure out what he was hearing in front of him. Carrington could see him through a small hole the computer cords snaked through under the desk.

The guard held his radio up in front of him like some sort of radio Geiger counter and pressed the talk button firmly. The hidden radios squealed louder now.

It was time to make his move. His heart raced, and his fear wanted desperately to take over, but he had to confront these two men and he couldn't let this guard get in his way.

He rose abruptly, unintentionally banging his knee against the desk. Carrington's presence, the banging noise and the gun pointed at him startled the guard so much, he dropped his radio. When the guard saw that Carrington's hand was shaking, he had a shot of confidence. He stuck his palm out, while his other hand moved slowly toward his gun.

"Hold it, Dr. Reid," he said. "You don't want to do anything stupid." The crease of a smile on the guard's face told Carrington what he didn't want to know. "Now give me your gun," he demanded, moving his hand closer to his own.

Carrington knew there was only one way forward for him, and he was committed to his course. It was time to cross his own Rubicon.

He pulled the trigger.

The gunshot jolted her and her eyes popped open.

"What the hell?" Westerling said softly.

Lunder beckoned him back with his hands. "Shhhh." He drew his Luger and walked out of her view, toward the door.

She looked back at Westerling, who was withdrawing farther from the door, eyes fixated on the area around it. Maybe someone else was going to do her work for her. She just wished she could see past the damn furniture inside the senator's office that blocked her view. She watched him and listened.

Westerling stepped back a few paces, and then behind his leather chair. He seemed to shrink a couple of inches, as if he was about to duck to the ground.

The sound of a door opening quickly and then banging into a wall caused him to jump slightly. He lifted his arms in the air, as a sign of surrender, and displayed that false grin he loved to shine on people, the one that said "vote for me."

A familiar voice demanded, "Where is Lunder?"

Westerling tensed up like something was about to happen and then he ducked behind his chair and peeked over the edge.

"Right behind you, asshole," Lunder stridently announced. "Drop it."

There was a loud metallic *clank* and she saw Westerling stand up resolutely. He walked back to where he was standing before. Some other movement came into her view… as she feared, *it's Carrington!*

He walked toward Westerling, shoulders stooped in defeat. Lunder followed, holding his Luger and now a second gun on her husband.

Carr was caught.

"What the hell did you think you were going to do with this, Dr. Reid?" Lunder walked around him and wiggled his gun at him like a parent admonishing a child, before tossing it on Westerling's desk. It clanked and came to rest at the opposite side, way out of reach. "He killed Clyde outside your door," Lunder said to Westerling. "Shot him in the chest."

"Look who else we caught." Westerling pointed at the conference room on the opposite side of the floor-to-ceiling glass wall. Carr could see his wife tied up on the floor of a conference room, her eyes filled with anger and fear. "Little bitch tried to shoot me too. But we're smarter than both of you. That wall is hardened to withstand a rifle blast. So, she had a better chance of shooting herself than me. Now, we will pass sentence for your crimes."

Carrington was shocked to see her lying there. But, as hard as it would be for her, she had to witness this and she had to know what he knew. If only she could hear them.

Her voice crackled through a speaker above them. "Shouldn't we be together if you're going to judge us?"

"Shit, she can hear us," Westerling grumbled, wringing his hands.

"Doesn't matter; they're both dead," Lunder stated.

"Since we've already been condemned to die," Carrrington jumped in, hoping to stop Lunder from getting Melanie, "and since my wife can hear this, perhaps you can explain what you're doing with a fission reactor that is venting large quantities of gamma radiation into a volcanic vent?"

Lunder froze in his tracks, halfway between them and the glass wall. He started to walk back to Carrington. "How? How could you know this?"

"Remember, we're in the presence of the brilliant Dr. Carrington Reid." Westerling stepped to the bar area and poured himself a bourbon, and then sat calmly on the sofa facing him. "You've been poking around where you shouldn't have."

"What I don't understand is why? Why would you do something that not only puts your people and your daughter and granddaughter at risk, but puts the whole world at risk?"

"One word, Dr. Reid: control." Westerling took a sip, enjoying this almost as much as one of his best Cubans.

"A number of years ago, something monumental yet tragic happened. My wife and my son-in-law were killed by some two-bit hoodlum on the day of my granddaughter's birth. That changed me." He looked pained and paused for a moment.

"I was already working on the Bios-2 project, hiding its billion-dollar cost in multiple appropriations bills to keep it out of public scrutiny. But, B2 was only a carbon copy of Cicada at the time, using plans we had bought from Cicada's manager. My ultimate plan didn't materialize until the day after my wife and son died. You see, I realized then that society was broken; I was going to find the means to fix it, using B2 as the platform.

"It was fortuitous, then, that I told Lunder here my plan and Lunder handed me the means to carry it out. Together, we swiftly changed B2 to what it is today, all in preparation for the Event. I didn't know when the Event would occur, certainly didn't expect such a big solar flare, knowing an X1 or X2 would do just fine and those occurred all the time, as you constantly reminded us subscribers to your newsletter. But my waiting paid off and we were rewarded with an X45 flare; again, thanks for the warning. It was the big one that you and all the other solar scientists were dreading and few prepared for, even though it was inevitable.

"And so I executed my plan. It was a simple one, really. After a few years, I alone would have control of the world, scrubbing away the scum that once inhabited it. Sure, billions would die, but with them, so would the lazy bums who sucked off the tits of the working population. And in the end, I would give this new world to my surviving daughter and granddaughter. The world would be reborn in an image of my choosing. And I would have total control over it."

Carrington had suspected all this, but to hear it articulated so blatantly and with such disregard for human life was shocking, unimaginable. "So, you murdered billions just for control?"

"To quote from my favorite movies, but in my own way, 'The needs of the few outweigh the needs of the many.'"

"You're a monster."

He smiled and took another gulp.

Carrington turned and looked at Melanie in the next room. "Did you hear all of this?"

Tears streaming from her eyes and her head nodding confirmed it. She mouthed, "Yes."

"I'm sorry for what I'm about to do, my love. I hope you will forgive me. And if there is life after this one, I hope we meet again. I l-love y-you," he stuttered.

Her face contorted in confusion. "What are you doing, Carr?" Her voice was scratchy over the speaker.

Carrington turned and walked toward Westerling. "I knew this, but I wanted her to hear you, so that she could tell the others after I killed you two." He lifted his shirt and showed them that he was wearing a bomb strapped to his torso. "Goodbye, assholes."

Melanie realized what Carrington was about to do when he lifted his shirt. He was going to kill them, and he knew that she would be protected behind the hardened wall—and now she knew everything they did.

In quick motions, she sliced her bindings off and yelled, "Carr, don't!"

She stood up and saw that Lunder had already dashed toward Carrington and hit him with his entire body weight, knocking him down to the floor.

The room filled with light.

29.
Cicada

Max hobbled into his residence, exhausted and in agony. He hadn't slept for over sixty hours, and there was no way he was going to get any sleep soon. He tossed his equipment down in a heap in the living room, grimacing at the burn raging in his right bicep, where he took a bullet and his swollen left ankle, where he landed after falling from the rope.

He limped over to the bookshelves between the living room and office and stopped at the one garnering the most attention since his return. He called it his Decision Shelf, because he knew life came down to one of these two decisions: on one side of the shelf was a three-quarters-full bottle of tequila and on the other side, his military leather Bible. The bottle of tequila had lost most of its dust; the book was still covered by over a year's worth of neglect. He knew the decision he would make right now, even though the other offered wisdom and peace. He didn't want peace; he wanted justice. He wanted to seek revenge and had no desire to find peace or purpose in all of this.

Max swiped the bottle and a glass from another shelf and moved over to his desk. A healthy pour later, he slumped in his chair, deflated. He gazed at the amber liquid, its satisfying fragrance already greeting his nose, beckoning him to take a sip. He took a gulp as he mulled things over.

Senator Brian Westerling, the leader of Bios-2, a Cicada copy, was killing the world and probably didn't even know it. Yet this man, who convinced Preston to give up their building and design plans and to divert their scientists and who had killed two of his people today, seemed determined to kill them or make them suffer. And now Bios-2 had sent an invading army.

But why?

He took another gulp, his festering anger not at all tempered by the tequila's harshness, despite its spreading warmth. "And where the hell are you, Bill? Cockerell said you took the hovercraft. Did you really go on some stupid mission just to get intel while riding on some experimental blue toaster?" He hollered at the tequila bottle, as if it were responsible.

He cackled at the thought of calling Bill's mission stupid when his own mission was at best a fool's errand. How could he have thought that taking five people, four with little training, on an assault mission to a place they've never been to and had no intelligence on, all to turn off a nuclear reactor that was killing the planet, was anything but idiotic?

"How could you be so damned stupid?" he scolded himself. First Felix was zapped by some sort of lightning gun, burning him so completely, you couldn't carbon date him. Then Rob died while Max was carrying him back. And then there were Sue's and Pel's injuries, which weren't life threatening, but still serious. These casualties were because of his rush to judgement and poor planning. It was so unlike him. He always planned.

But lately he had been filled with rage; a frustration born from a desire to keep everyone safe.

He took another sip of the harsh liquid as he tilted back in his chair with his eyes closed.

Think Max, think.

"We have a mole." He sprang forward and glared at the bottle that held all the answers. "Westerling found out about our raid from the mole. No other way he could have known I was there and taken credit for my killing. And that's why they were ready for us. He was contacted by one of the people we trust. It had to be someone who has phone access, too."

He looked to the left of the bottle and noticed the portable hard drive and notebook he had taken from Sampson's lab on his desk, waiting for him to investigate. "Sampson, you must have been up to something, or why else would your apartment have been tossed? Someone, probably our mole, was looking for something, but what?"

Max booted up his computer, and while he waited, he slid the notebook to him and started to thumb through it. When the computer was ready, he plugged in Sampson's portable drive and then leaned back and looked at Sampson's nearly illegible handwriting, hoping he could make sense of it.

He was sure the answers lay within.

Sally King was grinning, babying the new-to-her copy of *The Stand* under her arm and gripping Max's monster flashlight as she emerged from Cicada's not-at-all-public Library. She was excited, almost giddy. Uncle Max was alive, and she had a date. Okay, maybe not a date in the normal sense of the word, but she was meeting Webber in Comms. He had just stopped by after the man-whose-name-she-still-can't-remember told her the news about Max. Webber told her not to worry about the invading army, as they had a plan, and he wanted her help in Comms because Magdalena was with Max in the infirmary. Afterward, they'd have some dinner at the Rec Facility. She wasn't sure if it was the tech or the man or both, but she was positively excited about this.

She strolled through the Library's grand doorway, its hinges not making a peep as it closed, and she practically skipped to the elevator.

She heard something and stopped.

The sound of a man's voice, muffled as if he was holding his hand over his mouth, perhaps in an attempt to be not heard. The disjointed mutter seemed to come from above, floating down from the concrete ceiling. It was a man's voice and it sounded familiar. She shuffled around trying to determine its origination.

The closet.

It was the utility closet, and besides Dr. Ron's laboratory and the Library, it was the only other door on this floor.

She was told that there were communications boxes and much of the network cabling running through there to other points in this building and out to the others. But currently inside this closet was a man having a conversation with someone, but she only heard the one voice, as if he were on a phone.

Max stopped at a note in Sampson's notebook, scribbled in almost illegible script, and read it twice:

There is one other on the inside, like me: he is IT.

Max thought about what that meant. This mole, who has been working under their noses this whole time, whose sole purpose has been to hurt us and was directly responsible for today's deaths of

Felix and Rob. It had to be someone he didn't know. It had to be someone who Bios-2 sent to them or they got to, like Sampson, although he still didn't understand Sampson's motivations. Perhaps this would be on his portable drive, but he didn't have the time or the desire to investigate someone's motivations. He was much more interested in their actions. The land they now lived in required decisive actions, with little consideration to the reasons why. And when someone committed a crime, the punishment needed to be quick and absolute.

Who could it be? he wondered. What the hell did he mean by *he is it?* He looked again and noticed that Sampson had written *I T*, not *it*; he meant the mole is an Informational Technologies guy.

Then he knew who it was.

"Yes, plans are in place," the muffled male voice said, much more clearly, her ear practically on the door.

Silence as the man must be listening to the other voice on a what? Phone? Radio? Probably not a radio because you couldn't transmit out of this building. It had to be a phone.

"When will it happen?"

Silence.

"What, in an hour?"

Rustling sounds, as if equipment was being moved. *He's leaving!*

"Okay, I'll be waiting for a sign—" *Click-click-click.* "—Operations, are you there?"

Then there was a louder click and more movement.

Sally softly bounced on the balls of her feet toward the Library, to a niche where she thought she could hide in the shadows. She saw the closet door open further, just as she slipped into the protective darkness.

The door closed and the man's footsteps moved away from her, to the elevator.

Tentatively, she stuck her head out, just enough to see him walking away. He was carrying a small orange case, the kind that might carry a two-way speakerphone butt-set, used to test and talk on phone lines. And… he was wearing a blue baseball cap, just like Webber's.

Max drained his tumbler in one gulp and slammed it down on the desk, almost breaking it. Grabbing his .45 and scabbard off the pile on the floor, he slipped both into his belt against the small of his back while moving to the door.

The burn of anger squelched his pain and fatigue.

Before he was out his front door, he examined the picture of the Kings and said to Bill's image, "Hang on, buddy. I need to kill an asshole traitor first before I can go out and find you."

30.
Bios-2

The blast was strong enough to blow back one of the glass wall's doors, propelling her backwards into the window-wall. Now Melanie felt like all the air was sucked out of her lungs. She breathed so rapidly that she was hyperventilating and near passing out.

Did this just happen?

Had she seen the man she loved kill himself and take out Lunder and Westerling?

She could only gape, dumbfounded and desperately trying to take in air. It was as if she forgot how to breathe.

Westerling's office was obliterated. Wires and pipes hung from the ceiling, water spurting from a severed pipe; sparks flew, arced and then dropped into the smoky air like fireworks; and ragged debris hung or piled up everywhere. The glass wall held up, with only one panel laced with cracks; thousands of little bits of glass still held together as one but threatening to fall into a heap of unrecognizable pieces like the rest of the office.

There was no other movement inside. After that blast, she didn't expect to see any. Carrington had been thorough, planning every part of this, and they hadn't seen it coming; neither did she. He wanted her to hear what that monster had done, to all of them... to the whole earth. She couldn't fathom that one man would kill billions of people just to have control over the surviving population.

"Well, looks like you can't control everything, asshole," she said glumly, finally regaining some of her breath.

She examined her arms and legs as if they were someone else's, seeing that she must have already sliced through her bindings. *Did I do that?* she wondered as she examined her boot knife, still clutched in her hand, as if it were part of her.

There was movement by the office entrance door; guards poured into the office, searching for survivors. *Good luck with that!*

She didn't need an invitation to leave; already on her hands and knees, she crawled all the way to the hallway entrance before finally getting to her feet and made it to the elevator without being seen. With further luck, all the guards would have left their posts to investigate the explosion or gone to Operations. She descended.

The elevator dinged. She waited, knife ready to take more blood, but she heard no one outside. The three guards she had killed earlier had been moved over to a wall, out of the way. Simon was gone.

She deliberated and then walked over to one of them. He hadn't drawn and she wondered if he still had his gun. He did. She snatched it and two magazines, slipping them into her front waistband and covering them with her shirt. Her handy boot knife she shoved back into her shoe. She stood up straight and gazed at her reflection in the painted-over outside windows.

Her eyes were swollen from tears, from dust and smoke. Her head had a splash of dark red, some dried blood where Lunder had clocked her; *retribution is a bitch*, she thought and smiled slightly. Her face sagged back again.

Before thoughts of Carrington could invade and ravage her emotions and take away her rage, she pushed them back, mussed her already-rumpled hair with her fingers and stepped out into the bright sun.

She had a new goal in mind: shut down the reactor that was killing the planet. She couldn't do anything about Cicada. They'd have to fend for themselves. But maybe she could save a few scientists by helping them escape, and she could save them all by destroying the reactor.

She walked briskly to their apartment, trying not to draw any attention to herself. Carrington had fashioned two explosives… the second one was built into a clock. She would use that device to blow the reactor to hell—the hell that she hoped Westerling and Lunder now occupied.

She rounded a corner, her building in sight, and looked back at the Observation Tower. She was now on the side opposite of where she'd watched them die. Smoke poured out of a couple holes in the forty-five-degree angled windows. And then she noticed something else, something she had only seen a couple times during testing and the firing of their EMAs. The EPF was down. Bios-2 was unprotected.

A guard brushed past her and yelled at his dead radio, "The field is down. Operations, can you hear me? The field is down."

Melanie grinned proudly. Carrington had given them all a chance now. "Thank you, my love. I will make sure your efforts were not wasted."

It was her turn.

John couldn't believe what he was seeing. He stood tall on the road leading to Bios-2 after one of his men told them there was an explosion. Black smoke billowed out of a gash in the large tower in the middle of the walled complex. But he also saw something much more important. Their force field was down.

The Teacher told him to watch out for treachery from the leader of Bios-2. He said it would lead to their downfall and that John should wait for a sign and be prepared. And there it was.

A dozen other red-robed men joined him on the road, gawking at the damage.

"Prepare the men for battle," John hollered. "We're attacking Bios-2 in five minutes. Meet outside my tent then." John dashed down the embankment and into the woods, his men following, yelling to others, "Five minutes. Meet in five."

31.

Cicada

She found him in Comms, just as he had promised. He looked up; the bill of his Cubs hat tilted at her as she stood in the doorway, staring curiously at him.

"Hi, Sally. So glad you could come."

She considered what to say, like an actress trying to remember her lines. "Were you just in the hallway in front of the Library?"

"Of course I was. Remember, I talked to you in the Library about meeting me here?"

"I mean right after that; did you go into the communications closet off the hallway?"

"No… I haven't been in that room in probably a month. Why?"

She looked at him carefully and then shook her head. "Oh, never mind. Now, please tell me why we don't have to worry about the invading army."

"In a minute; first, help me figure something out. Come here," he beckoned from the dark Comms room.

"Why is this room so dark?" Nervousness washed over her like a blast of cold air. She timidly walked around to the far end of the console to where Webber was now standing, his arms behind his back, like he was hiding something.

He didn't respond, just gazed at her.

She hesitated because she was starting to believe that it was, in fact, Webber who was in that closet; and if it was him, he was up to no good; and he then must have been lying to her; and if he was, then what was he hiding behind his back?

Fear rose up behind her and she took a step back into the darkness of the room.

His expression changed to a querulous one. "What's wro—"

A swift movement from the doorway, and someone jumped on top of Webber, knocking him to the ground. "You!" screamed the madman, who connected a roundhouse to Webber's cheek, knocking his head into the floor.

Sally screamed. "Uncle Max? What are you doing?"

Max sat on top of a dazed and only semi-conscious Webber, pulled his right arm back to continue the pummeling and grunted in pain. "Ugh…" He lowered his arm. "This man is a mole for Bios-2 and called them to let them know we were coming."

"Wha-what?" Webber babbled, eyes blinking. "I did-did what? No, not me… why would I da-da-do that?" He thrashed about in a feeble attempt to free himself from Max's grasp.

Max hit him again in the side with a left. "Stop moving or I'll beat you to death."

"Maxwell," yelled Preston from the doorway, coming in. "For God's sake stop. What are you doing?"

Max spun and looked at Preston bounding toward him. "Freeze!" he yelled, training his gun on Preston.

"Whoa-whoa-whoa. Hang on, boss. It's me; what the hell is wrong?"

"This… asshole," Max said, sniffling, "is the reason two more…" Max's head dropped down and he took a deep breath. "…of our people were killed. He gave Bios-2 intel…"

"Look, I don't know what you think you know, but I know this man. He is definitely on our side. He is not the enemy. And I am absolutely sure he is not our mole."

Max looked at Webber, blood trickling out of his nose, his cheek swelling, and then looked back up to Preston. Behind him, Magdalena and several others, were all staring at Max.

Magdalena flipped on the light switch and Max stood up. Webber squirmed away.

"I don't want to believe it either," Sally spoke, squinting at the brightness, "but I just heard the voice of a man who sounded like it could have been Webber, talking to someone in the communications closet by the Library. He said, 'plans are in place' and that something was happening within an hour and that he'd be waiting for a sign. The man was Webber's height and he was wearing a blue baseball cap, just like that one."

They all looked at Webber, now holding a tissue to his nose. "But you didn't see my face or my Cubs cap, right?"

They looked at Sally, who shook her head.

"Web, I gotta ask, what were you doing in Comms on your day off in the dark yesterday?" Magdalena stepped further inside. "I saw you had a phone in your hand, in the dark."

"I noticed the drawer was unlocked. The console drawer is supposed to be locked, and I was checking to see if there was any problem with the phone," Webber answered with rapid-fire words.

"Maxwell," Preston insisted, "is what Sally or Magdalena said what convinced you he was our mole?"

"No," Max hobbled to and rested against the console, "it was Sampson's journal. Sampson's room was practically destroyed by someone looking for this. His journal said, 'there is one other on the inside, like me: he is IT.' Who else could that be?" Max begged.

"Johnson!" Webber said decisively.

"The Dodgers," Preston added.

"What?" Max asked, partially because he thought he must have not heard him right.

"Johnson wore a Dodgers cap sometimes. It's blue."

Magdalena jumped in. "Of course. He's an IT guy, and I've heard Web and him argue all the time about the Dodgers. Where is Johnson?"

"He just left," a voice out in the reception area yelled out. It was a guard, marching up the stairs. "He was in a hurry and just rushed out."

Max righted himself and hobbled toward the doorway, about to trot after him.

"Hold on," the guard said, "more important than Johnson is what's outside. There are hundreds of fully armed men and women, wearing red robes. They look like they plan to invade us."

32.
Bios-2

"Get this shit out of my face!" he shouted.

"Sorry, Mr. Westerling. I'm trying but there's a lot." Dr. Robert Thornton stood beside him, carefully pulling glass out of his face, one tiny fragment at a time. The nurse immediately blotted the streams of blood, cleaned and bandaged the wounds.

"Sir, can't I put you under so it's not so painful?" He watched his patient writhe with their every touch.

"No way. I'm not going under until we get that bitch Reid who did this to me."

"I'm almost done. Looks like two more," Robert said. "Just be thankful you shave, unlike most every man these days. A beard would've made it much harder to excise the glass from your face. And you were lucky that your eyes weren't hit. Hell, it's a miracle you're still alive. From what I understand, they'll be finding pieces of Mr. Gufstafson and Mr. Reid for weeks."

Robert stopped, his nurse still dabbing at the blood. After each wound was cleaned, she applied suture strips, then gauze, and finally surgical tape to each of the spots where glass fragments were removed from his face.

"There, that's it for the glass. Now, let me fix your arm; you need stitches."

"Not right now, Doc," Westerling said, sitting up in the infirmary bed and swinging his feet onto the floor. "Throw some of those strips on it for now."

Thornton deadpanned his doctorly advice. "You might want to take it easy."

Westerling ignored him. "Reynolds?" he called, looking past the bandages. "Where the hell is Reynolds?"

"I'm here, sir," Walter Reynolds answered, bounding through the clinic's doorway.

"Tell me you found Mrs. Reid." He glared at him and then went back to buttoning a shirt someone had brought down for him from his apartment in the tower.

"Sir, I'm sorry; we have larger problems... Our EPF is down and it looks like we're about to be attacked."

A red signal flare screamed into the green evening sky at John's command. The gunshots began. To conserve ammo, the warriors were to fire at three locations, purposely not firing at the northern gate. This was to both see how Bios-2 reacted and if they would take guards off that location. It would be easier if they did. The first lightning cannon erupted, filling the air with the smell of ozone and burned flesh.

John had his suspicions about these things and used the older women—those less likely to bear children and not part of God's Army—to attract their fire. The second lightning cannon went off on the south side.

"Okay," he said to his two gunners, "take out the cannon with the .50 and you tap everything that moves on the wall." He pushed plugs into his ears and watched the north wall with his binoculars.

The third and fourth lightning cannons went off just as his men's .50 came to life, pummeling their fifth cannon with exploding tracer rounds, each one finding its target with a mini-explosion. The M4 simply spat out death upon anything moving, connecting successfully with three shadows before it fell silent. The .50 sat quiet as well, having successfully dispatched its target.

"All right, give me cover fire."

John waited for another warrior with an M4 to join in and now both took turns firing two or three rounds on semi-auto at the wall, even though there was no one to shoot at. He handed his binoculars to another warrior, who scanned for life signs, and John ran to the gate to place the C4 on the prime points to give them their entrance. He had no training in explosives, but when they found the military supply on their journey, he was able to torture sufficient "how-to" information from one of the military guards and found he was quite adept at the process.

After setting the charges, he dashed away from the gate, his people supplying constant fire on the empty wall, and ducked behind a berm fifty feet away from where the blast should be.

"Fire in the hole!" John loved that expression.

He pressed the button.

"I don't give a damn if the entire Army, Navy and Air Force poured over our walls. The priority is to find that bitch Dr. Melanie Reid and bring her to me alive, dead, or in pieces," Westerling roared to the five security guards fidgeting in front of him.

"Now!" he snarled, lighting a fire under their feet, and they scattered. He should have had more security, but they all seemed conspicuously absent.

Reynolds hesitated, not sure whether to follow or stay.

"Stay near me, Reynolds. You're now my Number One, since Lunder gave himself to save me. Keep your eyes open and report to me what you see outside, but hang within earshot."

He watched Reynolds shuffle out the door and immediately take on his role, giving orders to guards outside the door. Westerling sat in a comfy swivel chair in the Operations Center, in the same tower where his office used to be. Operations had lots of top-of-the-line communications equipment, but now that the EPF was down, very little of it worked. Even their cameras, like much of their equipment, were shielded but seemed mostly nonfunctional, at best broadcasting staticky images of murky nothing.

He thought for a moment about what had just happened. His entire body throbbed with searing pain; he found it hard to breathe, which was understandable with a broken rib or two, wrapped tightly by the doc; and his arm continued to seep blood—even with the suture strips—which dripped off his pinky.

How could he have been sidestepped by some geek scientist in a fedora and his bitch wife? Everything was going perfectly, and then they screwed it up.

He figured he would stay in Operations until morning, catching a nap or two until then, when he hoped to hear Johnson's voice on the phone, confirming Cicada was theirs. Lunder's plan would have to wait until his people sorted out the wires in the damage.

"Sir," Reynolds piped up as he popped his head in, "we're holding the invaders back on all walls. And one of our guards has a prisoner you will want to see."

"Okay, send them in—and Reynolds, please bring the doc here to finish his work on me."

Two guards, one on each side, brought in a man who looked more beat to hell than the senator was. He was semi-conscious and was only vertical because the guards held him up. They deposited him on a side chair at the back of the room. One came forward and spoke to Westerling in a low voice. "This is Bill King. He's from Cicada. He was doing recon on Bios-2 and crashed outside the north wall in a blue flying machine that is nonfunctional. We picked him up just before he was about to be eaten by the Outsiders. We think he has a concussion because he keeps mumbling something like, 'Max can't be dead.'"

Westerling rolled his chair over to where Bill was heaped in his chair, rolling in and out of consciousness. He was about to say something when an earth-rattling boom shook them.

A ceiling tile fell in front of him, but Westerling didn't flinch. He had a new plan.

"Connect me with Cicada right now," he bellowed to the lone Operations tech watching over the mostly inert equipment.

33.
Cicada

Max sat alone at the Comms console, sipping on a coffee, nursing the agonizing pain in every part of his body, but it wasn't his body that hurt the most. After many offered apologies, Webber was in the infirmary being tended to from the beating Max gave him. Johnson, the traitorous mole, was still at large. Magdalena, at this point, would have nothing to do with him. Tom Rogers was tending to their people, getting them ready for battle. There was a gigantic army, sent by a madman bent on Cicada's destruction, assembling outside their walls. And to top it off, his best friend was missing after taking an experimental hovercraft out for a test flight. "What else could possibly go wrong?" he asked the back of his eyelids.

The phone rang.

Automatically, he slid open the large drawer, as he had done before. But now he stared at the pulsating phone, like it was some object he had never seen before. He knew who was calling, or at least he suspected.

It rang again.

"Preston," Max shouted. He didn't need to yell, because Preston had a light in his office, as did Max in his, that flashed when there was an incoming call—but he did.

Max pressed the speaker button, picked up the receiver to silence its infernal ringing and put it to his ear. "This is Maxwell Thompson,

Co-Creator and Director of Cicada. Who is this?"

There was only static, barely masking the heavy breaths on the other side.

"You are by far the luckiest sonofabitch I have ever come across in my sixty-four years of life… As I'm sure you know, this is Senator Brian P. Westerling, Creator and Director of Bios-2. Pleased to finally make your acquaintance."

Max inhaled slowly and deeply. He tried to focus. He wanted to say something reasonable and unemotional. This man had power over them in ways Max was only just beginning to understand, and he had to be careful. But at this point, he didn't care.

"Listen, you prick asshole; I tell you at this moment that I have made it my personal mission to make sure you don't see sixty-five."

That felt a little better.

"I heard you were a bit of a hothead. Now, before you say anything else you might regret—Ow! Shit, doc, can't you wait till I'm done with my phone call?—Anyway, I have someone you'll want to talk to… bring him over here…" Murmured conversations in the distant background got louder; then the sound of a heavy chair being slid across a long floor grew as well, until it was almost too much for the phone's little over-modulated speaker.

Max looked up and saw that Preston, Lisa King and Magdalena were all inside Comms now, listening with him. There were several others outside the door.

"Hello…" a scratchy, but familiar, voice spoke on the other end. "Max?" It was Bill!

"Bill? Is that you?" Max hollered into the phone. "Are you all right, buddy?"

"Yeah, just a little bang—"

"That's enough," Westerling cut in. "Do you believe me when I say I have your friend Bill King?"

Max looked up and saw Lisa holding her mouth, eyes watery, nodding a confirmation he didn't need.

"Yes, I believe you. Now-what-do-you-want?"

"It's very simple. My army should already be at your doorstep. When they announce their demands, you are to fulfill them, without resistance. When my guy Johnson calls me to tell me that the army has taken over, without incident, I will release your friend Bill. That's all."

Max leaned forward on the console desk, his weight on his elbows; it was as if Westerling's face were in front of him and he was moving in closer to it. "Now, listen to me, you douchebag," Max said very calmly. "If you at all harm one hair on that man's head, I will make you suffer the most horrible death imaginable. And because you seem to know everything about me, you know what I have done to people and that I mean every word I say. Do we understand each other?" Max stood bent over and still leaning on the desk—his face pressed against Westerling's imagined one.

"I'll wait for my call. Remember what I sai—"

Max slammed the phone down in anger. "Ahhhh!"

He stood up and stomped past Preston, up to Lisa and hugged her.

Her words tumbled out. "Max. Ple-please don't let them hurt Bill." She pressed her head against his chest and sobbed uncontrollably.

A murmur grew into loud debate in the Comms room and in the reception room, until one of their guards burst through the building's front door and yelled to the crowd, "The enemy's made their demands."

Everyone held their breath, waiting for the guard to say more.

Max led Lisa out of the Comms room, onto the walkway outside their office and above the guard and the people in the open reception area. Magdalena followed, and then Preston, who called to the guard below. "Go ahead, Tony, what did they say?" Preston figured this concerned everyone anyway.

"They said that we have ten minutes to surrender Cicada or they will destroy it and kill everyone in its walls… What should we tell them?"

Everybody, even Preston, turned and looked at Max.

34.

Bios-2

Melanie knew that it wasn't in their apartment, but she had hoped that maybe there was another note or that Carrington somehow had time to get the second bomb back and leave it for her. No, that was asking too much and too risky. And one thing she knew about Carrington, he planned for every contingency.

Her luck was holding out, not that she believed in luck. Still, there were no guards to be seen anywhere on their floor. She glided quietly across the polished concrete like a figure skater, glad for her sock-covered shoes. There were no other sounds but her soft steps and the constant hum of the machinery below.

The door to S227 was open; several papers were resting haphazardly in the threshold and out the doorway. Looking in, she saw why. Their place had already been ransacked. Hopefully the goons hadn't taken everything. There were a few things she wanted before she left this place, their home for the past several months.

She shut the door and walked to the sofa, its foam-stuffed cushions ripped open and tossed aside. Reaching under, she found the two knives stored on the underside wooden lip. She had developed a love for knives. They were silent killers. She had learned how to throw them in Laramie, but in the last couple months she'd developed proficiency with them, practicing on the underside of their coffee table for hours.

She examined both blades. In their former lives, they had been steak knives. Now, each had another edge and better balance thanks to her repurposing. She placed both on the coffee table along with the two magazines and her pistol, a newer Glock confiscated from the guard.

She examined the rest of the apartment. Into a large backpack from the closet, she tossed items picked from clothing strewn on the floor: a shirt, her good jeans, her only non-holey tennis shoes and three pairs of panties. Standing in front of the bookshelf, she searched. It wasn't there. Her heart rose almost to a panic until she saw it, *Shakespeare's Sonnets* half-buried in with the other books tossed from the shelves. Unfolding the back cover, she saw all of his notes still there—and several new additions, taped to the book's final pages. This went in the sack too.

She dropped the bag at the bathroom entrance and attempted to bring some order to her disorder. She sucked down some aspirin, and then tossed the bottle on the bag—definitely coming with her. She did her best to brush the blood from her hair, being extra careful to not touch the sensitive area where Lunder had hit her. She slipped a band around her tresses and made a ponytail.

What else? Finally, she snatched a roll of toilet paper, her hairbrush and the surgical tape from their first aid drawer and tossed them in the bag.

From the front of the little desk, its contents on the floor, she snatched a piece of stationery like the ones he used to write his notes and sonnets to her. Her fingers curled around the elegant Mont Blanc pen, a gift from his daughter and his preferred note-writing instrument. Looking up for inspiration, she carefully wrote the note, mimicking his hand.

Satisfied, she walked to the coffee table and slid one knife and both spare magazines into the front of the backpack. The other knife she shoved into her waistband, trying not to stick herself with it.

Let's go get a bomb, she mouthed, not wanting to say anything in case someone was still listening.

She took one final look at their apartment—their home for many months—and said goodbye.

Matt Richards wasn't about to leave his post. The place may fall to invaders, but he wasn't going to give them access to Supplies without a fight. He had been given this post by the big man himself, after being the senior security officer in the senator's detail. After a stint in the Marines and then DC Police, he had been the first on the scene when the senator's wife and son-in-law were murdered by the two drugged-out miscreants. He shot one, who later died, but the other got away, stealing a few dollars and a bottle of Percocet. It was a tragedy for sure, but this tragedy had led to a much higher-paying job on the senator's security detail, as thanks for killing one of the perps.

It was like that with people. They all had it in them to commit horrendous acts. But without the law to keep them in check, most would take and kill for themselves. He wasn't about to let that happen here.

A very pretty woman entered, looked around, and then approached him.

"Hello, Mr. Richards, we've never met. I'm Dr. Melanie Reid; Dr. Carrington Reid is my husband. I'm helping him on a vital project for Mr. Westerling. He sent me for these things." She slid him the piece of paper she had written up in Carrington's handwriting.

Richards read the note twice and then looked at her. This one was very curious. He knew people pretty well, and he could sense she was hiding something, but he wasn't sure yet what it was. "Come with me," he said, holding onto the note and standing by the door that buzzed open. "I'm sorry, but I will have to pat you down, Mrs.—"

"It's Doctor Reid, sir. And you are not touching me, you understand." She stepped through the door and walked right up to his face. "I know for a fact you don't pat my husband down. You are not going to get your jollies feeling me up, buddy. Now, I'm running late. Are you going to show me where this shit is that my husband needs, or do we have to talk to Mr. Westerling?" She remained unmoveable like a statue, hands on her hips.

Poor SOB, he thought of Dr. Carrington. He knew who ruled this household. Smirking, he turned and said, "Very well, follow me then."

35.
Bios-2

"What about him, Doc, will he come out of it?" Westerling asked Thornton, who was changing a couple of the bandages on his face.

The doctor looked back at Bill King, now lying flat on the floor unconscious. "He has a concussion, but it's not too bad, couple of broken bones, and some superficial wounds. Like you, he should heal in a few weeks."

"I don't care if he heals—he'll be dead by tomorrow. I just want to make sure he can talk if I need him to."

Doctor Thornton regarded him for a moment, wondering how he was ever talked into serving this narcissist whose hunger for power was greater than anyone he had ever met—and after the collapse of society outside their walls, greater than he probably ever would meet. He knew Westerling meant what he said; the senator never filtered his words around the doc. It was as if Westerling believed that doctor-patient privilege had no boundaries, even post-apocalypse. He had no doubt Westerling would kill this man, who was just an innocent pawn in some real-life chess game, where every person, including him, was one of the chess pieces. In spite of the relative safety he enjoyed, he regretted his decision to be here, every day.

"Are we done, Doc?"

"Yeah, we're done." He collected his supplies and packed up his bag.

"Aren't you going to tell me to take it easy, and all that doctorly kind of stuff?"

"No, do whatever you want. I'm sure I'll be patching you up again soon enough." Thornton walked out.

Black pawn fixes black king, prepares to be moved again on the board at the whim of black king, he thought as he tried to leave.

Reynolds almost knocked Thornton to the floor, crashing into him in the doorway. He was frantic. "Sir, some of the invaders are on top of the wall."

BOOM.

Operations' walls shuddered around them and the floor rumbled, like in a small dull earthquake.

"They've killed some of our people near the northern gate," croaked an out-of-breath Reynolds.

White pawn takes black pawn.

"Well then, fire everything we have at them there. Where are our soldiers?" Westerling asked.

Black knight takes white pawn.

"They're keeping them off the other walls. And the invaders keep picking off every soldier who has tried to help at our northern gate."

White pawn takes black knight.

"Look, their attack is at the north gate. Focus most of our men and weapons there. Put nonessential personnel on the other gates. Give them a gun and tell them to fire at anyone who moves. Grab the scientists if you have to. Reynolds, we have to hit them hard, now." He looked over to the entry as another guard brushed by Thornton, still standing there. The guard tentatively walked in, carefully holding two bottles of the forty-year-old bourbon and a box of Cohibas.

"Put them over there." He motioned to a table against the wall near where Bill King was having a nightmare about falling.

Black king orders black pawn around.

"Thank God. Now we can be civilized during our battles."

Black king takes a drink.

"I need more C4," John called out to a runner, who took off to report to one of his generals. "Get two more on the wall and our .50 up there," he yelled to Peter, who signaled and two more red robes shinnied up the ropes they set up on the wall.

John stepped back and looked at the gate. This one was pretty strong. The blasts shook part of it loose from the wall, but it was held in place by the other door. Two more blasts at the other door and the middle should bring it down.

He quickly drew his sight on a head that bobbed along the top of the wall running toward the gate and fired two shots.

"Keep our cover fire, there and there," John pointed to either side of the gate. "Soon, they'll figure out our game, so we need to blast the gate while we have the advantage."

"Wouldn't it be better if we waited for Teacher and the other soldiers?" said a woman. Only her eyes were visible from within the oversized robe she wore.

John stuck his face up to hers and said loud enough that she could hear it above the gunfire and commotion, "If you don't leave this battlefield right now, I will shoot you myself."

As the woman left, the tail of her robe trailing like some macbre wedding train, the runner returned with the C4 and grenades.

John whistled to one of his red-robed people on the gate, a signal for "get busy shooting fish in a barrel." The man looked down and

John tossed up the grenades one at a time. He smiled at the irony of this. The leader of Bios-2 made a deal with the Teacher to leave and not bother Bios-2, giving him explosives and three .50 calibers. Now, they were using those weapons on Bios-2. He would have a good chuckle when their compound fell.

John looked up to make sure that only friendlies were on the wall and he set up the next blast.

Another explosion sounded, smaller than the previous one and without any corresponding earthquakes.

Westerling exhaled a large puff and waited for the next report from Reynolds. He had a sinking feeling in his gut and it wasn't the bourbon. He remembered this feeling during his first congressional election. All his people were telling him that he was up in the polls, but the exit data coming in from several locations said that his competitor was capturing the minority and female vote. Considering that district was composed of a large minority population and a majority of the voters were female, his gut told him that he would lose. He could feel the shift in his political winds. His people continued to reassure him not to worry, he would carry the night. He lost by two points.

He could sense the winds had changed once again. He took another healthy sip of bourbon and then signaled one of the guards to come over.

"Grab one other guard, go get my daughter and granddaughter and take them to the bunker. Get it prepared and don't let anyone in but you four. Are we clear?"

The guard nervously but decisively nodded. "Yes sir, I'll protect your family with my life."

"Great, go now."

Boom.

The building shook again.

36.
Bios-2

They stopped first in a vast room of various building materials, all categorized, sorted and resting in their appropriate places. Of course, the metal conduit she was looking for was at the back of the room and Richards was taking his sweet time getting there. She wanted to get in and get out, not sure how much time she had before Bios-2's security looked for her here. It was hard enough for her to remain composed when each time they turned a corner, Richards would shoot his skeptical gaze back at her to make sure she was still there since her footfalls were nearly silent.

From what she had memorized from Carrington's drawings—*he would never draw another one again...* She fought back tears. *Concentrate, Mel!* It was near impossible because everything reminded her of Carrington, and she had not allowed herself a moment to grieve. She needed to stay at the anger stage until she escaped this madhouse.

"Is this what you're looking for?" They were looking at an area of one-to-two-inch-wide metal conduit pipes stacked in shelves based on length. It was like going to one of those big-box home improvement stores, with everything laid out for you and their not-so-eager staff pointing you in the direction you wanted, while other consumers battled for your helper's attention. Those days no longer existed.

She glanced at the shelves and then of those nearby, and then saw it. "No, that's what he wants," she pointed to a lower shelf with two-foot lengths of one-foot-diameter pipe.

Richards didn't respond or budge, indicating that he wasn't intending on helping her pick up the item. *Yep, just like the big-box stores.*

It must have weighed thirty pounds or more and was bulky, difficult to carry. Richards was already impatiently waiting at the end of the aisle; that was his way of saying that he wanted to move along so they could pick up the final item and he could be done with her.

She tried to figure out how to lug the damned thing around, first trying under her armpit—*too heavy*; then in front of her—*too difficult to walk*; then behind her head, straddling her shoulders—*just right*. Now she marched onward, head bent forward, wondering how she would explain the clock to him.

She should have just written it down on the sign-in sheet. Instead, she listed "Broken black pocket watch in Misc. Area," knowing from Carr's instructions that this was in front of where the clock and its internal bomb were hidden. Since the clock was already "repaired," she thought listing it would be suspicious, whereas the pocket watch would be somewhat easy to explain. She just didn't expect him to be watching her every move, and now how would she explain wanting this?

"So, what do you need the pocket watch for?" he asked.

Shit!

"Look, if we're going to have a conversation, maybe you can help me out here. This damn thing is heavy." She grunted to exaggerate her efforts.

He said nothing, not changing his stride either. She could have sworn he was snickering, just a little.

When they had walked what felt like miles, they finally reached a section that was actually labeled *Misc. Area*.

Richards once again halted at the end corner of the aisle she needed, intending to stand vigil at his post. Melanie wasn't paying attention, letting her mind wander about Carrington, gazing at the floor just ahead of her, until suddenly he was there. The surprise caused her to jump and her forward inertia, pushed by the extra thirty pounds behind her head, caused her to tilt off balance. Two things happened at once: she felt she might fall over and had to counter-weight by spinning herself around a hundred-eighty degrees. She also felt the gun, which must have worked itself free of her waistband in the commotion, slide down her pant leg. It proceeded to pop out and skid along the floor until it came to rest at his feet.

In the long moment that followed, they both stared at the gun, considering its many implications. And they both reacted at the same time.

Richards glanced at her from behind a mask of surprise and reached for his sidearm.

Melanie did another half spin, grabbed one end of the heavy metal conduit and swung like a slugger attempting to knock it out of the ballpark. *Homerun!*

She was surprised how light it felt, how it connected exactly where she was aiming. Before he had even drawn his weapon, she heard the *bonk* and felt the spray of his blood. Both he and the metal pipe hit the floor to the thunderous applause of the thumping in her ears.

No looking back. She grabbed her gun and jogged to the shelf Carrington had told her about. Reaching back, she clutched the small clock radio right away and slid it into her backpack.

She hesitated over Richards, who was either dead or out cold. Then a sly smile crept onto her face. She drew her knife and bent over him. He would help her after all.

When she was finished, she picked up the pipe and hoisted it back onto her shoulder and hurried back to the entrance.

Just in front of Richards's desk, where he buzzed people in, she could hear several security guards calling for him, probably wondering where the man who never left his post was. They filed into the main Supplies room, and Melanie ducked behind the first shelving area. Two passed, jogging and calling his name. She slipped past the check-in area and then the exit and headed to B216, feeling what she was sure would be a short-lived sense of relief.

Just before she reached the end of the T-intersection in the hallway, someone yelled, "Hey you... stop!"

37.

Cicada

"Did Max actually tell them to go blank themselves?" Sally asked Preston, who was making rounds to convince everyone to take up arms or at least to hunker down and prepare for a fight. She had been keeping company with Webber while he rested on a cot in the infirmary. Sue and Pel, who were injured in the failed assault led by Max and Tom, were also there sleeping. Sally had *The Stand* open and resting facedown in her lap.

Preston couldn't help but smile at her self-censorship, refusing to quote the F-word. She was raised well.

"I'd like to fight," Webber offered, lifting his head and grimacing at his discomfort.

"No, son." Preston held his palm out to stop him. "You need to rest. You know you have nothing to prove to anyone."

"My face attests to that, right?" Webber's bandages lifted with his smile, but even smiling hurt too much and his bandages sagged back.

"Here." Preston rested the AR-15 Webs had been practicing with over the past months beside the cot. "Keep this by your side, just in case."

He looked to Sally and hesitated, knowing what a struggle it had been for her.

She glared back at him, feeling the debilitating fear flood back again, and then turned to Webber. "Webs, please tell me you weren't fibbing when you said we have a plan?"

The men flashed looks at each other. Either they had ESP or they shared a big secret and Webber hadn't yet received approval to respond the way he wanted.

"Sally, we do have a Plan B," Preston stated in his usual composed voice, "but until then, only if it's needed, you know how to shoot, don't you?" He held out a rifle for her.

She grabbed the M4, pulled back the charging rod and let it slide a round forward. Then she flicked the safety on and rested it on her lap, barrel away from them.

Both of them grinned.

Sally looked back up to Preston. "Uncle Max taught me. He said, 'Sally, it's easy. Just aim at the bad guy and squeeze the trigger.'" Of course, everything was easy for Uncle Max.

Preston chuckled at the obvious Maxism. Then he became serious. "So, you're staying here with Webber?"

"Yep," she confirmed.

"All right then. Keep your eyes open," he said to both of them. To Webber he added, "Listen for the air-raid horn, son." He waited for Webber's confirmation. "You may need to help these folks too." Preston motioned to the two sleeping in their beds.

"Got it, sir. And thanks for standing up for me." Webber smiled and offered his hand.

Preston squeezed it and laid his other hand on Sally's shoulder, then walked to the other two occupied cots to wake their occupants with the news.

"What horn?" Sally asked.

After he explained that part, they waited.

The night's green auroras were now rumbling like angry storm clouds, their illuminations making everything look jaundiced and sickly. It was an aerial mirror of how each of them felt right now gawking at what was coming their way.

After Max had delivered Cicada's reply to the three red-robed representatives—the red looked gray—of the army of men and women outside, they said nothing and left, blending in with their hordes. A few minutes later, he watched hundreds of red robes begin walking in a mass around both sides of Cicada's walls. Like puddles building up from raindrops, pools of red robes swarmed and clustered in positions around the complex. They seemed completely unconcerned about being shot, staying approximately five hundred meters from the wall, just as Cicada's flyers demanded. Perhaps he should have just had his people start shooting, but even with the advantage of their protective walls, this enemy had the numbers, and with numbers, there was a chance to overwhelm. Plus, he was curious what they would do next and wanted to play it out a little more first.

The moat of red-black stretched around the entire circumference of Cicada, now a narrow band as far as he could see. Max signaled for his guards to be ready by swinging a propane lantern back and forth. Fifteen of the sixty-four breathing residents of Cicada were on its walls.

He held the lantern up toward the Observation Tower and covered the glass with his hand. Then he uncovered it and then covered it and then uncovered it again.

A light flashed there, in similar fashion. Shingles was ready. Shingles was a scary-good shot, too; he literally could pick off a bird from the tree line, almost a mile away.

He had instructed all his people to not shoot until one of those red-robes had crossed the line, or if it looked like they were processing forward. The near-impossible part was keeping a two-and-a-half-mile wall secure with only fifteen people. On their side, the walls were very hard to scale, with razor-sharp barbs everywhere along the wall, which also had a slick coating, making it impossible to free climb. With grappling hooks, it was possible, but still difficult. And of course, everyone in Cicada knew how to shoot. It was a requirement that they train with an M4. First Preston had trained them, and then when Tom came on board, he took over. Each had their assigned M4, having stopped by Operations to pick them up on their way to the wall. And finally each had plenty of ammo, in spite of the enemy's large numbers. They just needed to be patient.

They waited.

Johnson crouched low and hid in the dark shadows cast by the Comms building on the soccer field. Every time he heard a set of footsteps, he pressed himself lower to remain unseen. In a way, he had been in the shadows all this time, operating as one of two moles in Cicada. After Sampson was killed, it had gotten pretty dicey for him. But the timing couldn't have been better, with the army preparing to attack; he would have to ask Westerling how he'd arranged that.

It wouldn't be very much longer until he could leave this place. He craned his neck up, waiting to see the sign that told him when to do his part. And when he was done, it would mean the end of Cicada.

The first shot rang out like the screech from a giant turkey vulture alerting the other vultures about a newly dead meal and the feast that awaited them. This vulture must have been nested up in the tree line, hidden from the auroral light.

Max spun around to the sound's location and searched for a sign of its target. Another shot from the opposite side, and he saw one of his people on the corresponding wall crumple and fall into a heap.

They had snipers.

"Take cover!" he bellowed through his cupped hands. "Take cover. They're in the tree line."

More sniper shots, followed by two white flares arced into the air toward them: one from the east and the other from the west side of Cicada.

That was their signal.

The throngs of darkened robes swarmed the walls. Where the walls were on a mesa, they scaled the rocks leading up to them.

The red-robes should have been easy targets, but whenever one of Max's people would take a shot, the snipers would fire and force them behind the protective cover of the wall.

They were being pinned down.

First it was just one… then two… then it was many. Grappling hooks clinked against the tops of their stone walls, many of them grabbing hold. *That's how I'd have done it. They're scaling the walls.*

Max yelled for them to cut the ropes as he hurried over to the closest sentry, but they couldn't. Guns, not knives.

Holding his .45 close to the rope, Max fired off three shots to sever it. He handed his knife to the sentry and signaled for her to cut the next one.

The sentry closest to them shot at the top rope multiple times, trying to hit it where it crested over the top of the wall while trying to stay behind the wall's cover, but he was felled by a sniper's bullet.

Max leaned over the inside of the wall and yelled down to a

woman on the ground, already bounding up the first steps of the stairwell closest to him. "Go grab all the axes and heavy knives or swords you can carry."

It was Magdalena. She nodded and dashed off toward Operations.

The others futilely attempted to shoot at the rope, or waited for help.

Max handed out axes and large knives to each sentry, who then raced, bent double below the wall's protection, to a rope that nested itself nearby and severed it. Magdalena was doing the same further away. When she had handed out everything, she occasionally stopped to cut a rope herself using the knife she always carried with her. Once, as they passed each other when she was slicing away at a rope, the M4 she carried loosely around her slipped forward and she had to stop and readjust.

Max asked, "Do you know how to shoot one of those things?"

"Yes, of course," she said and then stormed off, otherwise very calm under fire.

There were just too many of them. All their people were running around the walls, desperately trying to keep up with the newly appearing ropes and people climbing them, and so far they'd succeeded in preventing anyone from gaining the top of a wall. It seemed like this could go on forever. Then he realized this was their plan to keep them busy. He scanned the walls and noticed that no one was climbing the north wall, by the gate. It was all a diversion.

He ran toward that gate, at least half a mile away, hopping over a couple sentries sawing at the enemy's thick ropes with their knives. He was almost there when he glimpsed a cart being pushed by two red-robes toward the gate. He fired off a couple of shots while running, not expecting to hit them but hoping at least to slow them down. They were already running away from the gate; their job was done.

Max hollered to his people below. "Get away from the gate. Get away from the gate!" Knowing what was coming next, he tossed himself onto the wall's stony walkway. The bomb hit the moment he did.

The explosion nearly shook him off the wall and over the railing.

As with the previous strike, the gate tilted inward. Almost immediately, using the dusty haze and smoke from the blast as cover, a few of the red-robes were coming through. He fired a few shots as he bounded down the stairwell.

More and more trickled in; some were now coming over the walls.

He yelled to the wall sentries, "Retreat." They echoed his command and started down their corresponding stairwells out of the line of fire and headed for the Rec Facility.

This was their last line of defense before Plan B.

On top of the Rec Facility, their own sharpshooters fired at each person who slid over the wall, as still others were coming through the gate.

At that moment, Max realized Cicada might fall.

Johnson had seen the sign and dashed toward Operations. He passed panicked residents and sentries running to their backup position. But it would be no use for them; after he did his job, there would be no saving Cicada. It would fall within the hour.

38.
Bios-2

Melanie made sure she could wedge the piece of conduit in between the gamma radiation venting and what she suspected was another crucial piece of the reactor. The one thing Carrington hadn't left in his notes was any detail on where to position the conduit with the explosive inside, so as to focus the detonation and make sure the damage was absolute in those two places. But she figured any place was a sweet spot on this thing. And with Westerling and Lunder out of the way, she didn't think anyone else would attempt to rebuild it; who else in this world would be that monstrous? Further, based on the radioactive warning signs, and what she knew about nuclear reactors, she suspected her efforts might have the added benefit of making Bios-2 uninhabitable for everybody for a long time.

It looked like Carrington had set the detonator to the alarm switch of the clock; when the alarm went off, so would the detonator and its explosive charge, now concentrated through the conduit on two spots of the reactor. She set the alarm for 1:00, figuring that three hours should be more than enough time to get the scientists out and get clear of this area. After sliding it into the conduit and wedging the conduit in place, she examined her work. It looked like it belonged there.

She backed away and walked out of the room, feeling good about this. Now she would try to get the scientists out. She hoped Rush got her note under the rock by his door and took the rest of the scientists to the rendezvous point.

"Mommy, is Crapaw coming too?" asked Leanne, her hand fidgeting in her mother's.

"Yes, Leanne. Your Crapaw is coming," Deanna coaxed her with a smile and a soft tug, pulling her a little closer. Her daughter loved her grandpa. She just wished she could tell her the truth: that he was a horrible, evil man. She hated her father for so many things, many she didn't dare even think about because they were too awful. At least he would do anything to keep his granddaughter safe. She supposed that her keeping up appearances—even in a constant state of inebriation—was better than being outside Bios-2's walls. But, was it any better being a prisoner inside them? It was all too much to handle. She needed a drink, bad.

Her buzz was wearing out and, with it, the fuzzy memories of what her father had done were becoming clearer, like blurry images coming into focus in binoculars. Then there was the painful throbbing at the base of her skull, the distant thunder of an approaching migraine. She either needed to get away from these two guards so she could visit her purse, or get to the bunker, which had a fully stocked bar.

She turned to one of the guards. "Are we close?" She somewhat feared she'd never find her way if she ever left to use a bathroom. The hallways were a maze that went on forever.

"Yes ma'am; it's one more hallway down this way," the handsome guard said as he pointed.

Deanna's purse slipped and she let go of Leanne to keep it from hitting the ground. She had snatched a bottle of her father's bourbon, and she didn't want it to break and advertise her theft to anyone with a nose (and also ruin her chances of a drink).

"Whew," she said under her breath, glad she grabbed it just in time.

She heard a giggle behind her and saw Leanne was gone.

"Dammit, Leanne; you get back here right now!" she shrieked, but Leanne didn't answer.

She heard a door close down a hallway they had just passed and took off running, followed closely by one of the two panicked guards.

So far so good.

Melanie was surprised that there were so few guards around: none in the turbine room and none in the hallways. She was about to congratulate herself when she heard voices pouring down the hallway right in front of her. She didn't want to return to B216 and the turbine room, so she ducked into B233A and pulled on the door to speed up its closure, she added resistance at the end to keep it quiet.

Immediately she heard someone say, "I saw her go down this way. She really clocked you, Richards, and you're hand is bleeding a lot."

An older, deeper voice replied, just behind the door she held closed. "Let's continue this way," Richards said. "I have a feeling." Their footsteps faded down the way she had come. She cracked open the door, looked at the T she was headed to and then back, confirming that Richards—she had thought he'd have bled to death or at least be sleeping off her concussion-gift for hours—had in fact left. Feeling safe, she hurried back into the hallway and collided with someone small. It was Leanne!

"Hey, sweetie, what are you doing here?" Melanie had bent down to looked at the little face. She was still wearing the necklace she had given her.

Leanne looked behind her, and then dashed into B233A with a giggle. Melanie followed.

"Leanne, what are we doing in here?"

"I'm playing hide and seek," she stated as if it was obvious to the world, and then ran behind the cluttered desk in the small office.

Melanie knew she couldn't leave her, and she couldn't take her along. "Come on, Leanne. We need to get you to your mom—"

The door popped open and someone bounded in.

Automatically reaching for the Glock in her waistband, she realized just before firing it was Deanna.

"There you are, you stinker," Deanna said, barely regarding Melanie or her gun and walking over to the desk where Leanne's little face was sticking out. Deanna plopped herself down beside her daughter on the floor and propped open her purse in her lap.

"Great," Melanie said standing up, "now that you two are together, I can leave." She reached for the door.

"Hey, Mel." Deanna unscrewed the cap of a bottle of bourbon and took a swig, eyes rolling back. "Ahhhh, that's the ticket." Then as if nothing had happened, Deanna stated, "Oh it's just the two guards my dad assigned to me." She took another swig.

"Shhh," Melanie pleaded, her hand flapping like a bird. She held the door open just a crack, her ear only slightly exposed to anyone walking by. She heard several men running their way. She closed the door and scurried to Deanna and Leanne, who were sitting together, watching her.

"I told you," Deanna said too loudly, "it's just the two idiots protecting me. Hey do you think—"

"Shhhh," Melanie flapped both hands at them, one holding her Glock.

"Yeah-yeah," Deanna whispered. "But do you think Buddy—you know, the hunky guard—is cute?" And then she was quiet as several men's voices came from the other side of the door.

"Sir, I'm sure they went this way."

"If you lost my daughter and granddaughter, I will fillet your skin off and feed you to the cannibals myself."

Westerling! Melanie thought. Her mouth popped open, head fell back, eyes shuttered. *That bastard is still alive?*

She held her gun up to punctuate her resolve and rose to finish it once and for all, when Leanne spouted, "It's Cra—" Deanna's hand clapped over the child's mouth.

"Did you hear that?" said one of the other voices, outside the door.

"Did it come from an office or down the hall? My damn hearing is still ringing from the explosion," Westerling groused.

"Down the hallway, sir, I think," said another tentative voice.

Multiple footsteps ran away and down the hallway.

"You're leaving, aren't you?" asked Deanna. She stood up, holding Leanne's hand, her bottle back in her purse. "Please take us with. We won't be a bother. I just have to get us away from my father. He's an evil man, you know?" *Oh, sister, you have no clue, do you?* thought Mel.

She was tempted to leave them, hunt the bastard down and finish the job Carrington started. But twice, Deanna had asked for her help to escape. And Melanie wanted to make sure the other scientists got out. What difference did it make if there were two more? Besides, it would really piss off Westerling, and this place was about to become radioactive. She couldn't leave them.

"Fine, let's get moving. But both of you need to be quiet."

They slipped out the door and hurried down the hallway toward their way out.

"Brother John," announced Ben, another apostle of the Teacher and a good warrior. "We have taken Bios-2. The occupants are running and hiding. But, otherwise, we are meeting only little resistance. A few men reported some of the guards going into that building." He pointed to one of the taller structures they were standing near. "Do I have your permission to hunt them down?"

Two other leaders of the one-quarter of God's Army that the Teacher had left him listened attentively, waiting for John's commands.

"Yes, Brother Ben, find them." Then to all three he said, "If anyone resists or has a weapon, shoot them; no exceptions."

They all left John, who eyeballed the complex, which was so much larger on the inside than it looked on the outside—and it looked huge outside.

If the Teacher was successful with Cicada, perhaps he would let John command Bios-2, his own little kingdom. In a way, just as he had been trying to convince the Teacher and all the Teacher's followers, he was like a god. Even if his own heaven was a beat-up giant complex and a few hundred people, he felt godlike at this moment.

He beamed, full of pride for his success.

Westerling was beside himself with anger. Bios-2 had probably already fallen to those heathen barbarians. And yet the only thing that mattered to him was that his daughter and granddaughter had been lost by his two incompetent guards. He had to find them quickly and then get back to the bunker, where he'd left a guard and Bill King. They had come around and were almost back to the bunker, just before the turbine room entrance, but there was not much more to search. They were running out of options and time, as he suspected the barbarians were already celebrating their spoils and would be down here soon enough.

"Should we double back?" asked one of the incompetents as they turned the corner and hoofed it down the hallway to the bunker near the end. The other three looked at each other, unsure what to do next, and none wanting to stick his neck out and get killed by their crazy boss.

Westerling and the others halted. "Am I seeing correctly?" he asked.

They watched Melanie Reid come down the end of their hallway and start toward them, beckoning others to follow. It was Deanna and Leanne. *They're with that bitch!*

"There they are! Get them!" Westerling bellowed, spittle spraying, bloody face bandages fluttering, crooked finger protruding.

Reid turned her head in alarm to see her worst nightmare: Westerling definitely still alive sending guards their way, and herself babysitting two kids, one big drunk one and one little one.

"Oh shit, he looks pissed," Deanna said with a slur.

They were about to run back the way they had come when they saw a group of men wearing red robes marching their way. One of the red-robed men called out, seeing them, "She has a weapon, sir. Should we shoot even though there is a child?"

"You have your orders," said another.

They were stuck at the elbow of these two connecting hallways.

"No choice," Melanie said. From her pack she yanked a folded bandana and once more she unwrapped their security key.

"Eww," Leanne shrieked pointing to Melanie holding up Richards' severed thumb.

Melanie pressed it up against the plate and the door clicked open. "Inside," she demanded.

When they were in, Melanie laid out three shots down each hallway before she slipped in and closed the door.

Muffled shots were volleyed from both directions of the elbow.

"Arghhhh!" Westerling bellowed his frustration.

One of his men reached the B216 door and tried to pull it open. He was torn to pieces by multiple shots coming from the other hallway.

The other guards, running full out but seeing their fellow guard get mowed down, slid on the concrete floor as they tried to stop. Two were cut down; the other, barely protected by the hallway wall, spun and ran back toward Westerling. "The invaders are here!" he yelled, joining Westerling in the bunker.

They sealed the door.

39.
Bios-2

"It's hot in here. And I have to go pee," Leanne whined.

"I know, honey. It will get cooler in a little bit, and I'm sure Melanie knows where the bathrooms are." Deanna's look said, *Please confirm this, would you?*

Melanie held up at the base of the stairwell, waiting for them to get down safely. She looked to Leanne, being tugged by her mom down the last couple steps, and said, "There's a bathroom right over there, sweetie." She pointed to a door inside a little nook, beside the stairwell.

"You have two minutes," she instructed Deanna. "I don't know how long the senator will be occupied with the invaders." She watched them go into the unisex bathroom and was glad for the moment to think. She had to figure out what to do next. She obviously needed to disable the bomb, for now, but then what? Best she could figure, they were stuck down there. They could wait it out, but for how long? The invaders must have taken Bios-2. They weren't going to go away. She needed a way out.

She heard some sort of rumbling above; it was like muffled automatic gunfire, but from something very large, much higher caliber than from a regular rifle.

"Come on, we need to go now," she said, stepping their way. Something caught her eye. It was a notebook lying on the floor, just inside the shadows of the nook. She bent over to pick it up and thumbed through it. She bolted upright, a burst of adrenaline pumping through her blood. "It's Carrington's!" she sputtered.

He must have been taking notes of the guards' comings and goings, because it had guard names or "Guard #2" and "Guard #3" where he didn't know a name, followed by the time he saw the guard and when they had left. But there wasn't much more. She started again from the front of the notebook, intending to look more intently. On the second page, she held up and examined a scribble in his handwriting.

She drew the notebook to her chest; its pages pressed up against her, and she closed her eyes feeling his warmth, as if he were there showing her the way. She would have loved to stop and take some time to relish this, one of the last things he had written. She wanted to savor it. But there was no time.

Mel looked at the scribble again, rubbing her eyes with her sleeve, and sniffed in a breath. Best she could make out, it said, "Shaft Room door! Where does it go to? Looks like old tunnels. Guessing to other areas of complex and maybe out? Need to explore!" Above this was an infinity symbol, their symbol. This note was meant for her.

Looking up and past the turbine room, she could see a big area where the giant steam pipes exited into the turbine generator in the middle of the floor before her. That must be the shaft room.

Directly above her, a loud clatter sounded. No longer muffled sounds; this was inside, just above them. They must have broken through because now she heard the rattle of multiple footsteps on the metal grating of the walkway above.

Melanie ducked in further to gather the two girls as they popped out looking a little more refreshed.

"Quick, we gotta run for it. Be quiet." Melanie grabbed Leanne's hand and took off toward the Shaft Room. Deanna raced to keep up.

Ben and his men had broken through the hardened security door. He stepped in, his men right behind, and they were at once blasted by moist heat and awed by the vastness of this room. They walked up to the railing and looked down. This must be where Bios-2 generated its power. This was an important area they needed to protect.

"There they are!" one of their warriors yelled. He lifted his gun and intended to shoot, but Ben grabbed the gun before he could fire.

"You idiot. If you hit something vital, we may lose power. We will need this place when the Teacher returns. Go down and get them," Ben commanded, and the men raced down the ladder single file.

He watched the woman combatant—that's what they had called them in the US military, so long ago—dragging a small child behind her as she and another woman ran into a large room with big pipes coming out of it.

"Looks like they cornered themselves," he announced proudly, and then followed the last warrior down the stairs.

"Here," Melanie said to herself as much as she did to Deanna and Leanne. It was a single door, its paint peeling from the steam. To the left of the doorknob was the infinity symbol, roughly scribbled in pen. It must be the doorway Carrington had written about and maybe their only way out. "Okay, this should lead to an old tunnel; go in there and see what you can find, but don't come back out. I'll be along in a few minutes."

Deanna was hesitant. "Please don't leave us," she begged.

"No worry there. I just need to make sure the ones in red don't follow us in. Please go." She scooted them through the door, and then turned to address the problem. She had maybe two minutes before they would be down the stairs, and maybe another thirty seconds to clear the floor and get here. She needed more time. *Think, Mel, think!*

Then she saw it, but she needed a diversion or something to keep them back while she worked. She ducked in the door and yelled, "Wait" to Deanna, who was only a few footsteps away—they hadn't moved. To Leanne she said, "Stay here." Grabbing Deanna, she barked "Come" and dragged her to the door. "Listen. Your life and your daughter's life depend on you." Deanna looked scared but was also trying to pay attention. Melanie thrust her gun into the woman's hand, and Deanna's fingers automatically wrapped around it. "You see someone move, aim here and here,"—she pointed to the sights, thrust her arm out and demonstrated—"and squeeze the trigger only once. Stand here." Melanie placed her behind the wall's edge. "You have eight bullets, shoot only one bullet a minute. Got it?"

Deanna nodded, now looking more alert than Melanie had ever seen her before.

Melanie grabbed a crescent wrench she had had seen earlier and jumped on top of two-foot-thick pipe, which ran horizontally about a foot off the floor. She touched another pipe that ran from it vertically upward to an elbow-joint about even with her head. It then ran sideways out of sight. It was hot, but not too hot. If she guessed correctly, this one was a vent pipe, used only if needed for getting rid of excess steam. All she had to do is detach the pipe at the elbow and turn on the valve and no one would be coming that way for a while.

Deanna fired her first shot and yipped when she did. Melanie wasn't sure if it was fear or excitement.

"I think I peed, just a little," Deanna chortled.

Melanie worked on the first bolt, putting literally her entire body weight on it, when it finally came loose.

Second shot.

"This is fun!" she yelped excitedly.

"Mommy," screeched Leanne, just inside the tunnel door.

"Not right now, baby-girl. Your mommy has a job to do."

Shots erupted from inside the turbine room.

"Oh my, they're shooting back. Now what?"

"Keep shooting," Melanie grunted, working on the second bolt. "Remember, one bullet every minute."

She fired her third shot.

"Mel, what if there is more than one of the red-robed people... person?" Deanna half-whined and half-giggled.

Melanie cringed, and got the third bolt loose.

"Shoot the bastard, will you?" Melanie hollered.

She pulled on the fourth bolt, her arms already tired. She wasn't going to make it in time.

Bang-bang-bang.

Melanie looked out to the room and saw two invaders in red on the floor.

"Ha! I got two of them. Take that, suckers," she taunted.

The fourth bolt came free; the fitting felt loose already. *Only one more to go.*

The fifth bolt unscrewed easily. She quickly tried to remove each of the bolts, now that they were loose.

Bang-bang.

"Umm, Melanie. I think my gun is broken. Can you get me another?"

Melanie got the last bolt out and stared at Deanna, who pointed the gun at her. It was empty. Damn, the backpack was on the other side of the door, with Leanne.

Melanie didn't waste any time. Using her shoulder and head, she shoved against the underside of the elbowed-pipe. Her neck burned instantly. She pushed with everything now, including her hands; with the rush of adrenaline and panic, she didn't feel them burn.

More gunfire. Lots of it from the turbine room.

"Melanie, they're coming."

"Push!" she goaded herself.

It broke free.

"Melanie?" She was whining now, backing away toward the tunnel door.

A red-robed figure sprang from the doorway and bounded toward Deanna. Melanie didn't think, her reflexes working perfectly in spite of her fatigue. She yanked the knife from her waistband and heaved it at where the invader would be, an inch or two in front of Deanna, finding the man's face. Deanna screamed and bolted for the tunnel door.

Close enough!

Melanie hopped down and kicked the valve lever, opening up the vent. Steam billowed out in great rolling torrents. Its heat and sulfur smell already burned noses and eyes.

She dashed to the door.

Someone screamed behind her. It was a cry of agony.

Melanie slammed the door, but just before it closed, she could see two men on the ground. One was writhing in pain, and she was sure his face was sliding off.

Westerling did not want to be stuck down in his bunker with Bill and two guards forever. He could barely stand being down here much longer. Besides, although the bunker was designed for weeks of hunkering down, it was only another layer of protection to allow his troops to secure the complex. There would be no securing Bios-2. He knew it was lost to the religious nutjobs who had crawdadded him.

He reached behind the short bar, grabbed a bottle—one of about a hundred bourbon bottles lined up—unscrewed the top, took a big satisfying drink and screwed it tight.

"Give me your weapon and hold this," he said to one of the two guards, who took the bottle and handed the senator his sidearm. Westerling could feel his face leaking blood, but he didn't care at this point. He was alive, but he had to figure out some way to get his daughter and granddaughter out. He hated that bitch, Reid, but knew that she was so damned dogged about things, she would probably protect them with her life. That would have to do, because there was no way back through the way they came, nothing waiting except their deaths.

He stepped around the bar and from behind the cabinet he pulled on a lever. The bar slid sideways, uncovering a stairway down into darkness. Westerling grabbed two flashlights and gave one to the guard with the bottle and the empty holster. "You'll need this; it's dark down there."

He started down the stairwell, flashlight on, and pistol pointing the way.

"What do I do about him?" the other guard asked. "Do we leave him?"

"No, he may be useful."

"Where are we going?" the flashlight-and-bourbon-toting guard asked.

"The way out!"

40.

Cicada

As he scuttled to his residence, his hobbled left ankle screaming with every other step, Max couldn't help compare their current situation to his battle in Basra, just before the first Gulf War: just as then, he was on autopilot. A bullet ricocheted, tearing away earth directly in front of him, driving home the sensation. Although, he seemed to hark back to his time in Basra every time he went into battle, comparing and contrasting the battle. *Perhaps it was like this with every soldier.*

Saving Cicada now seemed hopeless. There were simply not enough of them to hold back this horde of invaders, who were still coming over the wall and through the break in their gate. Still, he was reluctant to surrender to Plan B. He wanted them to make one final stand. He knew their rifles on several of the roofs and Shingles in the Ops tower were making the enemy's job difficult as they attempted to scurry over Cicada's walls. Max hoped if they could put more firepower on the breach in the gate and pick off the occasional red-robe that made it to their grounds, maybe they would have a chance.

As he ran, he told everyone he saw to meet Tom in Ops, where he would get them a weapon if they didn't have one. He dashed through the fencing that surrounded their compound.

Max ignored the angry pain in his twisted ankle, his shot-up bicep—he felt the suture open up earlier—and the pulsating throb in his head. After pounding past Ops and Comms, for a moment, he popped out into the open—he could almost feel some of the rifles on the wall train on him—as he sprinted to his residence. More bullets were directed his way, but all were missing the moving target. They appeared to him like heavy raindrops churning the gravel or dirt each time they struck harmlessly around him. Answering each raindrop, albeit much slower, was the thunder of Shingles's Barrett from the tower, finding each shooter.

As Max slid in the gravel to his door, jarring his ankle even more, he saw several people huddled for cover against the First House next door; they were waiting for Plan B to be called, no doubt wanting to be first in line. He waved them forward to join him. They were at first tentative, but as fear fueled them, they rushed and then clustered around Max as he opened his door and left it open for them. None had seen the inside before and they all welcomed the invitation to its safety. Max was already opening his Toy Room, its overheads blinking illumination on its many guns and gadgets. He pulled down from the wall all five of the M4s, loading each, and then handing one each to two of the five standing in his living room. They were the only ones unarmed.

"Aren't we going to Plan B?" pleaded one of their scientists—it was something like Dr. Stich or Switch, he couldn't remember. He looked somewhat surreal in a white lab coat with a military rifle slung around him.

"No!" Max answered, tossed the other loaded M4s and some extra magazines on the couch and went back in for more supplies. He put on his tactical vest and stuffed it with two M4 mags and two spare AK mags. He loaded both his AKs, slung one around his neck and tossed the other onto the coffee table with extra magazines. He took two grenades, but left the rest; every resident may have been trained in using a rifle but not in using explosives. Finally, he opted for the Glock 17 Gen4, rather than his favorite .45, which he laid on the table inside the Toy Room. He needed capacity more than stopping power. After loading one magazine and attaching his rig, he shoved two more mags into his tactical vest. He was ready. But he still grabbed more pistols and loaded them.

"We have to go to Plan B," Preston yelled as he bounded into Max's, out of breath and surprised to see the others in the living room. They parted to let him in and two nodded in affirmation of Preston's own call to action.

"Here." Max shoved an M4 and two magazines on him, seeing he was unarmed. "We may be there soon, but not yet." To the others he said, "Let's not give up our home so easily yet. I think we have a chance if we can focus on the breach in the north gate and get the stragglers who make it down the wall. They haven't won yet." He threw the loaded pistols he was holding onto his coffee table.

Lisa and Magdalena came in next, both disheveled, but otherwise opposite sides of the same scale. All eyes turned to them. Lisa was frantic and out of breath. She seemed ready to burst with anxiety and fear. Magdalena, on the other hand, looked calm, as though she had been in many battles. Only Magdalena had a weapon, if you could call her little paring knife much of a weapon against guns. He handed each an M4 and an extra magazine.

"But, what…" Lisa couldn't think of what to say.

"You five"—he pointed to the group of huddlers—"you focus on the west wall and anyone that makes it down. Keep behind the perimeter fencing and you'll be safe. Please be sure you don't shoot one of our own. Go!" They hesitantly shuffled out and around Max's residence, most happy that he kept them close to the rendezvous point if the horn sounded.

"Everyone else, come with me," he said and bounded out, M4 scanning. A robed man was running on the wall, toward their nearest stairwell. Max squeezed off one shot, dropping him, and headed to the Operations tower gate. The others followed behind until they all lined up behind one of four gates in the large perimeter fence that surrounded much of the compound, separating it from the remainder of the complex.

Max stood on a picnic table and announced, "This is the demarcation line. If the enemy makes it here, we'll call Plan B."

Shots were being squeezed off just above them and Max smiled when he saw it was Tom already set up on the roof of a single-story supplies building, next to Residences. He was firing over the fence at the breach in the north gate, where one red-robe at a time was trying to break through the opening. Most were cut down, but some were making it through and running for cover.

"This is where we make our last stand," Max yelled and fired off shot after shot.

Johnson ascended the spiral stairs of the Operations tower. He could hear Shingles's .50 cal Barrett booming above him every thirty seconds or so. With each blast, two or more shots were returned, pinging the outside metal shell. Most ricocheted off but some penetrated. They would eventually silence him; Johnson was going to make sure it happened quicker.

Johnson pushed his head out of the opening in the middle of the floor and watched. Shingles was firing, positioning himself in another of the tower's four windows, reloading, finding a target, firing and moving to another window. He had been a pillar of Cicada, having joined two years before the Event, but he never saw what was coming next. Johnson pulled out his revolver, aimed and fired one round at the back of his head. That was the end of Shingles.

Johnson bounded up the last few steps and shimmied across the floor. The last thing he wanted to do was get killed by friendly fire after waiting so long for this moment. When he was at the south-facing window-wall of the Operations Tower shack, he reached up to the lever right below it and tugged it from left to right until it clicked into place. The *clack-clack-clack* of the gate assembly didn't sound immediately because of the distance between the tower and that gate. So he chanced a peek to confirm his success. On the other side of the largest gate in Cicada that opened out onto the main access road, Johnson saw hundreds of robes waiting, for him.

At first he wasn't sure it was opening, thinking it was the auroral light playing tricks with his eyesight and the distance. But when he saw the first robed warrior press through, he knew he'd done it.

"I'm out," cried Lisa.

"Me too," Magdalena said.

"I'm out too, boss," Tom hollered from the roof a few feet away.

"All right, I'm calling it; time for Plan B. Tom, would you do the honors and make sure Shingles hits the horn and gets down safely?" Max peered up to the tower, worried a little because he no longer heard the boom of the Barrett.

"Sure thing, Max." He hopped down off the roof of the building and jogged to Operations, his sidearm drawn and leading his way.

"Preston, take Lisa and Magdalena with you and go get those in the infirmary. I'm going to make sure there are none just behind us here. I'll meet you in the designated spot." Max turned back around and fired off automatic bursts from his AK. Each distinctive discharge felt like home compared to the smoother volley of his M4, which was empty, as were any serious attempts to save the complex.

They would lose Cicada.

41.

Cicada

Tom was certain something was wrong when he entered Operations, and it wasn't the lone bloody boot print. It was the silence above. He could no longer hear Shingles firing that beautiful Barrett. Tom was sure Shingles must have bought it at the hands of one of the enemy's snipers. He was hesitant to go up and check on him, but the need to sound the horn was far more pressing than his reluctance to learn of his friend's fate. The lives of most of Cicada's surviving people rested upon Tom's shoulders. He had to blow the horn. Now.

He bounded up the spiral stairway, three steps at a time, his Glock pointed forward in case it was needed. Tom ascended these steps daily, checking up on this strange dude he called a friend. Their friendship was born from their odd status within this community, as neither were scientists and so not part of that clique. Shingles—Tom never knew his real name—was small and almost misshapen, as if he had had polio as a child. They shared a passion for weapons and shooting. Shingles was by far the best shot he had ever seen, and he knew he wasn't bad himself. He also had an almost encyclopedic recall of gun facts, as if he were reading directly from one of Jane's many publications. Often, Tom would bring him lunch and they would share stories—his were combat-related and Shingles's were weapons details. Mostly, he liked the guy, who was completely unassuming and genuine.

Below the western window, he found Shingles's crumpled body in a puddle of his own blood, a black slick that had a strange yellow shimmer from the auroral light pouring through the windows. Based on the spray on the wall, he knew someone had taken him at close range, from behind. The boot prints leading away and down the stairs confirmed this. Regardless, there was nothing he could do for his friend and he had a far more important matter than finding the bastard and seeking revenge.

"Goodbye, little buddy," Tom whispered, and then hopped up onto the floor. He reached into the shadows for the big red button. There was no mistaking it, and in the sunlight it plainly read "Alarm." He pushed it as he looked out the south window. He blinked once, thinking it was his old eyes playing tricks on him. It wasn't.

"Oh my God!"

Johnson was the first person to enter the old adobe house, minutes before the horn's blare. He pulled the warped door closed. Its ancient hinges screeched their disquiet, like some angry animal anxious to get back to its long uninterrupted slumber. Once it was closed, he latched it from the inside to make it more difficult for them to enter.

He was supposed to go to Comms first and make the call to Westerling, but a couple people were already there and his cover was already blown. He didn't have his phone box either, but it wouldn't matter because there were only two other places to connect: the utilities closet by the Library and in Research. He wasn't about to take a chance on either. This was the safest place—well, it would be soon enough.

It was pitch black inside the windowless house, but he knew where to go next, having practiced this many times in similar darkness. His footsteps were heavy on the concrete floor, the only improvement to the house in the last ten years. Then from the blackness, there was a sound of a thick object on rollers being pulled across the concrete. Its echo was hollow, the adobe and wood roof absorbing most of the sound. It sounded once more and then it was silent.

The house again appeared vacant, slumping slightly from a few centuries of gravity and the elements. It awaited the rest of Cicada's dwindling population.

When Max had emptied his last AK mag, he dropped the gun and switched to his Glock. When the horn finally blared to all of Cicada, he planned on staying only a couple of minutes before he tried to find the stragglers. He looked back several times, hearing the footfalls on the gravel behind him, just to confirm they were friendly. At least the enemy made their presence obvious in their red robes.

He wished he could see to the First House and count the numbers that passed, but the Rec Facility blocked his field of view. He'd give it another minute and call it. Beyond the fence gate there were three shots, maybe less than twenty meters from him. The fence blocked his field of view for the first five feet below it. He watched the gate creak open and a single red-robed head tentatively edged through, looking back and forth. When he assumed there was no one around, he beckoned others in. Max waited as two, then three, then several quietly walked through; he was hidden by elevation. He heard a set of running boots coming from one of his own people and saw the lead robe lift his weapon. Max emptied his Glock, rammed in another magazine and finished them off.

He hopped off the roof, watching to make sure no one else was coming through. Before closing the gate, he peeked outside to see what it looked like and now saw thirty or more shapes approaching the gate. He closed it and then dragged the bodies against it. "Thanks for your help, guys."

It was time to go.

The Teacher was jubilant as he sashayed into the front gate of their new home, Cicada. It was just as the forked-tongued devil said it would be. The Senator had told him they would resist at first, but he had a plan for this. Francis set up five of their best sharpshooters in the trees at specific points outlined by Westerling. They would supply cover fire for their people, who would go over the walls and through the gate on the north, damaged by the explosives they were given. They should commit one-quarter of their troops to this endeavor and have the remainder wait on the other side of the main gate to the south, which would be opened, letting them in.

But the Teacher didn't tell his people the plan because he wanted them committed to trying to make it in over the walls or through the damaged gate. This would add to the diversion's effect. And the diversion worked perfectly as their men and women walked in without any resistance through the main gate; all the gunfire seemed to be concentrated on the other sides and the far end to the north.

When the horn blared, the Teacher was told that meant they were giving up. That they would throw down their arms and wait at some designated spot to be captured.

It reminded him of the air-raid sirens from the movies. It was all so exhilarating.

"Teacher, they seem to be running. I think we've won," one of his female warriors said. She was one of the prettier ones, and one he had spent some evenings with.

"Yes, sister, Cicada is now ours."

Max stopped at his residence, seeing a large congregation of people at the First House. He wondered why they hadn't gone in but saw Tom arrive and knew he would figure it out. He needed to take care of a few matters at home first.

The door was still open and most of the guns picked clean: good, less for the enemy. He closed the door, wanting to not be interrupted for the next couple minutes. He hurried to the Toy Room and shoved the last remaining mags of .223 and 9mm into his vest and added one more grenade. Then he secured the door.

Now for a few personal items and a present for the home's newest occupant.

He grabbed his SOC Gear Long Range rucksack, already filled with his bug-out gear and hydration water bladder, and lumbered to his bedroom. His injuries were catching up to him, the adrenaline starting to fade. On his bedside table, he snatched his last Frankenstein flashlight and slid it into his sack on the floor.

He pulled out his clothes hamper, a wicker basket he bought in Mexico some years ago. He lifted the top off, walked over to the bed and peeled back the sheet and covers, unused in over a year even after the last three days. He dumped the basket's contents onto the bed and pulled the fabric over the now very angry rattler. Max grabbed some clothes from the closet and tossed them on the bed to provide cover to the moving lump underneath.

"I think that's a nice housewarming gift."

He slung his sack around his shoulder, lumbered into the living room and stared at his Decision Shelf, feeling surprisingly clear-headed after so little sleep and so much stress on his body. But his injuries were taking their toll and he was completely exhausted. Yet he felt sure of this decision. He reached up, grabbed what he wanted, and without hesitation thrust it into his sack.

One final consideration, he thought. He examined the three pictures on the entry foyer wall. Originally, he was going to take them all. After all, there were no other pictures of his grandfather or Fatima. But they were in the past. He reasoned they should stay with the house. He closed his bag, put it around both shoulders and fastened the clasp, already rearranging his weapons. He was ready.

Before exiting his residence for perhaps the last time, he looked at this place he so rarely used. It wasn't really his home because it was empty of people that he so stridently kept out of it and therefore out of his life. He didn't know any of them as well as the Kings, but he felt a duty to protect them all. He realized just then that he couldn't protect everybody; he could only do what he could do and, with God's help, many of them might survive this thing.

Looking up to the heavens he said, "If it is your will, O Lord."

He shut the door but left it unlocked, not wanting to keep its new occupants from receiving all of the benefits of living here. A sly smile filled his face. It was probably the first time he had really smiled in the three days he had been there.

Commotion at the First House drew his attention, the noise rising from maybe thirty people clustered in front, waiting. Tom was at the door, shaking it, but it appeared to be locked. Tom raised his weapon, fired off a couple rounds and the door swung inward. Preston thrust a propane lantern inside for light and Tom went in to find who had locked the door.

Max could see that Sally and Lisa were propping up Sue, injured in the failed assault on Bios-2. Pel was beside them in a cot, still unconscious, as he was when Max carried him back. Webber, still a little wobbly-looking from the beating he'd given him, held onto the other side of the cot. Max counted the others, who were desperately waiting for word that it was safe to go inside. There were only twenty-eight of them. He hoped there were more alive and just late in getting here. He had counted eight taken down from the attack, but he suspected their losses were worse than this. It was a far cry of the four hundred Cicada had been built to house for many years.

Tom popped out of the door and announced, "All clear, folks. Watch your step."

There was an explosion by the southern perimeter fence entrance and billows of smoke. This elicited shrieks from a few of Cicada's remaining residents, most of whom pushed to get through the door and out of harm's way.

"Whoa, people!" It was Magdalena. "One at a time," she demanded. She saw Max watching her and smiled at him. He walked over to her, not feeling the anxiety that most did from the enemy obviously blowing the perimeter fence open. They were less than a minute away.

"So happy to see you're in one piece. You look pretty good, considering." He smiled again.

"You too, but you look pretty awful."

"Thanks." Then to Preston and the others still outside, he asked, "Who are we missing?"

"Shingles bought it," Tom said, coming over to them. "I think that little prick-mole Johnson did it, and I think he locked this door too."

"Any sign of him?" Max asked.

Tom shook his head.

"Where are Dr. Ron and Dr. Monty? I see their wives here, but not them," Max asked, head turning to find them.

"They're in their laboratory!" hollered Preston as he carried Pel in with Webber, almost tripping at the threshold.

"I'll go check on them," Tom offered.

"Thanks. I think I need to lie down for a bit," Max responded and shook his hand. He looked him in the eye; they grinned at each other and nodded... "It's been an honor."

"Max, for me as well." Tom let go and darted to the Rec Facility's side entrance, his rifle raised and ready.

Magdalena stepped in and Max followed. He was the last one in. To his right, he saw some red-robes flooding onto Max's Boulevard and walking their way. To the left he saw dozens, marching in their direction from the breached fence. He closed the door and secured it as best he could. It was fairly quiet inside, other than a whisper or two and the hiss of the lantern's propane flame. The mud-adobe brick was a pretty fair insulator.

"Shhh," Max whispered. "They're almost here."

"Teacher..." Frank ran up to him, still a little winded after having run the mile-plus distance from the other end of the oval complex.

"Francis." The Teacher warmly shook his hand. "So glad you made it. You and your warriors have done a masterful job. What are our numbers?"

"We won't know for sure of our losses till morning, but I'm guessing about two hundred," Frank answered. He took a knee beside the Teacher, resting. He could walk tens of miles without losing a breath, but he wasn't used to all of this running.

"That's not bad at all, less than what I expected. What about Cicada's occupants?"

Frank's face turned sour. "I'm sorry to say, Teacher, we could only find fourteen bodies and no survivors."

The Teacher's face sank like the Titanic. "What did you say about prisoners?"

"None. We could find no one here alive."

"Where did they all go? Did they just disappear in the air like some fart in the wind?" Anger filled his features.

"Teacher! Brother Francis," Stanley called to them. "Come here."

They walked briskly to Cicada's First House, the plaque on the door saying just that. It was like some museum. Its door was open. Stanley turned to the Teacher before entering and said, "Several of our warriors said they saw people walk into here, just before we arrived…" He then stepped inside. The Teacher followed.

Someone handed the Teacher a lit oil lamp, and other than the concrete floor, he felt transported back into a small home from the late 1800s. In fact, it was probably just as it looked back then: a small table and three chairs where the family would have dined; a kitchen area with washbasin; a fireplace with a pot hanging over it; and three straw beds in the back corner.

There was no sign of anyone, besides his men.

Stanley finished, "…but as you can see, if anyone was here, they're not any longer."

Epilogue
Cicada

"This was probably the manager's residence." Frank stood in front of the open door. "It's the largest one, so we thought you might prefer this for your home, until a suitable one could be built for you, Teacher."

"It's just fine Francis, thank you." The Teacher strolled inside, first examining the three pictures, just beyond the door, and then moving into the living room.

Frank hesitated outside. "Teacher, my men have swept the place, and of course it is empty but a little unclean, and the door to the public bathroom is locked, but... we'll get someone in to clean up shortly, but I thought you might like to rest. Can I get you anything?"

"Yes, Francis; bring me a couple of my companions, and find me Cicada's survivors."

"Yes, of course, sir." Frank bowed and then closed the door.

The Teacher ambled through the living area and then to the bookshelves, examining each of the books there. He slid out *The Flames of Rome* by Paul L Maier, about Roman Emperor Nero, and blew the dust from the top of it. Something else caught his eye on the next shelf over. Alone on the shelf was an old bottle of tequila and two glasses. The shelf they rested on was layered in a year of neglect, except in one area. A rectangular void, cut out of the dust, told him that the previous occupant had just taken something from the shelf; another bottle, or a book perhaps? It didn't matter; he had what he required.

He wanted to be prepared for his companions when they came. He seized the bottle of tequila and both glasses, and strode with his new book under arm into the bedroom. It was a little disheveled, as if the occupant had left in a hurry, but otherwise, it would do. He rested the bottle, glasses and book on one of the bedside tables. He removed his robe, placing it on the end of the bed, and dropped his boxers, stepping out of them and settling onto the bed. After propping the pillows behind him, he relished the comfy feel. He slurped from the bottle of tequila, enjoying the burn as it slid down his throat. The bed needed to be straightened before Francis brought his companions by.

He put the bottle down and pushed the previous occupant's clothes off the bed onto the floor.

There was something under the covers too; probably more clothes.

He slid his legs under, relishing the feel of the sheets; they were clean. He swiped the bottle once more and took another gulp, happy for all the developments. He was a god. He had control over all of his people and the world around him.

Another gulp.

He threw back the bedspread and sheet and saw a bundled up shirt and pants. He leaned over, and with his free hand, he tugged at the bundle, just beyond his feet. It had considerable weight for being nothing but clothes. Maybe there was something of value in there. He pulled it closer to him, about midway between his feet and groin. Whatever it was, it started to slide out of the garb. He clutched the clothes tighter and gave it a yank, dislodging the object right between his widespread legs.

He focused on the object, which seemed smooth, with a diamond pattern on it.

And it moved.

When it rattled, the whole thing was so perplexing, he bent closer to look.

SNAKE!

In shock, he froze, and in horror, he watched it rear up.

It struck.

The story continues…

REMNANTS

(Book #4 Stone Age Series)

COMING SOON

Did you like CICADA?

Please leave a review
http://stoneageseries.com/book3

Reviews are vital to indie authors. If you liked this book, I would really appreciate your review.

Thank you!

Want to join in discussions about CICADA?
http://stoneageseries.com/cicada

Thanks and Acknowledgments

It's been said that if you sit enough monkeys down in front of enough typewriters (substitute with "computers" for those under 50), and given enough time, one will eventually pound out a Shakespearean Sonnet. This monkey is no Shakespeare and it took more than just time, luck or a few bananas to get this book into your hands; I had lots of help. Here's a brief list of those who have been invaluable to me in bringing *CICADA* to life, all of whom I am eternally grateful.

To my wife, Lisa... You're my anchor, my rock, my everything. You were the one who encouraged me to write, even when my writing became a damned mistress who schemed to suck away much of my time. Why you put up with both of us is a mystery to me.

To my editor, Karen... Even though I must make your eyes bleed and your head swell, you have diligently worked to "flesh out" what I wanted to say, sometimes far better than I could have said it.

To my cover artists, Alisha & Damon... Thanks for creating a thing of beauty that immediately stirs up emotions, and draws potential readers to that first page.

To my formatter, Jason... Thanks for untwisting the words from my awful Word-coded copy so that readers are less likely to curse my name.

To my proofreader, Sara... You're the last person who is tasked with the heavy burden of making this grammatically perfect. Thanks!

To my Advanced Copy Readers... Thank you for your words of support and even the occasional criticism. You guys (and gals) rock!

Finally, to my readers... I am humbled that you have invested your most valuable time and a little money into something I've written. I've done my best to make your experience enjoyable and thought provoking. I hope our journey together doesn't end here, but continues for many years to come. I promise if you bring the beer (substitute beverage of choice) and popcorn, I'll do my best to provide the entertainment.

About ML Banner

ML Banner founded more than a dozen companies over the past thirty years, before he found his passion for writing in 2014. Quite unexpectedly, his first book, *STONE AGE* became a #1 Amazon Best-Seller in Post-Apocalyptic & Dystopian Fiction. Since then he has written five other books within two series, including two more #1 Amazon best-sellers, and one a 2016 Readers Favorite gold medal winner & Kindle Book Review Sci-Fi Finalist. His books have been featured on Amazon's Daily, Monthly, and Big Deal.

He and his wife split their time between Tucson, Arizona and Rocky Point, Mexico. If he is not penning his next novel or short story in apocalyptic fiction, you might find him on the beach reading a Kindle, with his *toes in the water* (the name of his publishing company).

Want more from ML Banner?
www.MLBanner.com

Receive FREE books &

Apocalyptic Updates - A monthly publication highlighting discounted books, cool science/discoveries, new releases, reviews, and more

Keep in Contact – *I would love to hear from you!*

Email: michael@mlbanner.com
Google+: google.com/plus/+mlbanner
Facebook: facebook.com/authormlbanner
Twitter: @ml_banner